PRAISE FOR CATHY YARDLEY

Role Playing

"Singular characters and genuine emotion make this a broadly appealing romance."

—*Kirkus Reviews*

"This delightfully quirky romance . . . is a charming celebration of the many ways connections can develop."

—*Publishers Weekly* (starred review)

"Yardley does an excellent job writing realistic characters who still manage to be swoonworthy . . . Full of funny and heartfelt scenes with fierce yet kind protagonists."

—*Library Journal* (starred review)

"*Role Playing* features one of the most endearing couples I've read in a long, long time. Aiden's kindness, warmth, and patience make him the sweetest cinnamon roll hero possible, while Maggie is the cranky, fiercely loyal heroine of my dreams. Yardley doesn't shy away from difficult family and friend dynamics, but that only makes the way Maggie and Aiden help and defend one another all the more satisfying. And the earrings-removal moment at the wedding reception? Absolute gleeful perfection."

—Olivia Dade, nationally bestselling author of *Spoiler Alert* and *Ship Wrecked*

Love, Comment, Subscribe

"Yardley brings humor and humanity into the cutthroat world of online influencers, showing the realm's pleasures and pressures. Both protagonists are delightfully flawed, and Yardley seamlessly weaves their backstories and details of their Asian American heritage into the fast-paced narrative. This smart, sexy tale of fame and friendship is a charmer."

—*Publishers Weekly* (starred review)

"A fun, lively romance mines the insecurities common in people transitioning to adulthood."

—*Kirkus Reviews*

"Cathy Yardley is the queen of modern love stories. Her books are clever and swoony and unputdownable!"

—Penny Reid, *New York Times* bestselling author

"*Love, Comment, Subscribe* is so. Much. Fun. Cathy Yardley wrote this modern romance with just the perfect amount of humor and heartwarming moments that I was all in for Lily and Tobin's collab, both in business and in love."

—Tif Marcelo, *USA Today* bestselling author of *It Takes Heart*

Gouda Friends

"It's palpable how much Tam and Josh care for each other . . . Yardley's fans will gobble up this gentle but steamy romance."

—*Publishers Weekly*

"Yardley's prose is summery and light—you'll get swept up as Tam and Josh breezily fall right back into place as the lovably cheesy duo known as Jam. A mouthwatering romance."

DO ME A

Favor

OTHER TITLES BY CATHY YARDLEY

Ponto Beach Reunion

Love, Comment, Subscribe

Gouda Friends

Ex Appeal

Smartypants Romance

Prose Before Bros, Green Valley Library book 1

Fandom Hearts

Level Up

Hooked

One True Pairing

Game of Hearts

What Happens at Con

Ms. Behave

Playing Doctor

Ship of Fools

Stand-Alone Novels

The Surfer Solution

Guilty Pleasures

Jack & Jilted

Baby, It's Cold Outside

Role Playing

DO ME A
Favor

CATHY YARDLEY

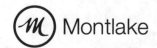

Published by Montlake, Seattle

www.apub.com

Amazon, the Amazon logo, and Montlake are trademarks of Amazon.com, Inc., or its affiliates.

ISBN-13: 9781662517105 (paperback)
ISBN-13: 9781662517099 (digital)

Cover design by Faceout Studio, Molly von Borstel
Cover illustration by Leni Kauffman
Cover image: © Valentina Vectors / Shutterstock

Printed in the United States of America

To my husband, Joe . . . against the odds, and worth
every single minute together. Love you, always.

CHAPTER 1

It was, unironically, a dark and stormy night.

Willa wasn't sure how long the clattering had been going on, but by now the sound was loud enough to be heard over the thunder. She catapulted up in bed out of a dreamless sleep. Her heart pounded like a taiko drum, fast and driving, and her breath was a captured gasp.

Her brain, on the other hand, snapped into crisis mode like a LEGO. She grabbed her cell phone off the nightstand and tossed off the covers in a well-practiced motion before she was consciously aware of it. Then she sprinted forward, rushing to address . . . well, whatever needed addressing.

There were a few problems with this approach, she quickly realized.

First: this wasn't her house.

Or rather, it *was* her house. Now. But she'd only lived there a grand total of three days, it had come furnished, and she wasn't familiar with it at all.

So she promptly stubbed her pinkie toe on the bed frame, which had her barking out a curse as pain shot through her.

Second: that slight, pain-induced pause was just enough time to remind her why she didn't need to rush.

It's not him.

He's not here.

It's okay.

It had been two years. It wasn't like she wasn't *aware* of her husband's absence. That she no longer had to be on high alert to anything he might need.

But sometimes, especially on nights when she could finally beat back the insomnia, a noise would trigger it all over again.

Muscle memory. The ghost of coping. The way everything crystallized as she held the phone in her hand to check the blood sugar monitoring app or to call 911 if need be. The cold clarity as she assessed: *What do I need to do?*

She heard the clattering again, although it was difficult to recognize over the raging storm. She turned on the hallway light and headed down the stairs in her bare feet.

She had no idea if storms like this were the rule and not the exception in the Pacific Northwest. Rain beat down on the roof in steady sheets, and the windows rattled from the wind. Each bolt of lightning preceding the thunder was like a blinding paparazzi flash, so seemingly close she was surprised she couldn't see the strike on the lawn.

The noise was coming from the adjoining garage, she realized, straining to hear it. An . . . animal noise, maybe?

She grimaced as a recent conversation with her parents crossed her mind.

Washington State? What if you get eaten by a bear?

Her mother had thrown out that plaintive question, just before Willa had moved up to claim her great-aunt's inheritance on this small island in the middle of Puget Sound. Of course, her mother had lived in Southern California for most of her life, and in Vietnam before that. At this point, anything outside of Irvine might as well have "Here Be Dragons" written next to it on Google Maps as far as her mother was concerned.

Willa trudged to the mudroom, listening at the door. The sounds were louder. There was definitely something in the garage.

Well, shit.

Taking a deep breath, she looked around for a possible weapon. Whatever was in the garage, she could chase it off, couldn't she? It was probably a raccoon or something. A coyote, maybe. They'd had a ton of those when she and Steven lived in San Mateo, before the restaurant had shut down.

Even if it was a cougar or a bear—or an intruder, or hell, even a zombie—she couldn't quite bring herself to feel fear. Now that the panic had subsided, she could barely muster curiosity.

What was it going to do to her? Her bank account was minuscule and her future uncertain, and while she'd been diligently chipping away at the medical debt . . . let's face it, she was bailing a battleship with a teaspoon.

At this rate, a bear might be doing me a favor.

"Stay positive," she said out loud to herself. She was pretty sure that self-hype wasn't supposed to sound quite so reprimanding, but it was better than nothing.

A few little things like debt, or bears, or being in her forties, technically unemployed, and alone . . . none of them were going to stop her.

Finally she grabbed an enormous umbrella and opened the garage. "Hey!" she shouted.

More metallic clanging. And a . . . whimper?

Then a short, sharp bark.

She turned on the light.

There, trapped in a bunch of what looked like aluminum ducting and hoses, was a trembling, growling dog. It was muddy, and soaking wet, so it was hard to tell what color its fur was. She couldn't tell one breed of dog from another. Whatever it was, it wasn't that big, although it was stocky and muscled, with a squarish head.

All things considered, she probably should have been scared of it. It was growling . . . *at the hoses?* . . . and, if she had to guess, about the size of a twenty-gallon flour storage bin. Also, probably capable of gnawing a hole in her.

But it also had the most adorable underbite she'd ever seen, one that allowed a little pink tongue to loll out as it panted. Its eyes looked at her with misery and just the slightest glimmer of pleading.

She'd never fallen in love at first sight before. (Steven had been a near thing, but even then, it had taken a few months.) Then again, she'd never had a dog before either. Her heart melted like white chocolate, her adrenaline washing away in a syrupy wave.

"Ohhhh." She slowly put down the umbrella and approached the animal. "Sweetie. How did you get in here?"

Another crack of thunder, another round of barking. The dog looked hopefully to her after each bark. Like somehow, she'd be able to shut off this terrible noise and make things better. She reached out her hand, slowly, carefully, like she'd always seen people do in the movies.

It finally sniffed her knuckles before giving her a teeny tentative lick.

"That's it, sweetheart," she reassured it. "C'mon. Let's get out of this garage and get you dried off."

She helped clear things out of the way. The dog was way too uneasy and a bit too big for her to pick up. It kept barking when the thunder rumbled, which was continuously. She tugged gently on its collar, easing it as best she could into the house.

The windows were double paned, at least, so the house had more of a buffer against the noise of the storm than the attached unfinished garage did. "Stay," she said.

Of course, it did not listen, but she couldn't bring herself to care. She went to the downstairs half bath and grabbed a mishmash of hand towels she'd hung on the racks.

The dog was shivering. She wasn't sure if it was because it was cold from being wet, or because it was scared due to the storm, or both. She instantly sat on the floor and cozied it up, drying it . . . *him*, she realized. While wet dog and mud probably didn't combine to make the most pleasant scent in the world, his snuggling up to her more than made up

4

for it. She wrapped him up, even grabbing a lap blanket and cocooning him. He grinned a doggy grin at her.

She grinned back, feeling the constant knot in her chest ease, ever so slightly.

"You lost, puppy?" she murmured, giving him a quick dry-off. "How did you wind up in my garage?"

He wriggled happily, burrowing into her arms as the storm continued.

She took a deep breath. While it wasn't a full-blown emergency, she had to admit that the situation—a problem that needed a solution, something that needed care—had been strangely calming. It certainly beat the hell out of all the tossing and turning she'd done prior to finally falling asleep.

What time *was* it, anyway?

She glanced at the grandfather clock before realizing she hadn't wound it and it was permanently frozen at seven o'clock. After petting the dog, she pulled out her phone and checked.

Eleven thirty. Not that late, really. Somehow, she'd thought she'd gotten more sleep than that!

That's what you get for trying to hurry tomorrow up. She should've known better than to try to get to sleep early, and wondered if she would be able to get any sleep now that she was awake again.

She ignored the upsetting thought as she snuggled the dog. Yes, she was getting mud all over her blanket. She didn't care. His doggy kisses and her lowered tension were worth it.

"You got a name?" she mused, slowly twisting the collar. The dog was obviously a pet, and a well-socialized one at that. He'd trusted her almost immediately. She glanced at the name etched on the silver disk hanging from the collar. "Noodle, huh?"

He let out a pleased little chuff.

She really, *really* liked this dog. She'd always wanted one, but her parents had absolutely turned her down (too expensive), and while

Steven had liked dogs in theory, he hated the idea of being tied down. He loved the ability to just pick up and go, anytime, anywhere . . .

. . . until he couldn't.

She bit her lip, then flipped the collar tag over. As she'd suspected, there was the owner's phone number.

Noodle let out a little sigh, climbing into her crossed legs and leaning heavily against her chest, even though he was too big to really be a lapdog. She felt tears welling up, and she knuckled them away before they could fall.

It was exhaustion, she reasoned. Stress. Not because this vaguely stinky, soft, cuddly, not-so-little creature seemed happy to be taken care of by her.

I could just keep him until morning.

It was late, after all. Who would want to drive out in the middle of this mess? She could just . . . clean him off some more. Maybe feed him a little, if he was hungry.

She could let him curl up with her in bed, even, and bundle him in her blankets, and keep him from getting scared.

But surely his owner was worried out of their mind. No matter how much she liked this dog, they had to love him, and the dog had to love them. She couldn't be selfish. She needed to do what she did best: the right thing.

After a long second (and a brief daydream), she called the number on the tag.

Whoever they were, they didn't pick up—not surprising, considering they wouldn't recognize her number, and it was nearly midnight. Still, if she were missing her dog, she'd want to know that he was safe. They might be driving in this mess, frantically searching.

So when prompted, she took a deep breath, then said clearly, "My name's Willa, and I believe I have your dog."

CHAPTER 2

Hudson wiped his hands off after he scrambled out of the crawl space connected to the water-heater closet in his customer's house. "Everything's taken care of, Mrs. Tennyson. You'll be able to use the sink now, and everything's draining fine."

"And the pipe . . . ?" She was wringing her hands a little. "So I won't need to call Kenny?"

Hudson hid his frown. Kenny was Marre Island's only plumber—and a total dick, because he knew he was the only game in town. If you had any kind of plumbing emergency after the ferry stopped running, you were stuck, and he used that as leverage. He also knew that a lot of plumbers off island didn't want to haul their shit out here, and the ones that did charged an arm and a leg. So Kenny charged just a little less—like a hand and a foot—and you were fucked.

Which was why, over the years, Hudson had gotten a hell of a lot better at plumbing and added at least the basics to his handyman services, stuff that didn't require permits. It helped for small jobs like this, even if it was kind of miserable work, especially when it was cold. Or when it was rainy, like tonight.

"Nope. All good," he quickly reassured the little old woman, who beamed. "Just don't dump any more grease down the drain, okay? It's not good for the septic, either, and that's something I *can't* fix."

"Right, right," she agreed, even though he had sincere doubts about how truthful she was being. Still, it'd take a while before he had to be out here again for a clogged pipe. He hoped. "Thank you, thank you! I don't know what we'd do without you."

We. Meaning the inhabitants of the island, where he'd lived his whole life.

Days like today, he wasn't sure what they'd do without him, either, to be honest. He hauled up his tool bucket and box, feeling every ache from squirming around in the damned crawl space. When he'd started this business, he could put in a full day and still feel ready to head out to the city, drink, flirt, dance for a few hours, or pick someone up for some mutual fun. Now, at forty-two, he found that a long day crawling around in the tiny area between a packed dirt foundation and a house's floor just hit different. He felt filthy, his arms ached, and all he wanted was to grab a beer and a shower—*beer* in *the fucking shower, hell yeah*—and maybe a sandwich after, then collapse into bed.

"Well, you have a good evening, Mrs. T," he said, one hand on the doorknob. "I'll send the invoice, okay?"

She waved him off, and he stepped outside. The storm was kicking up strong, so he was rapidly getting soaked, which basically made the dirt he'd gotten streaked over himself thanks to the mud in the crawl space just cake on more.

He hurried to put his tools in the back of his truck, then climbed into the driver's seat.

Thankfully, home wasn't too far away. (Technically, *nothing* on the island was that far away.) Despite having lived here his whole life, he knew to just drive slow and careful, because the storm was a beast, and he didn't want to go off the road due to exhaustion and overconfidence and mud.

But before he could, his phone buzzed with a text, and he groaned as his shoulders squeezed together like they were in a hydraulic press.

"Please don't be an emergency," he muttered. He did not feel like running out and dealing with somebody's generator failing or a tree branch crashing through somebody's window. He'd probably still go, let's face it. One way or another, they helped each other on the island.

Not that anyone kept track, but just about every single person who lived there had gotten him out of a pinch at some point, and it seemed the least he could do to do the same if they needed it.

Instead, he saw "Jeremy" . . . his son's name.

He panicked briefly, because it was nearly midnight, and he didn't care who you were—when your kid called at midnight, you panicked a little bit.

JEREMY: Noodle got loose again.

"*Fuck*," he muttered, even as relief flooded his veins.

Not that there was anything wrong with dogs in general, or Noodle in particular. As far as Hudson was concerned, Noodle was a helluva a lot better than the goats Kimber was intent on collecting. But Jeremy and his live-in girlfriend had been fighting, and he'd asked if "the family"—meaning his grandparents and sister, and of course Hudson— could watch Noodle at the farmhouse until "things settled down."

Hudson could've told him immediately that things were assuredly *not* going to "settle down," because Jeremy and his girlfriend were like Mentos and Diet Coke, but the kid was twenty-three. Consequently, he knew everything.

Hudson smirked a little, shaking his head. *God, I miss knowing everything.*

Still, this was obviously a problem—and Jeremy knew his father loved dogs *and* his son enough to go out, late, in this shitty weather, to make sure the dog was okay and bring him home.

Before Hudson could text him back asking for more details, he got more texts.

JEREMY: This lady called me, said Noodle got into her garage

JEREMY: Can you go pick him up? I'll bet he's scared

Hudson groaned, wondering briefly, selfishly, if the woman wouldn't mind hanging on to the dog until morning. But Noodle was a small-to-medium-size pit-boxer mix, with a bunch of other random breeds. He was also an escape artist, and he had a tendency to get into things as well as out of them. He was cute, so he usually got away with it, but who knew what this lady was like? It was a big ask. Also, if it was somebody from the island, Jeremy would've said so. There were some new people moving in, though. Maybe Noodle had found one of those.

He texted back: Where is she?

Jeremy answered with an address.

JEREMY: Looks like she's our new neighbor. Moved into Ms. Caroline's house?

At least it was close. He quickly texted back.

ME: All right. But you'll owe me.

JEREMY: Cool thanks dad

Jeremy's quick agreement meant he thought Hudson was kidding. He wasn't. He just needed to think of a proper repayment. Maybe coming home and mucking the barn or something. Or dealing with the goats.

He started the truck, then put it in gear and cranked the wipers to high before starting down the slick road. This was going to suck, but the sooner it was done, the sooner he could get that shower and the beer, then go the fuck to sleep.

CHAPTER 3

"You look *much* better," Willa crooned to the now dry, marginally cleaner dog.

Noodle preened, or at least she thought he did. She'd essentially given him a sponge bath with the hand towels. Then she'd dried him with a fluffy towel from the linen closet. After a quick "what's safe for dogs to eat?" Google search to make sure it was all right, she gave him a bit of boiled chicken, hoping his owner wouldn't mind. It did distract Noodle from the storm, calming him a little. He wasn't relaxed, but he was definitely happier.

Now, he was resting on the couch with her, twisted on his back with paws in the air and his head resting on her lap as she rubbed his belly. His pink tongue would dart out to give her a thankful lick as she did, making her giggle as it unerringly hit the pit of her elbow. He looked at her adoringly. If there was a mirror nearby, she knew she'd see herself looking back with the same expression.

"I wish I could keep you," she said, rubbing his tummy until he shivered with pure doggy delight.

She quickly cut off that line of thought. The man on the phone who had finally called her back, Jeremy, sounded nice. He'd thanked her and was apologetic for the inconvenience, insisting that "someone from his family" would be right by, since they lived "practically next door."

She wasn't sure what that meant, exactly. She didn't think they lived in the Victorian house across the street, the only other house nearby on her part of the island. She'd only seen a man there, in passing, driving an Audi, and Jeremy made it sound like it was more than one person. Otherwise, it was as if she didn't have neighbors, not like when she lived in the suburbs. Her late aunt Caroline's property butted up against hay meadows and some rambling, wild forest, fenced in with wire.

No, this dog was just out and mischievous and had probably gone too far afield, and she'd bet his humans missed him terribly, because he was adorable.

"Maybe I can volunteer to dog sit," she told him, rubbing his ears and putting him in tongue-lolling ecstasy. "Or . . . I don't know. Maybe walk you for free? Dog walking is a thing, right?"

What does it say that I'm lonely enough that I'm willing to schedule essentially a playdate with a stranger's dog?

She gritted her teeth. *Positive thinking!*

If she just kept repeating it, surely it would stick, right?

Besides, the sooner Noodle was claimed, the sooner she could get to bed and work on that whole "get sleep" thing. She had that call in the morning with Vanessa, the editor she used to work with, and it was too important for her to be unfocused or exhausted. Right now, it was just a little past midnight. If she maybe meditated, or listened to one of those guided sleeping things on YouTube, she could get enough rest to be clearheaded. Then she'd be able to impress Vanessa. She needed that *way* more than she needed a dog.

She nuzzled Noodle's head, laughing when he licked her chin. *Even an awesome dog.*

The knock on the door startled her, and she grunted when Noodle twisted like a breaching shark before launching himself off the couch, somehow using her leg as a springboard. He barked at the door protectively.

"Shh! It's okay, it's okay," she reassured him before carefully opening the door so the dog didn't either jump on the person or make another wild break for freedom into the rain.

Lightning chose that moment to flash like a strobe, making everything seem to stop.

A man stood on her porch. Taller than her, not that that was saying much. If she had to give a one-word description, it would be *strong*. Not because he was bulky with muscle. If anything, he was lean, rangy. He gave the impression of rapier-like thinness. Like Timothy Olyphant, she thought absently, in *Justified*. Everything but the hat.

In that frozen moment, she also saw his T-shirt was drenched from the rain and clung to obvious muscle definition. The garment was somewhere between white and gray, she'd guess, streaked with dirt. There were a few holes in the fabric, presumably worn from age and use. His jeans were similarly filthy and similarly representative, not so tight that they were obscene but definitely and lovingly well worn.

Those weren't gym muscles. Whatever this man did, he'd earned every lean, corded line through hard work—she could just tell.

But the real shock was his face. Dark hair streaked with silver, cut medium length except for a messy, rakish drop of bangs that shielded eyes as blue and bright as a butane flame. Cheekbones you could carve marble with. Sharp jaw accentuated by a salt-and-pepper shadow.

She went absolutely, utterly still.

And of course, at that moment, the lights went out.

She let out a startled cry. In response, Noodle jumped against the door, slamming it shut in the man's face.

"Ma'am?" she heard him shout through the door, over the storm. "Ma'am, are you all right?"

"Yes! Just . . . just one minute!" she yelled back. Just like that, the lights flickered back on. She could feel her heart hammering in her rib cage, blood rushing in her ears, pulsing hard in her throat. "You're here for the dog, right?"

"Yes, ma'am."

She bit her lip. "What's his name?"

A pause. "Sorry?"

"What's . . . um, the dog's name?"

"Noodle," the guy answered immediately. He sounded . . . amused? Maybe? The important part being he didn't sound irritated or angry. Or scary?

Not that she felt scared of him. But she felt *something*, very big and weird and alien. She tried desperately to get a read on the situation, but frankly, she was at a loss.

Taking a deep breath and grabbing Noodle firmly but carefully by the collar, she pulled him back enough to get the door open.

The man was still there, still looking imposing.

Well, no, not imposing. That wasn't the right word.

Striking, her brain supplied instead.

"You okay?" he asked, stepping in and closing the door behind him, shutting out the roaring sound of the storm. That bright-eyed gaze pinned her. He smirked a little, revealing a dimple pitting his cheek, just over the stubble. The smirk wasn't mean spirited, but . . . yup. He was definitely amused. "Wanted to make sure I wasn't here to try and steal a dog at nearly midnight?"

Good lord. Here, in the relative quiet of the house's tiny foyer, the guy's voice was *ridiculously* deep.

ASMR deep.

Like, *audio porn* deep.

She could feel it like a rumble in her sternum. She shivered a little.

What the hell *is going on here?*

"Wanted to make sure who I was opening the door for," she answered with quiet aloofness. It was her front-of-the-house voice—neutral, polite.

His smile immediately fell. "Oh, shit. I'm . . . you're right. It's late. And you don't know me . . ."

"It's fine." She didn't mean to sound curt, but it seemed to come out that way. She bit her lip. "I mean . . . thank you. For coming. To get Noodle."

Noodle leaped at him, and he knelt down, letting out a little laugh as the excited dog immediately licked his neck and face.

"Okay, okay! Fuc—uh, frickin' Houdini," he teased, taking the dog's face in his hands and giving him a gentle little shake. "Why can't you just stay at the farm?"

She frowned as a detail clicked with that question. "The hobby farm?" she said before she could stop herself.

He glanced over at her as he petted Noodle, whose tail was wagging enthusiastically. "You know it?"

"It's down the road . . . ?" She seemed to remember a sign as she was driving here, meeting the real estate agent, getting the keys.

"Yeah." His smile was back, less amused, more genuinely happy. "Our property goes all the way to yours, though. We're neighbors. That's probably how Noodle made it over here." He sighed a little, pointing at Noodle until he focused. "Bad dog. You've gotta stop running away."

Noodle's ears went down, and his puppy eyes went wide and liquid, looking forlorn.

Her heart tugged. "I'm sure he didn't mean it," she quickly interjected. "He just got out, and the storm scared him, and he got lost. And made it to my garage, somehow. I'm glad he found me."

The man stood up. "I'm not . . . I'm not angry at him," he said slowly, studying her. "You know that, right?"

She shrugged, wrapping her arms around herself. She hadn't thought he'd been *angry*, to be honest. She just really liked Noodle and hated seeing him sad. Already the thought of him trotting out the door caused a pang.

Nonetheless, her reaction to the man standing there was starting to unsettle her. She wasn't afraid. She'd been ready to face down a frickin' bear in her garage with barely a blip in her heart rate. But this?

She still couldn't define it, but she definitely felt *odd*.

She wasn't sure if he believed her, but his smile was gentle, his movements slow. "My name's Hudson. Hudson Clark, of Marigold Meadows Family Farm." He held out his hand, then seemed to realize he had the leash in it and swapped. His hand was clean, but he had mud streaking up his wrists.

She straightened, releasing her inadvertent self-hug, and shook his hand. "Willa Lieu-Endicott," she said in a rush. It felt weird, saying it out loud, like it'd been ages since she'd talked with someone who didn't know her. Who wasn't somehow related to something official.

Real estate agent. Banker. Lawyer.

"Of . . . um, here," she finished clumsily.

He laughed. "You live here, then?" he asked. He shifted his weight to one foot, smiling at her, completely casual. Completely *comfortable*. Like he'd known her for years, rather than simply striking up a conversation with a stranger. "You buy the place from Ms. Caroline's family?"

She felt her eyes widen. "You knew my great-aunt?"

"Oh, *you're* her family." His smile widened. How? It didn't look fake or anything, or even overly jovial. But she just got an overwhelming rush of *more*. Like she'd somehow unlocked a conversational level she wasn't aware she was working on. "She was a great lady. She'd want us to welcome you. She was friends with my mom. They traded recipes all the time."

Willa made a noncommittal noise, since she wasn't sure how to respond.

"You should stop by and say hi," he added. "It's summer, so the farm stand will be open, and you can always just say hi to the animals. I'm sure Mom and Dad would love to meet you."

Why couldn't she *speak*? She nodded, feeling foolish and lost.

Then he took one step closer to her. He did the thing that taller people—taller *men*—sometimes did when they crouched to be eye level, studying your face.

"You sure you're all right?" he asked, with obvious concern.

The guy's voice was like getting a full-body massage with chinchilla mitts.

Oh, God, this is a problem.

She shivered again, then set her jaw and took a step back, her spine bumping against the banister.

"Just . . . tired," she finally said. "I, um, should probably get some sleep."

"Oh." He mirrored her action, taking a step back. "Yeah! Of course. It's late. Thanks for taking care of Noodle."

He unrolled the leash. Noodle looked back at Willa, and for a second, she wanted to see if this Hudson guy would sell him to her . . . or let him visit . . . or *something.*

She gritted her teeth and tried to ignore Noodle's plaintive look as Hudson clipped the lead to Noodle's collar.

"It was nice meeting you, Noodle," she said softly, forcing herself not to reach out and pet him one last time.

Noodle replied with a little *woof* and tail wag.

"Nice meeting you, too, Willa," Hudson added, and she felt heat flood her face.

"Oh! Well, yes." Then she covered her face with her hand. "I mean . . . you too. Hudson."

Oh please God kill me.

Hudson chuckled, just a brief, tiny moment. Like a perfect one-bite dark chocolate truffle.

Then he opened the door.

"Ma'am," he said, tipping an imaginary hat before walking out into the storm, Noodle in tow.

She shut the door and locked it, then all but collapsed against its wood surface.

What just happened?

She hugged herself again as she checked the house, making sure everything was locked tight. Her heart hadn't quite slowed down. She chalked it up to adrenaline. Same with the dance of nerves that seemed to flicker over her.

Too many new things all at once, she finally decided, before washing her feet and settling back into bed. She'd only been in the house for less than a week. She needed to make some hard decisions, and a lot would ride on her conversation with Vanessa the next morning. Add to that an adorable and unexpected dog and a . . . well, *striking* and somewhat imposing stranger who then took away said dog, and it was just an inordinate amount of new and unexpected and overwhelming.

She plugged her phone in, hoping that the power didn't go out again.

She then proceeded to not fall asleep for the rest of the night.

CHAPTER 4

Hudson slowly made his way downstairs, struggling to hide a yawn. "Morning," he called out before turning the corner and heading toward the kitchen. It was late for him—eight o'clock, when he was usually up by six—but he still felt wiped out.

He sighed, shuffling toward the smell of coffee like a zombie.

"Morning," his mother sang back. Her gray hair was pulled up in a high ponytail, and she wore a sunshine-yellow tank top, paired with jeans. She was making omelets at the stove, with veggies from the garden and plenty of cheese. His stomach rumbled. She turned. "What kind of toast—"

Then she got a good look at him, and her eyes widened.

"Sweetie, what happened?"

"What do you mean?"

His father sat at the kitchen table, eating an omelet and looking at his tablet, probably checking the Mariners' score from the game last night. Noodle sat at his feet, looking up hopefully. His father shot Hudson a glance, then quirked an eyebrow at him. "She means you look like shit. You getting sick or something?"

"You were out in the rain, under Mrs. Tennyson's house," his mother fussed.

He headed for coffee like it was a life preserver. "I didn't get that . . . *agh*," he grunted as she tried to pull the quintessential mom move, pressing her hand against his forehead despite being shorter than him. He dodged. "I'm *fine*."

She rolled her eyes. "Grumpy. Dad's right, though. You look awful."

"Didn't get much sleep," he admitted, finally getting a nice big ceramic mug of coffee and dumping in some sugar and creamer.

"Me either!" chimed in his daughter, Kimber, as she entered from the back door with a grin and a wink. "Seems like I had a lot more fun than you, though."

"Don't want to hear it." He glared at her, but without much heat. After she'd gotten her agricultural degree at UW, she'd pretty much had a bustling social life despite moving home to work with his mother on "expanding" the family hobby farm. "It's your fault I had to go get Noodle when he escaped last night. In the rain. At midnight. After fixing Mrs. Tennyson's clogged pipe."

"I am sorry," Kimber said, and to her credit, she did sound it. "I was still in Seattle, on my date."

"Date. Is that what the kids are calling it these days?" Hudson's father muttered under his breath, but fell silent when Hudson's mother then glared at him. Kimber and Hudson sat at the table, and she slid omelets in front of them.

"Thanks, Mom." Hudson took a long sip from his mug, feeling the healing power of caffeine kick-start his system. *Thank God.* He cut into the omelet. "Kimber, as long as you're safe and you were able to take care of those demon spawn—"

"The goats are adorable, and you know it!" Kimber yelped.

He ignored her. "—and didn't make your grandmother get up early to do your chores, you know I don't judge where you spend your nights."

"Of course I didn't make Gram take care of them." Kimber looked offended. "I always take care of the animals! I already got a start on the garden stuff too. I'm going to be picking blackberries for jam later."

"You're going to help me make soap, too, right?" his mom prodded her.

Kimber nodded, and the two of them chatted as Hudson got down to eating his breakfast.

A lot of people didn't understand how he could still live here this way at his age. They thought he was "trapped" with two parents in their sixties (not that he *technically* lived with them . . . they lived in the cabin on the far side of the property) and his grown twenty-three-year-old daughter. The only one of his immediate family missing was Jeremy, who had moved to Seattle. He still came back plenty often, though, for food and to do laundry, and his room was always waiting for him in case he changed his mind.

The thing was, the Clark family had been a unit for so long, sometimes Hudson wondered if he'd know how to exist any other way. It felt like perfectly broken-in work boots: functional, comfortable. Maybe not the most stylish thing in the world, but it got the job done, so who gave a fuck?

Kimber looked thoughtful, drinking some yerba maté—a beverage that made Hudson shudder in disgust. "You're usually a good sleeper. If you keep having trouble, I've got some fresh lavender oil. You know how that knocks you out."

"Oh! Or I've got melatonin," his mother added, sitting down with her own plate.

"I've got scotch down at the cabin," his father stage-whispered with a wry grin.

"Thank you, everybody," Hudson said, shaking his head and smiling. "But don't worry about it. I'm sure it's nothing."

"Are you worried about the bid this morning?" his mother asked.

Now, all three sets of eyes studied him intently. He never should've told them, but he knew they'd be asking, especially since he was in relatively dressy clothes—meaning a clean, new polo and his best jeans and work boots.

"Actually, no," he said, although . . . well, he was a little nervous. Not enough to lose sleep over it, but enough to have some tension.

"Nobody could restore that Victorian better than you," Kimber said, and her unshakable faith in him made his chest warm. "Any bid he gets from someone off island is going to cost four times as much, and they're going to take at least twice as long. And they'll probably suck too!"

"Trust me, I'm going to be pushing that," Hudson said.

"Also, nobody loves old stuff more than you do," Kimber tacked on.

Hudson grinned. "Because I'm old? Thanks."

"No, because you love antiques," Kimber said with a patented eye roll. "I can only imagine what the inside of that house is like. You'd be in antique-geek heaven. They probably have all that funky, you know . . ." She made a weird wiggly motion with her hand.

"Scrolls? Ornamentation? Carvings?" he offered.

"That stuff."

He shrugged. "Well, the Bauers weren't exactly party people, so it's not like we got to see the inside often. I guess I'll find out today."

Kimber's eyes narrowed. "Wait a sec. I thought you grabbed Noodle from there last night?"

"Um . . . no." He suddenly started shoveling in eggs, avoiding their gazes. "Noodle had run away over to Ms. Caroline's."

"I thought it was still empty!" his mother said. "But it couldn't have been, if somebody called Jeremy. Was it one of those Airbnb renters?" The sourness in her voice said exactly what she thought about *them*.

"Actually, I met the new owner." He finished his breakfast and put his fork down. "She's related. Her niece. Grandniece? Great-grandniece? Something like that."

"I wonder if I've met her," his mother mused. "What does she look like?"

He acted like he had to think about it, when in reality, he didn't have any trouble at all picturing her. Probably because he hadn't stopped thinking of her, it seemed, since he'd stepped out of her house. He'd spent most of the night thinking of her, in fact. *She* was the reason why he hadn't been able to sleep.

"She's short," he finally said, smiling at the memory of her standing in the foyer with her sweatpants and large T-shirt, bare feet with high arches. "Small . . . well, compared to me. Black hair. Asian, I think. At least part."

"Asian?" his mother noted absently. Caroline had been some kind of eastern European originally, with crepe-thin wrinkled white skin and soft silver curls. He remembered his mother talking about it with the older woman, since the Clarks were also eastern European, as well as Italian, Irish, and possibly Brazilian. "I don't think I've ever met her, then. But Caroline only lived here in the past ten, fifteen years or so. Did this niece look young, then?"

Her voice was deceptively casual.

"Was she *pretty*?" Kimber translated, with a note of mocking as she glanced at her grandmother.

Hudson thought again of the woman in the house.

Her shoulder-length ink-black hair was cut in a style so razor-straight he could've cut himself on it. She hadn't been wearing makeup, he was pretty sure, which, considering she was ready for bed, made sense. She had big brown eyes with long black lashes, arched eyebrows. A round face that would be friendly when she smiled, probably hiding dimples. The fullest lips he'd seen, possibly ever, so deeply pink they looked cherry stained.

But there was something else that he couldn't quite shake. A feeling he'd had before.

He'd been six years old when his grandfather had shown him his first antique clock, an Atkins mantel version in walnut with brass details. It didn't work, so Hudson hadn't seen what the big deal was, and said as much.

"Yeah? Check this out," his grandfather had said, and then opened the case.

Hudson's jaw had dropped. The clockworks were like something out of a dream or a cartoon or something, all gears and wires and tiny little hammers. His grandfather had then pulled out some impossibly small screwdrivers from a special case in his workshop and done a few adjustments, and the clock had slowly ticked to life.

From then on, Hudson had been fascinated by clocks—by the complexity that hid under a simple, clean, luxurious design.

Something about Willa hit him like that. Even mussed and messy from Noodle-wrestling, there was something classy about her. Something complex, hidden under the surface. Maybe it was in her eyes, or her manner, or her quiet voice. Whatever it was, it was like that first moment he'd seen the inside of a clock and his world had opened up.

"You really are asleep," his mother repeated, but it was almost a question. There was a note of worry there.

"Sorry," he quickly said, then finished the coffee and got up for more. "She's maybe my age, I guess? It was hard to tell, and it was late. I didn't really talk to her much or anything."

"You found out that Ms. Caroline was her whatever-aunt," Kimber pressed, eyes bright.

His daughter was too smart sometimes. Took after her mother, he thought, and he meant that in a good way. "We did talk. I told her she should stop by the farm, that we'd been friends with Ms. Caroline. She seemed nice."

Now they all exchanged glances, seconds before Kimber started laughing. "You *like* her!"

"What? I literally talked to her for less than five minutes," he protested. His mother was shaking her head, grinning smugly. On the other hand, his father was rolling his eyes.

"Like I always say," his father tacked on gruffly, "don't shit where you eat. If you're going to get mixed up with a woman on the island, you'd better be serious."

His mother playfully smacked his father's shoulder. "I, on the other hand," she said over Kimber's quieting chuckles, "have said it's past time for you to have another relationship. Would you say she's in her forties . . . or thirties?"

He tensed, his jaw clenching. "No, Mom." The words weren't harsh, but they were firm.

She sighed softly. "You can't blame me for asking."

"You've got two grandkids already. Don't be greedy." He paused. "Although . . . I was thinking of stopping by, to make sure she's settling in okay."

Which set Kimber crowing again. "You *do* like her!" She got up, doing a little victory dance, wiggling her butt, which Noodle enthusiastically approved of, dancing around her as if it were some kind of precursor to his getting fed. "Don't tell me: she batted her eyelashes at you, said she loved a big, strong handyman, and then asked if you could maybe fix her pipes?"

His parents laughed as Hudson finished off his coffee, annoyed. "This isn't a porn," he snapped. His father cleared his throat in warning, and he huffed out a quick, "Sorry. But no, it's not like that."

"Really." His mother sounded unconvinced. "Because you take after your father. You're a handsome, charming devil." His father grinned, leaning over to kiss her cheek and waggle his eyebrows at her. "I think half the single women on this island under sixty would jump in your bed in a minute—and the other half would take fifteen minutes, max."

"Some of the married ones too," Kimber added cheerfully.

He grunted. The damned thing was, he knew, on a certain level, it was true. Not because he was some gorgeous guy or whatever. He stayed in shape because his job was really physical, and he'd always had a good metabolism. Beyond that, he was blessed with good genes. His mom was still stunning in her sixties, and his father had been a heartbreaker, from everything Hudson had heard—his mother wasn't kidding there. Hudson had his mother's bright-blue eyes and ability to dance, and his father's devilish smile and lean build.

Added to that, Hudson knew he piled on charm. He liked flirting, with or without a desired outcome. He flirted with anything and anyone. More than one hook-up had told him he had a voice made of pure sex . . . which tended to work out, since he liked sex.

But he hadn't flirted with Willa.

Maybe it was because it was midnight, and maybe because he'd been exhausted and wet and punchy. But the minute she'd let him in, with Noodle dancing at his feet as she'd stood back and watched, she'd just given off this aura of . . . *something*. Something he couldn't put his finger on. Something that warned him she wasn't open to flirting, harmless or not.

"Trust me, she wasn't charmed," he clarified.

"What, did she hate you or something?" His mother scoffed. "Because I don't believe *that* for one minute."

"Maybe she's being a pick-me," Kimber added.

"What the hell is a pick-me?" his father chimed in.

"You know. 'I'm not like other girls! I won't succumb to your charms, you handsome alpha male!' That kind of thing," Kimber explained. Or tried to. His father still looked confused. "Like she's playing hard to get, showing that you're going to have to work for it."

"I'm not saying I'm working for anything," Hudson protested. Then he took a deep breath. "It was . . . it was almost like she was scared?"

And *that* was the crux of it, although it still wasn't quite the right word, because the woman he'd met hadn't seemed afraid. She'd stood her ground without flinching.

This was vain, but it was weird enough that she wasn't charmed, and that she was throwing off a don't-try-it vibe over a six-foot radius. She wasn't just disinterested, or irritated, or judgmental. She seemed *removed*. Like she'd built an invisible wall.

He didn't know what was going on there, but some part of him wanted to reassure himself that she was okay, both in general and with him.

All humor fled the kitchen. "Well, it was late, and she doesn't know the island," his mother said quickly. "She doesn't know *you*. You wouldn't hurt anybody."

"Who didn't deserve it, anyway," his father added with a fierce nod.

"I was thinking of stopping by after the bid, actually," Hudson said, as the idea formed. "It was late and stormy last night. I can just check in and make sure she's okay, and, you know, kind of let her know that I'm okay and not scary . . . ?"

"No." Kimber's voice was firm. "That's stalker creepy, Dad. If she's nervous, you stopping by isn't going to make it better."

"I'm not asking her out, for . . ." He looked at his glaring mother, and sighed. "For pity's sake. I just . . . I don't want her to be scared of me. Or anything."

"Your heart's in the right place," his mother soothed, "but I have to go with Kimber on this one. You need to let her make that decision. If she really is scared of you, for whatever reason, you need to leave her alone until she does something. Going over there is *not* going to help."

"Maybe you'll run into her at the grocery store," his father added. "Everybody winds up there, right?"

Which was true. A reality of island living: there was just one grocery store, and you ran into someone you knew eventually. It wasn't great, but it was something. "Anyway, it's no big deal," Hudson finally said. "I'm going to get that bid."

"Break a leg," his father said, and his mother and Kimber both hugged him. He headed out toward his truck, his leather portfolio in tow.

They'd made great points. Besides, why should it matter if one woman didn't like him or was nervous around him for no particular reason? Why did he care? It wasn't an ego thing. It could've been, and he checked himself to make sure.

But it was a *concern.* She was wary, or distant, or something, and he didn't *think* he'd done anything to deserve it. Which made him wonder why she was so cautious—and if there was anything he could do to help.

He hadn't felt concern like this for anybody but family in a long time. That, combined with the fascination he'd felt toward her . . .

Jesus, get a grip.

So he did. He gripped the steering wheel and headed down the street, toward the Victorian . . . and toward Willa, just across the street, where he absolutely would *not* stop by.

CHAPTER 5

After a few cups of black coffee and a lot of cold water splashed on her face, Willa felt . . . well, not exactly *ready* for her conversation with Vanessa, her old editor from her cookbook ghostwriting days. But she was at least *awake*, and right now, that was about all she could ask for.

The phone rang ten minutes late, and Willa forced herself not to jump on it. "Hello?"

Act casual. Act normal.

"Willa," Vanessa said, her hyperbright voice sounding perky. "It's so nice to hear your voice!"

Willa smiled for a second, until Vanessa's follow-up.

"I so rarely, you know, *talk* to anybody these days. Authors do everything over Zoom or text or even Discord. Or email. But you're old school!"

Old, Willa's brain emphasized.

"Well, you know me," Willa demurred. There was a pause, and she figured she might as well go for it. "You said you had—"

Vanessa was too quick, though. "I was so sorry to hear about Steven."

In a blink, the conversation jumped the tracks, like those treadmill-fail videos where someone inevitably went flying off the back of the belt and plowed into drywall.

"Ah. Thanks." She'd learned there wasn't anything else to say to the sentiment, and it was the quickest way to head off uncomfortable or awkward questions.

"I meant to get in contact with you earlier," Vanessa said, not quite moving on but at least not digging deeper, "but you just seemed to have so much going on, and you hadn't written for us in a while . . ."

Willa could almost feel the guilt rolling off Vanessa like a Chicago cold front. "It's fine," she said, her own voice brisk. "It's been two years, and I was . . ." She hunted for a word. "*Busy* before that."

"Busy" didn't even come close to describing it. But then, she didn't have that kind of relationship with Vanessa. Even if her parents hadn't drilled professionalism and "no blurring lines" into her since college, she knew this was business, not friendship, and it was better not to muddy the two. Especially not when she needed this contract so badly.

"I'm ready to get back into the swing of things," Willa continued, confidence picking up. "You said in your email that you had a project that I could maybe go for. I'd love to hear about it."

Vanessa sighed with obvious reluctance, but shifted gears. "Things have changed since you've been in the game," she said, with more of the characteristic bluntness that Willa remembered. How long had it been since she'd last ghostwritten an actual cookbook? Five years?

No. Almost ten. She winced. Steven had some investments that they'd slowly cannibalized as he got sicker, and she'd taken some piece-meal projects here and there, menu planning for whoever needed it, doing desperation work that she could manage the deadlines for without too much of a problem.

Ten years was a lifetime.

Crap.

"Changed how?" she asked, still trying to sound positive.

"The fees aren't what they were, to start with," Vanessa said. "Hell, advances aren't what they were, unless you're a celebrity. 'Celebrity' meaning a TV-show or internet person, not like a Michelin chef, by the way."

Willa felt thrown, her stomach knotting. "How low?"

Oh, God. Can I not even make a living doing this anymore?

Vanessa threw out a number, and Willa tensed. She had been counting on this money to help her stay afloat. The mortgage on her new-to-her house wasn't going to pay for itself, after all, and there were still debts to pay.

Besides, this was a new start. She needed to get back into the pipeline. She needed Vanessa to start seeing her as a viable hire again. This was a stepping stone.

"But I do have this one project that pays more," Vanessa continued. She made a puffing noise, not smoking. Vaping, maybe? "One I think you could maybe knock out of the park. There are just a few little provisions."

Willa almost, *almost* felt her hope bloom at that . . . but her chest felt like there was a lead blanket on it.

Provisions. That screamed "red flag" instead, but beggars couldn't be choosers.

"What do you need?"

"One: your name can't be on it."

Willa shrugged, then realized Vanessa couldn't see it. "You know that's never been an issue for me." She preferred being behind the scenes, normally. She'd seen enough chefs, worked with enough in restaurants and pop-ups and things, to know that their egos could be both sensitive and oversize. She'd even worked on a few books for chefs who would've hated the idea that their "enemy" had used the same ghostwriter. Others didn't like anyone questioning whether their genius might've come from what they termed a "glorified stenographer." (Not that newer generations even knew what a stenographer *was*, but most chefs didn't know "Dragon software," so it didn't matter anyway.)

She wasn't under any illusions, and she knew what she wanted. Money was money. She wasn't going to be putting out her own cookbook, after all, even though her friend Nat had insisted years ago that she start "demanding her due" and get credited with her name on covers.

"Two," Vanessa continued, "it's due in two months."

Willa winced. That was tight. "That's . . . doable," she said, a little more slowly. "Depending. What sort of shape is it in now?"

"That leads me to three." Vanessa let out a nervous laugh. "This guy got a big advance, because . . . well. He's a social media guy."

"What does that mean?" Willa asked.

"You're not going to believe it." Vanessa laughed again, even more high pitched. "He does these short videos where he cooks . . . usually shirtless. Sometimes pantless. And he, um, licks things."

"He," Willa echoed, sure she'd misheard, "*licks* things."

"Yeah. That's his whole deal." Vanessa sighed. "The guy's got millions of followers or whatever on a number of different social media outlets, enough of a platform that they're offering him the money. No culinary school training, no restaurant background, but a pack of rabid followers who are dying for this cookbook, especially if we can get it out by spring."

Willa scribbled aimlessly across the top of her spiral-bound notebook. "What kinds of cuisines?"

"You think this guy has a set cuisine?" Vanessa sounded amused. "Based on what I just told you? His cuisine is *stripping with food*."

"Right." Willa grimaced. "What's the theme of the cookbook, then? What's the title?"

"No title quite yet, but his name is Sexy Chef Sam. So it'll be some play on that."

"So I'd be writing a book for a shirtless guy who licks things, and that's the only theme I've got to work with?" Willa blurted out before biting her lip.

"Doesn't matter if the theme is 'food without clothes,' the guy has an army, and we are going to sell them big, fat Sexy Sam cookbooks with full-color glossy shots of him sucking batter off his finger," Vanessa shot back. "Need to strike while the iron's hot, though. Before they find some new sexy guy with lots of followers. There's plenty of competition out there, and nobody stays popular forever."

"Got it. Does he have some recipes he wants to go with?" She grimaced. "I should meet him, I guess. Where is he based?"

"That is another thing." Another puff sound. "He's technically based in LA—almost all the influencers are, I hear—but he's going to be in Ibiza for some party thing, then in . . . I want to say Taiwan, to talk with people about licensing cookware. And/or possibly a clothing line?"

"A *clothing line*?" Willa said. "From the cook who doesn't wear clothing?"

Good lord. The game *had* changed a lot while she'd been out of it.

"Sexy aprons, for all I know," Vanessa said, and Willa could practically hear the eye roll. "Although I will admit, the guy's hot."

Willa felt a headache making itself known, pounding at her temples. She pushed at one steadily with her fingers as she held the phone in her other hand. "All right, I won't be seeing him. Maybe a phone call, at least? Or video chat is fine. It can even be in the middle of the night, but I need to get some sense of the guy."

"If you want a real sense of what we're looking for, I'll send you a link to his socials." Willa heard the sound of tapping. "It'll give you his voice and his style, if nothing else."

Willa frowned. "He doesn't even have a list of recipes for this, does he?" she murmured as the true dread of what she was going to sign up for hit her.

"No." Vanessa paused for a long second. "Okay, total transparency: no other ghostwriter wants to touch this. He is all over the map, and his food is . . . well, chaotic at best. He doesn't have any ideas. He just wants a turnkey cookbook that he can then work with a photographer to 'make sexy' and promote on his channels. So that's what I need you to. Come up with thirty recipes . . ."

"*Thirty?*" Willa said around a gasp.

". . . and make sure they're sexy. Or at least lend themselves to be eaten sexily. Or cooked sexily. Or something." Vanessa sighed.

Willa flinched.

"Sexy?" she finally echoed, her voice sounding hollow to her own ears.

"Well, make it so *he* can make them seem sexy, anyway," Vanessa added. "Which, honestly, could be anything. Donuts. Bananas. Figs. You see where I'm going here."

"Yeah, I see," Willa said, then straightened her spine. "Two months?"

"Two months."

"Half up front, half on completion?"

"Absolutely," Vanessa said, and the glee in her voice made Willa feel a little better. "I'll get the contract to your agent as soon as possible."

"No agent," Willa said, since at this point, she didn't have one. "Just . . . send it to me."

"Oh." Another pause. "Okay."

Willa was glad Vanessa didn't ask any further questions, but still felt it necessary to respond to the obvious curiosity in Vanessa's tone. "With Steven being sick the last few years, I was only doing the occasional freelance thing anyway," Willa said. "My agent and I agreed to part ways, amicably. She even said I could contact her when and if I decided to get back into the game. I think she retired last year, though."

"Happening a lot," Vanessa commiserated.

"Well, I've done enough ghost work to know the contracts, anyway," Willa said, hoping again that her voice sounded comfortable, casual. *Not weird.* "Once I get more contracts going, and am doing more work, I'll probably look around for another agent."

Hint, hint! I want you to consider me for more work!

"You slam-dunk this one, and I'm sure we can find you more projects," Vanessa said, and Willa bent a little against her countertop. "But I'm not going to lie. It's not going to be easy."

"Trust me," Willa said, her voice turning grim. "I can handle it."

Because she'd handled *not easy* for years. Trying to save a restaurant that was circling the drain wasn't easy. Losing their house and moving to a small rental at the other end of the state wasn't easy.

Watching her husband die, slowly, bitterly . . .

A pain-in-the-ass so-called "sexy chef" didn't even crack the top ten.

She could do this. She'd been up against the wall with worse disasters. She knew that she could cook anything, in theory, and reverse engineer any recipe. She knew big personalities. Sure, it'd been a while. But she could, without question, do this.

She'd just fake it until she made it.

"Okay!" Vanessa sounded relieved. "I will send over the links and the contracts. Can't wait to see the sexy stuff you come up with!"

"Thanks!" Willa chirped. As she hung up, though, those words finally sank in.

The sexy stuff . . .

That you come up with!

Willa stared at her phone, aghast.

"Oh, shit," she murmured.

Food, she could handle. All day long.

Sex . . . ?

There might be a problem after all.

CHAPTER 6

Hudson could usually tell whether a client was going to be a pain in the ass in the first five minutes of meeting them, and Patrick "tech dudebro" Ayres was definitely leaning that way.

Still, it would be a big job and would break in Hudson's new general contractor's license. So far, he'd only used it for a relatively small job, adding a room to the Sawyers' house, close to the school. It had been a good test run, but he'd gotten the license so he could sink his teeth into bigger jobs.

There was more money coming into the island. While he still had mixed feelings about that, there was no ignoring the way that people from Seattle, especially, were flocking to Marre, eager to make it a new Whidbey. That meant lots of remodels, rebuilds, even new housing. He knew the island better than any contractor who could be brought in. While it was always the client's choice, he hoped that he could maybe guide things so that they weren't building anything too monstrously gaudy, destroying the quirky local color the island had had for years.

"Great house, isn't it?"

Hudson nodded. "Gorgeous," he said, and meant it. Now that he was inside, he could see the details he'd wondered about. Intricate crown molding topped each room, details around the doorframes. Even parquet flooring in a herringbone pattern, scuffed though it was. He only got a glimpse of the ornate fireplace mantel.

"I want to keep it authentic, if I can," Patrick said. "I was lucky enough to cash out with our IPO, and that money let me buy this place, among other things. For me, it's more important to do it right than to cheap out, you know?"

Well, Hudson thought, that was encouraging, at least. He valued people who valued history and wanted to preserve it.

"Well, mostly authentic," Patrick amended as they walked down the dark hallway to the kitchen. "Some of the stuff's too over the top and will need to be replaced, and it's not like we're in a period piece, you know? I have to live here."

He chuckled, and Hudson shifted back to his original thought but held his tongue and opened his leather portfolio, getting his pen out and clicking it open. "So, first things—"

Patrick dove in. "I want a full kitchen remodel. I like cooking, it's a passion of mine, and I can't do that here as is. I mean, look at this stove. It's an *antique*."

Hudson couldn't stop staring. It was an antique, actually, and a gorgeous one.

"I can't imagine what the oven temperature's like," Patrick continued, "much less the heat consistency on the burners, and it'll be impossible to clean. I'm surprised the fridge doesn't use actual ice blocks, you know?"

He laughed at his own joke, and Hudson humored him with a smile even as he took in every detail. If they were still in working order, those appliances could be sold for a mint.

"Think they'll fit in the dumpster?"

Hudson's gaze spun to him. Was this guy kidding? But Patrick had stopped joking. Instead, he seemed to be mentally measuring the pieces.

"I want all new cabinets. Custom. New appliances," Patrick said, warming up to the topic. "Flooring . . . travertine, probably. Just that one poky old sink? Yeah, that's not going to work. And the window's way too small . . ."

"All right, I need to stop you for a sec," Hudson said, finally getting a word in edgewise. "Everything you're talking about? Is doable. No problem. But we need to get some details down first, okay?"

Patrick looked faintly irritated. "I know what I want, though."

"That's great," Hudson said, employing the charm he was famed for. "Trust me, it makes a difference to have a client that's not wishy-washy. But *I* don't know what you want, and there's kind of an order that will make that easier. Can I ask you some questions?"

Mollified, Patrick leaned against the countertop, nodding and taking the semicompliment.

"Starting with appliances: You know what you want? Specifically?" Hudson asked.

"A six-burner stove, easily," Patrick replied.

Hudson nodded. "Brand? Model number?"

Patrick blinked. "I'm just getting a bid from you, right?" he said. "Does it matter?"

Hudson had been ready for this. "Kinda, yeah," he said. "Because everything else is going to hinge on that. You want custom cabinets? It's easier to build around the appliances than try to fix and accommodate because we didn't get the measurements right. Also, it will impact the bid."

"I thought you'd offer me a selection," Patrick said with a sniff.

"I can do that," Hudson said, quickly telling himself that he'd add an asshole tax to this particular bid. "Six-burner, you said?"

From there, they hashed out the details. Complete gutting of the existing cabinetry, something that broke Hudson's heart a little, because while they were battered and could use some refreshing—new paint, or if he had his way, maybe just treating the natural wood—the cabinets were period authentic to when the old mill owner Karl Bauer had built this house in the late 1800s. There was a pie safe and matching plate rack. The frame of the window was wide, ready to accommodate plants.

Yeah, if you liked to cook, you probably wanted something more modern. But ripping out everything and tossing it away—including the beadboard, to be replaced with some god-awful who-knew-what—just felt wrong. Also, if this guy *did* throw everything out, you could bet your ass Hudson was taking it. It was no different from his grandfather scooping up that clock at the garage sale from people who were tossing what they thought was junk. Just because Patrick couldn't see the value didn't mean Hudson was going to let this stuff get destroyed.

After a lot of measuring, a long punch list, and some notes about who he'd tap for the more important elements of the job, he nodded. "Okay. I'll send along the bid with all your options," Hudson said.

"I spoke with some other people on the island who said you would be perfect for this job," Patrick said. "Which is good, because the last remodel I did cost way too much for what they did, in my opinion."

Hudson mentally upped the asshole tax on this bid. If he didn't love this house and didn't want a new project so badly, he'd have walked by now with some polite excuse.

"That said, I do have some experience with remodels," Patrick pointed out, his smile turning sharp. He shrugged. "So I know what it takes, and I know that it should be cheaper, seeing that you're local and all."

Hudson kept his temper, but his charm was starting to hit its limit. "You're absolutely right," he said, hoping his voice drawled out, calm and maybe a little amused. "Not only that, but I know the best electrician and plumber on the island, and if there's a trade that isn't available here, I know some great specialized contractors out of Tulalip and Mukilteo."

"Not Seattle?"

Hudson shrugged. "These are people I trust, that I've worked with before."

Patrick looked at him thoughtfully. "I'll be honest—I also heard you were a handyman."

Hudson's charm slid, and his tone turned cool. "That a problem?"

"*And* a licensed contractor?" The disbelief was clear.

"The general contractor license was recent," Hudson admitted. "Feels like the island's going to be in need of more of that kind of work."

"Have you actually *done* any work?"

"I have helped organize projects," Hudson said, feeling the back of his neck heat. It was worse knowing that Patrick wasn't actually wrong. He didn't have much experience, technically. Just because *he* knew he could do this didn't mean that Patrick ought to take him on faith. "And I've built an addition, here on the island. I've got photos on my phone, or you could go see it—the Sawyers would probably love to give you a tour."

"That's not necessary."

Hudson could tell from the pursing of his lips that he'd just fallen to the lowest tier of Patrick's candidates and felt the muscles in his arms tense. He put the pen in the leather binder, then closed it with a snap.

"I'll get you a bid by next week," Hudson said.

"That'd be great." Patrick's smile was polite and broad. He shook his hand halfheartedly, though. "Looking forward to seeing the difference between local and offshore prices, honestly!"

Which felt like a message: if Hudson wanted this job, he'd better come in rock bottom. If Patrick had so much money that it "wasn't an object," why the hell would he want to cut corners on so gorgeous a house? In his favorite room? If he was passionate about cooking?

Hudson tried not to fume as he headed out to his truck, but he slammed the door with more force than necessary.

This had been a total waste of time. Even though he felt angry, what was worse, he felt that little sting of pain, heard that voice from his past, that was always, *always* triggered in these kinds of situations.

I didn't want to stay stuck on this shitty island with a fucking handyman!

As he started the truck, he glanced over, across the street, to Willa's relatively small farmhouse. Compared to the imposing Victorian, it was a happy pale buttercream and looked cozy and inviting.

Just as well he'd decided not to see her, he thought. Because today, if she was withdrawn or wary, he probably wouldn't help the situation with his dark mood. He pulled out of the driveway and headed for home.

CHAPTER 7

By the time Hudson had made it back home, his father had gone off to work at the island's lone auto garage. Even though he was technically semiretired, he still showed up every weekday, just a bit later. Hudson could hear Kimber blaring music in the workshop by the milking barn where she took care of the goats, who were currently jumping around on hay bales and bleating at each other or munching on what grass they had. He walked into the kitchen, intent on getting some more caffeine in the hope it would improve his shitty mood.

His mother was drinking coffee, apparently having had the same idea. She pointed to the pot, and he grunted his thanks that there was some left. She took one look at him and sighed.

"Guess that didn't go well, huh?"

"He doesn't think I have enough experience." He stirred some creamer into the coffee, then thought *Fuck it* and grabbed the Hershey's syrup out of the fridge. Sometimes you just wanted sugar, even if you were forty-two. He dumped an unhealthy amount in, then put it back and stirred his coffee viciously, until a little whirlpool formed in the mug.

His mother bristled. "Everybody around here knows your work, though."

"Yeah, well, apparently that's not good enough, since he's had remodeling done in Seattle or somewhere, so he knows everything about it." He knew he sounded bitter. He *was* bitter. "Basically told me that if I didn't give him a bargain-basement bid, he'd be using someone else. To make it worse, he's got all this gorgeous period-original stuff—you wouldn't believe it, it just needs some love—and he's going to toss it all away to buy some fancy stuff that will look outdated in ten years and wear out in twenty."

"I'm sorry." His mother's face reflected the sentiment. "That had to hurt."

He gritted his teeth. It did, on a number of levels.

His mother set her mouth, then gestured for him to sit down. He did, puzzled at her suddenly grave expression. "Are you sure you want to go this route?" she asked.

"What are you talking about?"

"You've had a good run as a handyman, is all," she said, and he could tell she was picking her words carefully. "You have more than enough work, especially with Kenny being an ass about jobs. Most people here don't need a full remodel, and the ones that do, the ones that can actually afford to hire you, they're going to expect you to be there all the time. They're not going to understand that you have to run over to Mrs. Tennyson's to fix the rotten step on her back porch, or go to Dan and Kelly's because their son hit a baseball through the picture window."

He let out a defeated huff of breath.

"There's no shame in being a handyman, you know." There was some steel in her voice now. "There's a waiting list for fixes, from people who have lived here and have known you since you were a child. Even the new folk, the rich folk, have contacted you. It's steady work. You're making a good living."

"I know, Ma."

The damned thing was, he *did* know. He'd been doing odd jobs since he was in high school, and then when Amanda turned up pregnant just after graduation, he'd gone into overdrive and made it a true handyman business. He'd worked steady, bringing in enough to keep the kids fed and taken care of after Amanda moved out to go to law school. People on the island always needed things fixed. There were too many old houses.

But he didn't just want to fix plumbing endlessly because Kenny was an asshole on a power trip who charged too much and did a half-assed job.

Or patch up drywall because someone's kid had tried to golf in the living room.

Or finally replace the soffits that were rotting out under the eaves of somebody's house.

I didn't want to stay stuck on this shitty island with a fucking handyman!

He grimaced. He'd made his peace with Amanda, he really had. But that one sentence, the one that had finally closed the door on them, just seemed to stick with him, like a splinter you knew was there but couldn't see.

"So you think I should abandon the general contracting?" he said. "But there aren't a ton of old houses on the island—"

"No! No," she quickly said. "But . . . maybe you can just target building additions or things for a while? Or doing remodels that are more general? There isn't going to be a lot of call for restoring things, and I know that every time you see something—"

"Sure there are," he interrupted. "They're smaller, but we've got those Arts and Crafts bungalows, and the Cape Cods by the beach . . ." He trailed off at her irritated look. He should've known—she hated being interrupted. "Sorry."

"I'm saying, rather than doing the general contracting for older houses, why don't you do what you really used to love?" she said.

He looked at her. "Clock stuff?"

"You wouldn't have to limit yourself to clocks," she said with an encouraging smile. "You're like my father. You like tinkering, fixing things. I don't think there's a thing you couldn't restore, if you put your mind to it."

He made a half grunt. She wasn't wrong. There was a time when he would've really enjoyed being an antique restoration specialist. His family wasn't aware that he'd taken some courses in clock repair and restoration, in the city, over the past few years. Nothing terribly strenuous. He didn't know why he didn't tell them, other than he didn't want them asking questions. It was a private hobby, something that was purely his. Better they thought he was going to a club than that he was going to learn about pendulum quartz movements.

He did like restoration, though. It was gratifying. In a way, that's what he did as a handyman on the island. So many parts of it were old and broken or worn down, and he brought them back to life and use.

Restoration would be a nice side hustle, he had to admit. Less physically taxing.

Not that he was having that hard a time, but he could see his future if he kept up his one-man show: grimacing and grunting as he sat down in his recliner at night, popping ibuprofen for too-young-to-be-this-old aches instead of a partied-a-little-too-hard hangover.

Didn't mean he had to like it.

"Sorry," he repeated, only this time, it was for being grumpy. His mother meant well, he knew that, and he literally wouldn't have been able to do what he did, or take care of his kids, without her help. So he bit back any other curt words. "Maybe I'll go off island tonight. Blow off some steam."

Now she shook her head, and he groaned before she could launch into her usual tirade.

"No, Ma. I love you, but I don't need the lecture right now. I am a forty-two-year-old man."

"Which is my point exactly," she transitioned smoothly, as if he hadn't protested at all. "You're forty-two. Your kids are grown up. Do you really still need to 'blow off steam'? Haven't you outgrown this . . . this nail-and-bail stuff?"

"I don't know that twenty-three is grown up," he muttered, deliberately ignoring the fact that his mother had actually used the term "nail and bail." He'd be brain-bleaching that for weeks. "Especially when Kimber still lives here, and you and I both know Jeremy and that girlfriend of his aren't going to pan out."

"You were barely nineteen when you and Amanda had them," she said.

"And look how well that worked out."

Of course, that was when Kimber had to walk in. He saw her look of hurt and immediately felt like a complete shit. He got out of the chair, giving her a quick, hard hug. "I don't mean *you*," he said. "I meant how the marriage turned out. I love you, and Jeremy. I don't regret having you one bit."

"Thanks," Kimber said with her usual sarcasm, even though he saw the sting in her eyes. "That makes one of you."

He winced. "Come on. I can't speak for your mother, not really, but we both know she—"

"Loves me, I know, I know," Kimber said dismissively. "What's going on?"

His mother reddened. "Nothing, sweetie," she said. "How's the soap going?"

"The mix is cooling," Kimber replied after a quick suspicious glance between the two of them. "Then we'll start the stir for the trace."

His phone rang as they started babbling about what they were going to put in the thickening soap. He barely glanced at it, just eager to grab a lifeline out of this conversation. "Marre Island Fix-Its," he said, moving to the living room to get some quiet. "How can I help you?"

There was a momentary pause, long enough that he wondered if he'd somehow accidentally been butt-dialed. "Um, hi, yes," a woman's flustered voice finally said. "I . . . well, I think there's something wrong with my stove, and the woman at the grocery store gave me your number?"

"What's wrong with your stove?"

"If I knew," she said a little ruefully, "I wouldn't have called?"

He barked out a laugh. "No, I mean, what's it doing? Or not doing? Is it gas or electric?"

"Gas," she said. "And I don't hear it clicking, and the oven isn't heating. Since it's gas, I don't want to mess with it on my own. I don't smell anything, so I didn't call the gas company, although I don't even know how long it would take them to get here . . ."

"That's smart. Don't worry, you did the right thing," he said to relieve his caller. "I'll be over soon, but in the meantime, maybe open your windows, wait outside? Where are you?"

"Ah . . . kind of next door, I think," she said. "I'm Willa. We, ah, met last night? I returned your dog."

He felt his smile spread. "Willa, right," he drawled, leaning against the wall as his chest heated. "Of course. Well, I'm sorry your stove's not working, but I'm happy to help. I'll be there as soon as I can."

"Thank you. I appreciate it."

"No problem."

He hung up. It was like his brain did a complete one-eighty. He'd been pissed and exhausted and frustrated when he'd walked through the door. Now, one phone call had managed to do what a full cup of sickly sweet syrupy coffee hadn't. He felt energized. Not just awake but pumped up, like he was ready for a night in a club . . . or a longer night, with someone equally enthusiastic.

Not that Willa is either enthusiastic or interested. He thought back to his mother's nail-and-bail accusation.

That at least sobered him up a little, but he was still grinning when he walked back into the kitchen. His mother noticed immediately, of course.

"Who was that?"

"The new neighbor, Willa," he said, and no matter how he tried, the smile didn't leave his voice. "Her stove's not working, and it's gas, so I'm gonna run over there and make sure it's okay. Ms. Caroline was so old by the end there, I think she wasn't using much other than her microwave and toaster oven."

"That's nice," his mother said, then smiled herself . . . something more catlike. "And she's your age, you say?"

"Again: knock it off, Ma."

"That's what Gram was getting on you about?" Kimber said, then rolled her eyes. "You're not still trying to get him remarried, are you?"

"He's only forty-two," his mother repeated with a shrug.

"Okay, I'm . . ." He stopped himself. "Actually, before I leave: Do we have any extra blackberry jam I could have? Or some soap bars?"

Kimber narrowed her eyes. "Bearing gifts, huh?"

"Welcome present," he said. "Don't worry. I'm not going to push her. I just don't want her scared of me. I figure if she sees me in daylight and I'm bringing some island stuff, she'll relax a little." He didn't know why it was so important that she feel at home, but he also didn't really care. He tried not to overthink that kind of thing. He just didn't want her to feel uncomfortable. About anything, really.

His dad was right: don't shit where you eat. He'd never dated anybody on island since the divorce, and he wasn't going to start now, no matter how sweet the neighbor looked.

"I'll get some of the lavender oatmeal goat milk soap," his daughter said.

"I'll get the jam and honeycomb," his mother said. "Oh! And we've got some Sungold cherry tomatoes. Maybe some vegetables?"

"Thanks," he said, and moved quickly to help them gather his peace offering.

CHAPTER 8

Now that the storm had passed, the morning's sky was a lovely Wedgwood blue. Willa sat on the hanging bench on the front porch, waiting for the man from last night—Hudson, the apparent island repair god—to come.

She felt a little nervous. Not about the stove, per se. It wasn't like she'd smelled gas in the kitchen or anything, though she knew enough about gas stoves to know not to mess with it. Even if rationally there wasn't much chance, better safe than sorry. It was practically a family motto.

Not that her parents considered any decision she'd made, pretty much since she'd gotten together with Steven, to be safe, if she was honest. This endeavor, thinking of moving to a small island in the Pacific Northwest, was just the latest.

"I don't blame you for hying off to the PNW," her friend Nat had said as she'd packed her car to the brim with kitchen stuff and clothes. "It'll be good to go somewhere new, clear your head. Figure out what you want to do next. Your parents still on you about how you're going to make a living? Any thoughts there?"

Willa had nodded, biting her lip with embarrassment. "It's been a long haul, and I've been busy handling the estate stuff."

First for her husband, then her great-aunt. She had probate lawyers on speed dial and could talk about trusts in her sleep.

Her uncle—her father's brother—had volunteered to "help her out" (read: take over) when it came to executing her great-aunt Caroline's will, but Willa had refused, even though the man was Aunt Caroline's son. He was also shocked that she didn't simply liquidate the house. A small part of him might have wanted a bit of the money from the house, too, she realized. But she tried not to think about that. Her mother had also wanted her to sell, to *get the money* . . . because obviously, in her eyes, Willa needed to do *something*.

Nat had shifted her weight from one foot to the other, looking at her with concern. Willa was getting used to those looks from friends and family. Nat had flown down from the Bay Area to help her get packed, and she'd stayed at Nat's house as a rest stop on her way to the island. "You know you can ask me for anything," she'd said seriously.

"It's fine," Willa had assured her. "I appreciate you helping me out, but I could've done this by myself, you know."

"Of course you could. You are almost dangerously independent, you know that, right?"

Willa had grinned and shrugged, even though she knew it was a family tradition. From an Asian standpoint, or at least as far as her mother had told her, you didn't share family business outside the family, and you certainly didn't take favors. You'd owe someone, and they'd know that, essentially, you were weak. Willa's father came from sturdy Slavic stock, just a few generations emigrated. He felt the same. You counted on your family, and you didn't reach out for help if you didn't have to.

They also liked stability: steady jobs, no debt, tight budgets. Certainly not gig economy, hand-to-mouth, "frivolous" jobs like anything in the restaurant or food industry.

Willa actually had planned on being in a stable job, once upon a time. She'd gotten a degree in food science and probably would've wound up either in the FDA, writing guidelines and testing things, or working for a big corporate food conglomerate, making turnip chips taste like delicacies without revealing the trace amounts of things like sawdust they actually contained.

Then Steven had blown into her life like a comet, and she'd followed in his wake. She couldn't regret it. He'd introduced her to a dazzling array of culinary geniuses, and she'd learned more with them than she ever would have at a culinary school.

She could still remember eating fresh abalone with Chef Perry Park, back when you could still harvest it in Northern California. He'd taught her about flavor combinations, the perfect balance of heat and sweet, of salt and sour, and the punch of umami that made everything better.

She'd learned how to make perfect sourdough from the eccentric Berkeley baker Chef Lei D'amato. She'd learned how to make miso-caramel ice cream from the chef's girlfriend, pastry chef Phyllis Galanis.

Finally, she'd learned how to combine everything together under Marceline Dumonde, one of the most fearsome, brilliant, and wonderful people she'd ever known. Under her fierce but comprehensive tutelage, she'd found not only a mentor but a friend.

In those years, Steven ran what amounted to a culinary salon of chefs, restaurateurs, and investors. She'd helped organize their events. She'd cooked at their pop-ups. That was how she'd gotten into cookbook writing. It was flexible, and with the strange hours she worked, it made it easier.

When Steven had wanted to open a restaurant, it genuinely hadn't occurred to her that they could fail, with all that talent and energy around them. She'd been starstruck and optimistic. So had Steven, if she thought about it. She'd loved that about him. When it seemed like she'd always been tentative and confused about her future, he'd been fearless and focused. His confidence was one of her favorite things about him.

But they hadn't made it, and the house had paid the price, as well as their credit. And, ultimately, Steven's health.

She didn't want to blame that for the spiral that seemed to occur for the next few years. Steven was a type 1 diabetic, after all, with whatever genetic trigger that kicked in the disorder hitting him without warning. His bon vivant lifestyle hadn't caused his condition. His lifestyle was his way of rebelling *against* his condition. Where others could indulge in sugar and food and alcohol until their bodies were battered, his had been trying, in immune-compromised error, to kill him . . . in a slow process that had started when he was ten and would pick up speed until it finally won.

She'd married him when she was twenty-three and he was thirty-two, just one year after she'd graduated. He'd warned her at the time. She didn't care. She was in love, and she'd thought she knew what it meant, to commit to what was coming.

Now here she was. Alone and scrambling for some kind of security in a very unstable world.

She needed this cookbook. She needed to somehow get back to her life. It was easy to feel creative and to pull work out of your ass when you were twenty-three. Forty-six? Yeah. That was a lot harder.

At least she had the house as a backup. Yes, her parents would love it if she simply sold it, used it as a nest egg while she moved back home and got back on her financial feet. That was a last resort, though.

She turned on her tablet, opening up to the chef's short videos. If she was going to have to create a cookbook out of whole cloth, then she was going to have to click back into the mindset of a ghostwriter. She needed to know who this guy was and what he was about. Hopefully, with enough videos, she'd see a pattern. Then she could choose a theme, or at least sections, and flesh them out with recipes that made sense. That couldn't be that difficult.

Or at least so she thought . . . until she saw the first video.

Sam was a good-looking guy, no question there. He wasn't wearing a shirt, which she'd expected. From an objective standpoint, she felt the little stir of *Hey, he's pretty good looking.* He had muscle definition, but wasn't like bodybuilder-on-steroids bulked up. He had dark wavy hair that was tousled artfully. He smirked, revealing a deep dimple pitting his left cheek.

Everything about the guy screamed sex.

"Hey, gorgeous," he said to the camera, his tongue doing the world's quickest slick along his bottom lip. "Hungry? Me too. I thought I'd make us something yummy . . ."

She frowned. He had a decent voice, she supposed. And again, he was good looking. But he was making . . .

Wait. What the hell *was* he making?

"Asian pork belly tacos," he said, his hazel eyes twinkling.

"What the heck?" she muttered, backing it up.

In less than a minute, she saw a sped-up montage of him "being sexy" while cooking tacos. From what she could tell, it was just him flexing while squeezing lime. Shaking his butt (with rhythm, she'd give him that) while chopping onions, tomatoes, cilantro. Wiggling somehow and then licking his finger while making some kind of Asian dressing with soy sauce, oyster sauce, way too much ginger from the looks of it. (*And* hoisin and five spice? Did this guy just hit the ethnic aisle at his grocery?)

When he actually *slapped the pork belly*, then gave a little *ooh* sound, pursing his lips at the camera, she couldn't help it. She burst out in hysteria-tinged laughter.

"Oh, God," she whispered to herself, putting a hand on her face. "This is going to be *awful.*"

But it was the job. She'd just grit her teeth through some more of his videos and see if there was something she could pull out. Even if it was ridiculous, it was how she made a living. She'd make him seem like a sexy Michelin chef if she needed to, now that she knew what his shtick was.

She was thinking that as the truck pulled up. She quickly shut off her tablet—God knew she didn't want the guy seeing it and wondering if that was what got her hot and bothered. Actually, she didn't want him wondering *anything* about what made her hot and bothered.

It rolled to a stop. She stood up, putting the tablet down and smoothing her skirt. Which then made her frown because . . . why?

"Hey there," he called out as he left the cab of the truck.

His voice was just like she remembered: deep, rich, smooth. Like Swiss chocolate, the real stuff, not the stuff here in the States. It was almost hypnotic. The "sexy chef" on the videos *wished* he sounded like this guy.

She frowned. Not that it mattered, of course.

She was still pushing that invasive thought away when he stepped around the front of the cab, opened the passenger door, then pulled out an absolutely enormous gift basket.

"What's *that*?" she yelped.

He grinned, his expression full of mischief. "This," he said, holding up the basket, "is a welcome present."

"Why?"

His grin stretched into a full, amused smile. "Because you're new here? And we're neighbors? And you saved Noodle? Dealer's choice, really."

"Oh, you didn't have to—" she quickly protested, but he handed it to her, and she would have had to drop it if she refused. It wasn't light either.

"I know," he said. "My mother and my daughter helped, though. Welcome to the island, from Marigold Farm."

She thought about Nat's comment, about her being dangerously independent. He seemed nice, granted. Still, she could only imagine what this guy might want in exchange . . . and if she was honest, what paltry gift she could offer in return.

Not that he'd want anything, she internally scolded herself.

Not that she'd be interested in what that might look like.

She bit her lip, forcing herself to focus. There was no way she could graciously turn this down, she realized. Maybe she could overpay him for fixing the oven? For the first time, she hoped that a local tradesman *would* screw her over in the estimate.

"Now, why don't you show me the oven, and we can figure out what's going on there," he said, gesturing to the front door. Baffled, she lugged the basket, letting him open the screen door for her in a courtly gesture. His smile was still there, more gentle than anything . . . even if there seemed to be something more in his eyes, maybe? She wasn't sure what. She didn't think he was making fun of her, though. On a gut level, that didn't seem to be the case.

God. She'd kept her head down for so long, she didn't know *what* was the case anymore. She was out of practice hanging out with anyone but her parents, some lawyers, an accountant, and the few friends she kept in touch with. That wasn't helping *at all*.

"Come on in," she mumbled, and then walked into the kitchen, wondering how she should proceed.

CHAPTER 9

He followed Willa into the house.

She was wearing a sundress with reddish-pink flowers on it, he noticed, something perfect for an old house without air-conditioning in the Pacific Northwest in June. Her hair was cut about shoulder length, and in the daylight, he could see it was a glossy blue-black, mixed in with a few threads of gray . . . not a one out of place. If she was wearing makeup, he couldn't tell, other than that her full lips looked rosy again. Yet as casual as the whole getup probably was, he still had that impression of . . .

Quality. That wasn't quite right, he realized, and he'd never been much of a word guy anyway. But she was quality in the way that porcelain was, or cars. Or clocks. They didn't need a whole lot of bells and whistles to be amazing. His father always told him that cars like Rolls-Royces, or Maybachs at this point, weren't flashy like sports cars, but they were expensive because of the details. Every "quiet" bit of them was made with loving care, the highest attention to detail, the finest materials.

That's what he felt like, seeing her.

A lot of it might have had to do with her expressiveness. Her wide-eyed shock at the basket, for a starter. Her affection for Noodle. Her soft voice. Her quiet caution.

It was the caution that reminded him to be careful around her. One of the main goals of his coming over here was to make sure she wasn't uncomfortable in any way. He hated the thought of that, especially if he was the one who was triggering it.

Which was when he noticed she was lugging the too-heavy basket, and he felt like an ass. "Sorry," he said, reaching for her and grabbing the handle. "Let me—"

"No, that's fine," she rushed out, her voice soft and sweet, with an underlying note of stubbornness. "I've got this . . ."

But by that point, he'd already lifted it a bit. His fingers brushed against hers accidentally on the thick wicker handle, and she made a tiny little *meep* sound before letting it go.

"You okay?" he checked in.

She made a noncommittal noise, then cleared her throat. "Thank you. What's *in* here, though?"

"Things from our farm, or things that people make with things from our farm," he said. He put it on the sturdy pine kitchen table, noticing that it was the same—that it was Caroline's. "We raise some goats—my daughter, Kimber, does—and we sell the milk or use it to make soap, so that's in there. We've got some beehives too."

She glanced over her shoulder. "Really?"

"My mom's expanded her garden too," he said, seeing that she was engaged, the words sort of tumbling out. "And my daughter's looking to grow it even more. It's early in the season, especially for the west side, but we've got established cane berries: blackberries, raspberries, even some loganberries. We've also got some cherry trees. Sour and Rainier."

"There are Rainiers in there?" She stared at him, brown eyes shining like tigereye.

He couldn't help but smile back. Not that he did a lot with the farm, other than maintain things and do . . . well, whatever his mom or Kimber needed done, just like his dad did. But Willa was looking at him like he'd somehow given her gold.

Guess she likes cherries. His brain made a small note. "Yup," he said proudly. "And some veggies . . . again, little early in the season, but some beets, asparagus, stuff like that. Maybe radish?" Honestly, he hadn't been paying attention at that point, as Kimber and his mother had gone into hyperdrive and gathered the basket together while he made sure he looked okay, despite having *just* gone on a client quote.

Which he'd think about later.

"This is too much," she protested again, obviously flustered. "You . . . you can't just give me all this!"

"Why not?"

She spluttered. "Because . . . it's too much? Do you know how much Rainiers *cost?* And all that stuff!"

"We have a huge tree, and we don't mind sharing. We count on each other on the island," he said with a shrug. Then laughed. "Which doesn't make us sound like a cult at all. Guess you're not used to a small town?"

"Not at all," she admitted, with a small smile on those dusky-pink lips. "Grew up in Irvine, then moved to the Bay Area after college. Always a city . . . or a big suburb, at the least."

"Small towns are different," he said, then wondered if he sounded like a hick. He cleared his throat. "Islands especially. We're at the mercy of the ferry, unless you've got a boat of your own, and even then, nothing's really *easy.* We get used to taking care of each other. Your aunt was like that."

"Did you know her well?" she asked, and he detected a note of . . . he wasn't quite sure. Nostalgia, maybe? Or regret? Discomfort?

"Until she moved away a few years ago, sure. She'd been to a bunch of our barbecues, and I fixed stuff when she needed it. Ms. Caroline made the best cobbler on the island," he added as memory hit him. "Maybe western Washington, even."

Her smile was worth coaxing out. "She's the one who encouraged me to cook, taught me the basics. Even baking."

"Did she teach you how to make those cream cheese cookies? Because those were my favorites, behind the cobbler, anyway."

He was rewarded with a little laugh, and his chest warmed. *Hell, yeah! Progress!*

Then his brain did a double take.

Progress?

Dude! This wasn't happy hour at some dive bar, and she was just starting to trust him. Was he *trying* to screw this up?

She shifted her weight a little. "So . . . um, the oven . . . ?"

"Right!" Right. The whole reason he was here. He shook his head, like that would somehow help him focus. "Let's see what's up."

He started to pull the oven back.

"Oh! Um . . ."

He paused and looked over his shoulder. She was biting her full lower lip and looking anxious again.

"You okay?" he repeated.

"Don't . . . um, hurt yourself?"

He forced himself not to grin. "It's okay. I move heavy stuff all the time." Did that sound like bragging? Jesus. He really needed to get it together. "It's kinda part of the job. Sometimes. And stoves aren't actually that heavy."

"I knew that," he heard her mutter, but it didn't sound like she was annoyed with him. More at herself. Then she spoke up. "I'm more used to commercial stoves."

He noticed her fidgeting with her hands as she explained it, even though her expression was calmer than it had been.

She's a worrier.

He smiled, hopefully with reassurance.

He pulled it farther out, then looked at the gas line. It was an older appliance. He now vaguely remembered Ms. Caroline complaining about the oven. Hudson had volunteered to fix it for free, but before he could, Caroline had been moved to an elder living facility. The son hadn't even bothered to buy a new oven, instead renting the place out as an Airbnb.

Yet another reason to be glad that Willa had moved in.

He frowned. The gas shutoff valve should've been right there, behind the oven, but it wasn't . . . and the line led to a hole in the cabinet. He huffed out a slight groan, barely an exhalation.

"What is it?" she asked immediately. "What's wrong?"

"Nothing," he quickly said. "Just gonna have to go into one of the cabinets to find this valve, that's all. Do you mind if I empty this?"

"No. Do whatever you have to do."

He quickly pulled stuff out of the cabinet: old Farberware pots, ancient Tupperware. The CorningWare square things, white with blue flowers, just like his mother owned. When the cabinet was empty, he pulled a small flashlight out of his pocket and shone it around. Sure enough, covered in dust, there was the red metal valve . . . in the perpendicular shutoff position. He tugged at it, and it twisted easily back into the on position. He went back and tested it. The stove lit with a quiet *fwump*.

"Really? That's it?"

"Yup."

"Why was it shut off, though?" she asked, peering into the cabinet. "Do you think there's anything wrong with it? The oven, the stove? I don't want a gas leak."

"Let me look it over."

He opened it up, looking at the tubing, sniffing carefully and looking for any potential splits or weaknesses. After about fifteen minutes, he closed the cabinet, then turned on every burner and the oven. "The range is kinda dirty," he admitted. "That could be blocking some of the gas. But I don't think that's a big problem. Still, if you smell any gas, you let me know, and then go outside, okay?"

She nodded solemnly, tucking her hair behind her ear. "Why *do* you think he shut off the gas stove?"

Hudson grimaced. "When she told me there was something going on with the stove, her son had been hanging around a lot. He was"—he was about to say *an asshole*, but then remembered that Willa was this guy's niece—"concerned about Ms. Caroline's ability to cook. I think he brought his own repair guy, from Seattle or wherever."

She sighed. "You think the repairman shut off the gas? Maybe so my great-aunt couldn't cook anymore?"

He had his own suspicions, but he wasn't sure of his place on this, so he shrugged.

She looked sad.

"I'm surprised none of the Airbnb people complained, actually," he mused after he'd shoved the stove back in place.

"He *rented this place out?*"

Hudson studied her. "Well . . . yeah?"

"No wonder she left this place to me," she muttered. "And made me executor of her will. Uncle Harold was *so* pissed when he found out I was, not him."

Hudson felt his shoulders tense, his hands balling into fists before he knew it. "Did he give you a hard time?"

She looked surprised, and he supposed he'd growled it a little. He winced, hoping he wasn't scaring her.

Instead, she gave him a little smile. "Don't worry. I was raised by my mother to respect my elders, but I was raised by my father not to back down either. Uncle Harold's more bluster than actual bite."

Hudson shook the tension out of his hands, acknowledging what she'd said. Of course she was capable. Just because she was fine didn't mean she was fragile—quality had strength to it too. Hell, a lot of times it was built right in. So of course she wouldn't need him to, what, protect her?

A white knight in torn jeans and patched boots. *Yeah. That makes sense.*

He knew that the work was done, but he didn't want to leave immediately. That said, he also didn't want to wear out his welcome. He liked her, and she no longer seemed scared of him. That was probably as much of a win as he was gonna get.

"You've got my number," he reminded her, "and if anything else comes up, please reach out."

"Of course," she said, and he could've sworn her cheeks and the tips of her ears went pink.

He grinned. She might be polished and pressed and all, and she screamed "cultured." She might be a bottle of fine wine next to his beer can.

But when she blushed—holy shit, she was cute.

Too bad he doubted she'd take him up on the offer, unless something was *dire*.

He started walking back to the front door, passing the living room. He hadn't paid any attention to it when he walked in, too focused on her. Now, he got a look at the room, and he yelped.

"What the *hell*?" he breathed.

She walked into his back with a slight *oof*. "What?"

"Sorry," he quickly said, but walked into the room regardless. "Oh, crap. *Tell* me that your uncle isn't responsible for . . . for *this*."

When he turned to her, he noticed that she looked around. "This doesn't look like it did when I visited during summers," she agreed slowly. "I just figured her tastes had changed?"

"Hell no," Hudson said. "Trust me. She would *never* have agreed to this. This is to make it look good for those rental pictures," he added darkly. "He took out the built-in bookcases so he could fit in two pull-out sofas. And that mantel? What kind of prefab gaudy monstrosity is that, and what was he thinking? This is more of an Arts and Crafts house. It doesn't go with the stair banister, or the window frames . . . Seriously, what the hell?"

He winced, shutting up immediately. He'd come all this way to show her he wasn't scary, and being pissed about a slapdash shitty "remodel" was probably going to make her think he had anger issues.

"Sorry," he said, contrite. "I don't mean to . . . I'm not *actually* angry. Other than the fact that I think he took advantage of Ms. Caroline."

To his surprise, her eyes were blazing, and she nodded. Not a shrinking violet, he noticed with approval. "*I'm* angry," she said with a short, decided nod. "Aunt Caroline would've hated this, I think."

"I know she would've," he said with a sigh. He smiled. "The stuff in here was gorgeous. The woodwork, the built-ins, everything. This whole house could be a showpiece, but it was even better as just a home."

"I love that," she said.

They stood there for a long second, just smiling in agreement.

And his heart double-beat for a second, just a second.

I like this woman.

A whole lot.

He nodded. "Come stop by the farm anytime," he invited. "If you want more of anything in the basket."

"Oh! The basket," she said, startled. "Let me empty it, and you can bring it back."

"Nah." He winked at her, and she looked like he'd goosed her. "You can return it whenever. Just pop by."

With that, he retreated, getting into his truck. He was gratified when she stood on the porch, looking at him, her head tilted.

He waved, and after a second, she sent him a shy wave back before returning to the house.

This had all the hallmarks of a bad idea, he thought as he started the truck. But damned if he didn't like this woman.

Besides, like the saying went—just because it was a bad idea didn't mean it wasn't gonna be a good time.

CHAPTER 10

Two mornings later, Willa found herself pulling up the pitted dirt driveway of Marigold Farm. It had a cheerful wood sign, so she knew she was in the right place. She could see a dark log cabin off at the edge of the lawn area, a cute farm stand that was currently closed, and the yellow main house beyond. The barn was off to one side, weathered red with peeling paint, by the areas that she had to assume were the paddocks or whatever, where the goats ate grass and maybe some blackberry brambles . . . she could see a large cluster of the fruit choking a corner of the property. What she assumed were vegetable gardens were closed in with chain-link fencing, probably to fend off deer. It looked like it held the produce she'd received in her basket, in a cheerful, somewhat haphazard layout.

The chaos of it would've driven Steven nuts, she thought with a bittersweet smile. He was into aesthetics as well as actual product. The memory caused her only a small pang at this point, as so many memories of him did. It was like smacking your shin on the same coffee table you've hit a million times but you've never moved the table, because you were used to the pain.

She was nervous, and she wasn't sure why. Hudson *had* told her to stop by, after all. Besides, she was here for a specific reason: to return the basket and to pay him back for fixing the oven. He'd refused to take any money, since he'd insisted it wasn't actually "fixing" anything, just turning a knob. Still, she'd felt indebted by both the action and the food, and the thought that the scales were imbalanced made her skin itch.

She carefully pulled up to the farm stand, which was shuttered. It looked like it would open in an hour or so, although the posted hours said "more or less" next to them in an amusing hand-painted font. She parked, unsure of where they usually had customers or even guests park. Finally, taking a deep breath, she took the basket out of the passenger seat and then, straightening her spine and squaring her shoulders, headed for the farmhouse.

She hoped he was home. Or at least, she thought with a grimace, she hoped *someone* was home. This wasn't the kind of gift that she could leave on a doorstep, and she suddenly realized with irritation that that was poor planning on her part.

She admitted that the majority of her decision to return the favor was out of sheer procrastination because she was having a really hard time getting into the cookbook. She had stayed up way too late the previous two nights, trying to figure out what to do to start. She'd watched almost all the videos that "Sexy Chef Sam" had put up. There was simply no rhyme or reason to them. The only unifying factors were him and a lack of clothing. She'd even considered calling the cookbook *Things to Cook Practically Naked* but felt it was maybe too on the nose.

She rubbed at the inner corners of her eyes. Who was she kidding? Marketing would cross out the "practically" and slap it on the cover. With a glossy photo of his olive oil–greased torso, photoshopped Hawaiian-roll abs rippling under veiny crossed arms. Maybe a strategically placed chef's toque covering his no-no parts, somehow miraculously staying up without help. Sam, the Human Hat Rack.

Okay, maybe you're a little punchy there, Willa.

She had gotten a grand total of four hours of sleep the previous two nights. She'd also messed up a bunch of ingredients, which didn't help. At least they were small experiments. Finally, she'd decided to make her payback gift at around three in the morning. Now she was wielding several small restaurant to-go boxes (cardboard containers that she'd saved from Steven's restaurant, part of a plethora of things that she really ought to toss) filled with cherry-and-rhubarb cobbler, and a plastic container of goat-cheese-and-honey ice cream. She was pretty happy with how it had come out—which is more than she could say for the cherries jubilee recipe she tried for the cookbook, which was too painfully derivative . . . a cursory Google search could provide the same thing. While originality might not matter, this was the only way she could get back into ghostwriting cookbooks, and just phoning it in, tight deadline or not, probably wasn't going to help her cause. While the guy didn't seem to do anything particularly taxing, neither of them could rely on such painfully basic material accompanied by some cheeky hot-guy calendar shots.

Although maybe they *could*. Photos were the lifeblood of cookbooks nowadays, as far as she could tell, and some cheesecake shots of a sexy guy couldn't hurt.

She frowned. Also, she ought to consider including cheesecake, now that she thought about it.

She felt the beginnings of a headache starting, and she sighed. She'd take some ibuprofen and then get back to work.

She heard the barking and felt her heart lighten as Noodle came barreling out of the house, running straight at her and jumping.

"Hello, beautiful boyyyyy—" she started, but he was too excited. He rammed into her, sending her ass-over-teakettle onto the grass. She grunted, but he started licking her face. "Oof! No licking! Noodle!"

He seemed momentarily chastened, but his tail was still waggling, shaking his entire butt with excitement, so she couldn't feel that angry about it. Still, he'd spread everything everywhere, so she quickly picked the boxes up to put back in the basket. They'd be a mess, but at least they were cobblers . . .

As she started picking up the ice cream and tried to maneuver herself back onto her feet, she looked up.

There, right in front of her face, was a bearded, narrow visage with prominent teeth and eyes with vertical pupils, studying her.

With a yelp, she dropped the ice cream. It hit just right, the lid popping off and ice cream spilling onto the dry grass.

The thing *screamed* at her, and she jumped back with a scream of her own, almost tripping over her own feet.

"Goat," she muttered to herself, finally registering what she was seeing. It was about as tall as her waist, maybe her chest, with a thick barrel stomach and gray-beige fur going darker around its face and legs. It had a stub tail that wagged. Noodle seemed to give it a wide berth, hiding behind her, and frankly, she couldn't blame him.

The goat stared at her, completely unfazed. Then screamed at her again . . . and promptly bent down to start digging into the carton.

"Oh, no!" she protested, reaching down to try to stop it. At which point it glared at her, chin pointed aggressively, as if to say *I wish a bitch would try*.

Willa, absolutely that particular bitch, would *not* try, because she had a sense of self-preservation. Instead, she backed away slowly.

The goat screams had apparently been a combination warning and invitation, as two other goats came trotting up, bouncing like basketballs. They were smaller and black, and in a different frame of mind, she'd probably think they were cute. But by now Noodle had abandoned her and was bolting for the house.

"Now, now . . . nice goats . . . ," she tried, holding the basket up as the original goat unrepentantly dug into the ice cream. "Nice goats . . . nice *goooooats*!"

One of them, that actually *looked like it was smiling*, headbutted her immediately, knocking her on her ass again. Some of the boxes she'd just rescued slipped out.

NOPE. Nope nope nope nope nope . . .

They were between her and the farmhouse, and the cabin seemed miles away at this point. So she made a break for some hay bales she saw by the barn.

She didn't think that goats had a prey response, so she suspected that they thought she was playing with them. Which was probably why they then sprinted at her heels.

She was squealing very loudly, she realized on some psychological level, but she couldn't seem to help herself. The basket swung around as she made it to the hay bales and started to climb.

Of course, her brain immediately, if somewhat belatedly, provided her with a fact she'd gleaned from some long-forgotten documentary. Or possibly *Heidi* or *The Sound of Music*.

Goats are really good at jumping and climbing.

They immediately bounced by her side, intent on mugging her.

"Oh, *come on!*" she wailed as they tried to stick their heads in the basket to retrieve the remaining two boxes. "No, no, no!"

"Beelzebub! Satan! Knock it off!" a deep voice shouted.

She looked over to see Hudson walking over, a fierce look on his face. Behind him was a young woman wearing jeans and a tank top, her hair dyed blue. She rolled her eyes impatiently. "Midnight! Shadow!" she called, glaring at Hudson. "You need to call them by their *actual* names if they're going to respond, Dad." Then she held out something.

The agile thieves obediently made little goat noises, skipping off to the new offering. Obviously this woman was their favorite. She scratched them, and they nudged her with encouragement.

"You okay?" Hudson asked Willa, holding a hand out to her.

Her heart was racing. "I . . . yes. Sorry."

"For what?"

She took his hand, and he tugged her to an unsteady standing position on the hay bale. Then she squeaked when he let go and put his hands on her waist, lifting her easily before placing her on the ground like she weighed nothing.

"Oh. Sorry," he quickly echoed her, yanking his hands away like he'd just grabbed a cast-iron pan straight from the oven. "You okay?" he repeated.

She nodded, then looked at her basket. Only one small box remained. "Oh! Crap!" She looked up to see the young woman—his daughter?—grabbing what remained of the boxes, but the food was done for, and her heart sank. "Damn it," she muttered.

"I'm glad you came by," he said, and his voice was warm, but his expression was embarrassed. "Should've warned you about the goats, though."

"No, I'm sorry," she automatically responded. "I should've called, given you a heads-up." *Or just given you the food from my car, a quick handoff.* But it was all a bit late for that.

The goats had made short work of her thank-you-payback present. "Whatever it was, it looked good?" Hudson said, with an edge of teasing in his voice.

"It was cobbler," she said, now feeling bad again. "Cherry rhubarb. With, erm, goat-cheese-and-honey ice cream."

His eyes widened. "Wow. Sounds fancy."

Was it? Oh, God. She probably seemed like a snob. "Um . . . well, I had both fresh . . ."

"It sounded good," he reassured her, with a slow grin that made her insides warm.

"Um . . . well." She shoved the basket at him, then closed her eyes at her own clumsiness. "I figured you'd need the basket, and you'd given me the fruit and stuff . . ."

"It was nice. Thoughtful."

Gah. This was *way* more awkward than it needed to be. "Well, I hope you enjoy what's left!" she quickly rushed out, then started walking to her car.

"If you've got a minute," he said, making her slow in her tracks, "I'd like to introduce you to my family."

She winced again. What was *wrong* with her? She'd managed to charm restaurant investors, schmooze with reviewers and influencers, once upon a time. Was she really that out of practice?

"Of course," she said, and followed him.

"This is my daughter, Kimber. She raises and milks the goats and makes the related products. Also, she's our beekeeper."

Kimber smiled from where she had grabbed the (now empty) boxes and ice cream container, giving her a nod.

"I'm so sorry," Willa said again. "It won't hurt them, will it?"

"Did it have garlic or onions? Meat? Chocolate? Alcohol?"

"No," she said, describing the contents. Kimber shrugged.

"Should be fine. I'm sorry I'm missing out on the ice cream, though."

"I'll make some more," Willa promised.

"Grandpa's at the shop, and Gram's grocery shopping," Kimber said, "but I'm glad we got to meet."

Willa shifted uneasily from foot to foot but smiled back. "I, er, ought to get going. Thank you for the welcome basket." She looked at the remains of the food that the goats were gleefully lapping up. "I feel like I still owe you, though."

"I told you, we don't keep track on the island." Hudson's eyes gleamed, and the corner of his mouth kicked up.

That dimple's lethal.

It was weird, how she could see Sexy Chef Sam practically bare assed but one little divot peeking out near the corner of Hudson's upturned lips made her heart stutter and her breathing go shallow. She tucked her hair behind her ear, then frowned. She knew that was a nervous habit.

Why was she so nervous around this man?

"But if you're feeling bad, I'm sure we can come up with something," he said.

Her eyes widened.

"Kidding! I'm sorry, that was terrible," he said as his eyes widened in response. Kimber, on the other hand, burst out laughing. "I genuinely was . . . I am so . . . that wasn't what I meant!"

"He meant please feel free to stop by anytime," Kimber said, amusement still plain on her face. "And if you've got ice cream, hey, I'm not saying no."

Willa felt herself relax a fraction. Then she nodded and fled while she still could.

CHAPTER 11

Hudson nursed his pale ale while surveying the crowd. He'd taken a ferry over to Seattle, making his way to a bar/club that he'd been going to for about a year or two. It wasn't anything particularly special: a brick building with a door painted black, a plain bar with the usual mixed drinks and a few beers on tap. Still, the music was a good mix: nothing too pop, nothing too trendy or EDM, just a steady stream of sorta-Latin-sorta-alternative-but-still-danceable. Even country on some nights, not that he particularly cared for that. Not his kind of dancing. But it accomplished what it needed to: the crowd wasn't a bunch of college kids. The bar was close enough to an office complex that it was usually people trying to blow off steam after work.

Much like he was.

He was wearing his favorite jeans and a black T-shirt that was just tight enough to get second glances. He'd left his face unshaven. He knew that, especially for office workers, the "rough and ready" look played well.

He was here to get laid, point blank. He didn't feel particularly bad about that.

He'd used dating apps in the past, but after a few instances of that going wrong fast, he'd abandoned them. One time a woman, who obviously *should not* have been on any sort of dating site, wound up weeping about her ex for a solid hour as he'd bought her delivery dinner and listened. He got her to call her best friends, then fled. Another time, he'd had a woman who wanted him to tie her up and choke her . . . and then wanted to "switch." Which, hey, he wasn't going to yuck anybody's yum, but he'd literally just met this woman. There was no way in hell he was doing *anything* like that, from either angle, without some level of trust or even a simple heads-up, especially since nothing had come up in their messaging.

Now he did things the old-fashioned way: meet at a bar, size each other up, go back to someone's place (hers, obviously, since he didn't bring anyone home, and even if he'd been inclined, the island was very inconvenient for anybody from the city). Occasionally a hotel.

Have some fun, sweaty, athletic sex. Get off, leave happy. They didn't exchange numbers.

It wasn't that he hated relationships or anything, although he imagined that's what it looked like from the outside. He'd had a good role model with his parents, who had been married and in love for over forty years now. But his marriage to Amanda had been a mistake, for a number of reasons. She'd been his high school sweetheart (okay, senior-year sweetheart). But they shouldn't have gotten married when she got pregnant. It'd made sense at the time—it was the only way things *should* go, as far as the small town was concerned. (Well, except for her family. They were pissed enough to kick her out and then move off island.)

Since they'd divorced and he'd become sole guardian of the twins, those two kids had been his total focus. It might seem clichéd, but they were his whole fucking world. It wasn't just that he wanted to protect them from getting attached to someone who he might break up with, although there was certainly that fear, and he had some history there too. It was just that juggling actually caring for the two of them with being self-employed in order to care for them, and making sure he wasn't burning out his folks . . . that was already too much.

He didn't go off island often, and the women he got with understood very clearly that it was just sex, or least he tried to emphasize that idea as clearly as he could. It might make him a dick, but better to hurt feelings up front than essentially take advantage and then cause resentment later—or at least, that was the best he could come up with.

The problem was, he was *tired*. Getting dressed up (or at least dressed to fuck), then taking the ferry and a cab, paying a cover if there was a live band and the price of the drinks . . . meeting the women, seeing who was interested in just what he was, making sure they were at least somewhat compatible . . . the older he got, it just seemed to get more exhausting. And empty. Sometimes, he wondered if he wouldn't be happier just jerking off and sleeping. It'd certainly be cheaper.

His fatigue wasn't helping his current frame of mind. He knew that as he shook his head when the bartender's raised eyebrows and nod asked if he wanted another beer. He glanced down the bar, his gaze locking with a woman with sandy-blonde hair and a wide, mischievous smile. She had eyelashes so long and thick, he wondered if they were real, then silently cursed Kimber for telling him fake lashes were even a thing.

Still, he got up, making his way to sit next to her. "Hey," he said. *Really suave, asshole.*

She didn't seem to mind. "Hey, yourself," she said, leaning close to be heard over the music and, possibly not coincidentally, letting him get a good look at the cleavage that was presented in a sky-blue top. She looked up at him coyly through those thick eyelashes. "What's your name?"

"Hudson." He smiled. Damn it, he knew how to do this. "I was wondering if I could buy you a drink."

"*Were* you?" Her smile was flirty back. "Just a drink, hmm?"

"Depends on what else you're interested in."

It was all just a routine at this point, and he felt like he was going through the motions. It felt empty, like when you weren't hungry but you ate a whole damned bag of cheap potato chips in a flavor you weren't even crazy about because they were there and they were good enough.

I want to have an orgasm or two with a fun woman who also just wants to have an orgasm or two. Then I want to go home and sleep.

He winced at himself. He wasn't even sure if he was convincing himself anymore.

"You okay?" she asked, looking a little concerned, and he shook it off.

"Yeah. Just a long day."

"What do you do?" she asked, still flirty.

"Handyman," he said without thinking.

He saw the exact moment her interest waned. Those blue eyes dimmed and quickly looked elsewhere in the bar. "Oh! I think . . ."

"Your friend just got here?" he supplied, since that was the usual response when someone lost interest. She latched on to it, and he shrugged, giving her a friendly smile and nod before turning away. It didn't hurt. He didn't even know her.

Maybe he ought to just throw in the towel. He took another long sip of his beer. He'd just finish this off, and then . . .

"Hi!"

He glanced over his shoulder at a red-haired woman, who looked back at the two women flanking her, giggling and nodding encouragingly. Her friends, obviously. The redhead was probably in her thirties, on the younger side. "Hi," he replied.

They giggled again en masse. He suppressed the sigh. The young end of thirties, and acting even younger. He hoped she wasn't late twenties. Twenties was a deal-breaker for him. He refused to sleep with women who were closer in age to his kids than himself, thinking of how he'd feel if the situation was reversed with either of the twins.

"You're hot," the woman said without warning.

He grinned. It was the grin that he knew was, as a previous hook-up had said, panty melting. "You're not bad yourself, darlin'," he said, laying on the vaguely sexy drawl thick. Her responding smile was like a ninety-thousand-lumen flashlight.

At that moment, the DJ shifted to a song that had a good beat, something sexy but still kind of fast. He glanced over.

"You dance?"

"You asking?" Her expression looked like she was trying to challenge him, but the excitement was still there.

He smiled back, then led her to the small dance floor. There were a few other people—it was Wednesday, after all—but he got into the beat, moving easily. He'd gained his love of dancing from his mother. His father grumped about it sometimes, but Hudson knew, deep down, his dad liked dancing too. Sometimes the two of them would groove in the backyard during barbecues. His dad would smile at her like they were still twenty, meeting at some concert, falling head over heels. And while he'd never admit it, it made Hudson happy to see it. Hopeful.

It might seem weird to other men Hudson's age, but even when he couldn't get laid, he genuinely *liked* dancing.

He gave her space, watching her as he sank into the song, gauging her interest.

Dancing also told you a lot about a person—especially how they'd be in bed. He guessed by the way her gaze ate him up that she knew this already, and she seemed to like what she saw.

Unfortunately, he also saw what *she* was doing.

For one thing, she was all about acting sexy, which meant either she was more than a little tipsy or she was interested in getting laid. The second, obviously he was okay with—he, too, had that in mind. The first one, absolutely not.

Beyond that, she was off rhythm and, worse, seemed to hope that the gyrations and the shimmies and flaunting of her boobs would help him overlook that.

Honestly, with most men, it probably would. Even for him, it wasn't exactly a hard pass. But he got the feeling she'd be either over-enthusiastic or . . . well, *off rhythm*. And while he didn't mind doing the bulk of the work, or *all* the work, when it came to sex, he couldn't help but wince a little, especially when she decided to move up on him, rubbing her pelvis against his and running her nails up his chest.

He sighed, mentally smacking himself. *Get it together! What is wrong with you?!*

But he knew what was wrong with him. He still liked sex, but at this point, he didn't want to go through all this trouble just to get horizontal with a woman who he wasn't really all that attracted to. He was getting tired of hookups: the anonymity, the fast-food convenience, and the similar feeling of dissatisfaction and emptiness afterward.

Not that this was about her—he was sure she was a perfectly nice woman. It was him. He finished the song with her, hoping that she didn't notice he hadn't chubbed up. Was it an age thing?

Fuck. He hoped it wasn't an age thing.

They headed back to the bar. "Can I buy you a drink?" he tried again. He'd come all this way, after all, and she seemed pretty and amenable. Besides . . . if he was burned out on convenient sex, what did that leave? Relationships?

He didn't have a great track record there, and he wasn't going to start here, that was for damned sure.

"You really want to?" Her smile was more of a smirk, and her friends were watching like hawks. "Or do you wanna . . ."

Before she could finish, his phone buzzed. "Sorry," he said quickly, glancing at the display.

Willa?

It buzzed a couple of times—a few texts. He found his heart fluttering, just a little, in his chest, and the smile he'd been forcing all night turned suddenly, reflexively real.

"Gotta take this," he added, with what he hoped was an apologetic smile. She shrugged, a little irritated, and turned away from him.

He went outside, even though he didn't need to, the air cool compared to the bar's sweaty enclosed atmosphere. He scrolled through Willa's texts.

Willa: Hi. It's me.

Willa: You actually know it's me. Anyway. I would like to get a bid for fixing the living room? What Uncle Harold did was hideous, and I want it back to what it was, especially if I decide to flip it.

He grimaced. He immediately knew, in his gut, he didn't want her to flip the house.

For reasons.

Willa: Anyway, you seem to know the house, but if you need another visit to get the particulars, please let me know, we can schedule something. Thank you for your help.

He reread it. There was literally nothing in the text that could be taken as flirty. He could hear it in her voice: that soft, smooth, gentle tone. Yeah, it was purely professional, just this side of formal. There was that candor too. Like they were in this together, fighting the world of tacky remodelers like her uncle. He also liked that she appreciated his knowledge, seemed to respect what he did. Lots of people on the island trusted him to fix their homes. She didn't need to look at his portfolio or get him to undercut "actual" contractors or any of that.

She was something, someone, valuable. She treated *him* like she thought he was too.

He looked back at the bar, all interest gone.

Maybe he was getting tired, or old.

Or maybe . . . maybe he just wanted to get back on island.

For reasons.

CHAPTER 12

"Okay. Think *sexy*," she ordered herself in her empty kitchen.

So far, she'd come up with maybe a few tentative dishes, but there still wasn't any cohesion. She'd gone for low-hanging fruit, culling the best potentials from his existing material. They hadn't told her she *couldn't* use his videos, after all, and Vanessa had actually pointed her to his social media. Of course, she wanted to test the recipes themselves. In a lot of them, he didn't offer measurements, or the ones he did use seemed off.

That was the food scientist in her, though, not the ghostwriter of sexy cookbooks, she thought doggedly. She didn't have any time to waste.

She frowned at the blank page and thought about some of the ingredients she'd bought at the local grocery. It was small but surprisingly well stocked, even though their produce wasn't nearly as good as what she'd gotten from Marigold Farm. If she hadn't made such a spectacle of herself—and if she hadn't still been wary of the goats—she'd have gone back and cleared out the farm stand.

Maybe she'd put in an order with Hudson, she thought. Then felt her ears heat.

Stop that.

She sighed. Then she picked up her cell phone.

Nat picked up after a few rings. "Hey there. How's island life?"

"Pretty good," she prevaricated. "Getting my bearings, you know?"

"Still planning on living there?"

"I'd like to, maybe? I mean, it's still early, and I don't know if I'll like living here in winter or anything. But right now, in summer? It's beautiful," Willa said, doodling on the paper in front of her. She sketched the few Rainiers she had left, washed and ready for her to eat in a plain white bowl. "You wouldn't believe the fruit and vegetables out here too."

"Really?"

"Seriously. *Yum.*"

"I'll have to come up and visit," Nat said, the smile clear in her voice. "That's a hint, if you missed it, by the way."

Willa smiled back. "Let me get a little time under my belt. I'm still not sure how long I'm going to . . ."

Last here.

". . . stay here," she finished.

Nat paused. "Don't tell me. Your parents ever-so-helpfully suggested you sell and move back to Irvine."

Willa winced. They *had* had a brief conversation that afternoon, or at least she'd spoken with her mother. (Her father would rather be forced to jump out of a plane than talk on a phone, to anyone.) Her mother had gently circled around her intentions: "You can't live on your savings forever," she'd hinted.

The joke being on her, since Willa didn't really have savings, per se. The advance she'd received would carry her through the end of the summer. Then . . .

Well. Then she'd see what happened.

Her mother would be horrified.

"They'll get over it," Willa said, with a confidence she didn't feel. "I got a cookbook gig. Can't really talk about it specifically, but you won't *believe* what I've got to write about."

"Wait, wait, let me guess," Nat teased. "Purely vegan Super Bowl snacks."

"Nope." Although her mind started playing with ideas. It'd be hard, but that could be a fun challenge at some point.

"Okay, other direction. A hunter's guide to five-star cooking in the wild?"

"No."

Nat made a thoughtful *hmmm* sound. "How to cook hamsters?"

"What? *Ewww! No!*"

"All right, I'm out," Nat said. "What've you got?"

"I have to write a *sexy cookbook*," Willa said, laughing as she said it.

There was silence for a beat. Then Nat prompted: ". . . and?"

Willa's laughter cut off, and she frowned. "Let me restate that," Willa tried again. "*I* have to write a sexy cookbook."

"Still not seeing the challenge here," Nat said. "I mean, it's kind of boring, it's been done a billion times, I'm sure—like, every Valentine's Day—but what's the problem?"

Willa felt uncomfortable. She started sketching the water glass she'd been drinking from, half drained and sweating from the ice. "Well, there are some elements I can't talk about, like I said," Willa added. "But yeah. It's like everything's been done, and I don't feel . . ."

She stopped herself.

"You don't feel it, huh?" Nat's voice was gentle and understanding.

Willa sighed. "I really, really don't," she said. "Everything I'm thinking of seems either like a cliché or a stereotype. Or a joke."

And I'm really, really counting on this project to get me more assignments. She couldn't just phone it in. Not if she was going to keep working.

"That sucks," Nat said sympathetically. "But I know you, and I know you'll come up with something. Remember what Marceline always said?"

She had met Nat when Nat was a saucier at the Cloisters, under Marceline. Willa had staged there, to help her recipe process and because . . . well, because Marceline had not only been open to it, she'd *insisted*.

"Marceline said a lot of things," Willa pointed out fondly.

"She said that if things aren't working, or are boring, it's because you're thinking too small. You need to be bold. Bold flavors. Bold, unexpected combinations."

Willa remembered the woman's stern voice, her strong French accent only somehow adding to her gravitas, even if she was one of the kindest, most thoughtful people Willa knew. "Si tu as peur de merder," she murmured as the memory came back to her, "tu ne survivras pas dans ma cuisine."

"God, you even almost sounded like her there!"

Willa barked out a laugh. "Not sure if that's a compliment or not."

"Have you called her, since . . . ?"

Now Willa felt a burn of guilt. "No."

Nat sighed. "I'm glad that you still call me, that you trust me," she said. "But you know there are a lot of us that miss you, right? That you don't have to be alone?"

"I know." That was the worst part. She did. But for so long, she'd felt like part of a unit—Steven-and-Willa. He'd introduced her to so many of them. And then, when he'd died, she hadn't known how to reach out or what to say, especially in the face of incessant sympathy and plaintive, uncomfortable offers of help that she knew she'd never take.

"All right. Let's attack the problem," Nat said briskly, and Willa was grateful. "You said that you're not feeling inspired. So there's your answer. Get inspired."

"I've been trying," Willa said. "I told you, the ingredients here are—"

"Not with food, ding-dong," Nat scoffed. "Or at least, not just with food. Try focusing on the sexy aspect."

"Oh, *ugh*," Willa blurted out.

"So that's the problem," Nat said. "It's not just that you're writing a sexy *cookbook*. It's that you need to tap into your sexy side, period."

Willa felt her face flame. "You have no idea."

"All right. So, what turns you on?"

Willa laughed until she realized Nat was serious. "I can't talk about that!"

"Why not? We're all adults here, and trust me, I am impossible to shock."

"I'm not!" Willa protested. "I'm very easy to shock!"

"I'm not saying go watch a bunch of dungeon bondage porn," Nat said, and Willa choked on air. "I'm saying . . . all right, let's start smaller. Who do you find hot?"

Willa frowned. "You mean, like, actors?"

"Or singers, or whoever."

"I don't know. I don't really pay attention to that sort of thing. I mostly watch cooking stuff."

Unbidden, her mind provided a flash of Hudson in her kitchen, smiling at her over the ridiculously large welcome basket.

"I can't think of anyone," she squeaked, shoving the thought aside.

Nat huffed. "How about situations? When you watched movies, or from books you've read?" she pressed. "Anything?"

Willa thought hard, her mind scrambling to find something. "Um . . ."

"Seriously, anything," Nat said. "I'm not going to judge you, promise. This is brainstorming, so anything, no matter how bonkers, is a jumping-off point."

Willa felt her shoulders slump over. She drew a rough skull and crossbones. "I am so screwed," she finally said. "I literally can't think of anything."

"Oh, sweetie," Nat said, and it was tinged with sympathy. "Okay, I'm sorry to bring this up, but . . . does this have to do with Steven?"

God damn it. Willa felt cold flood over her.

"Because . . . everyone's grieving takes a different time period, I know that. I'm not trying to rush you or say you shouldn't be feeling anything that you're feeling. I'm just wondering if that's part of the issue, here?" Nat waited a beat. "That you haven't let go?"

Willa grimaced.

"It's not that," she said. "Not exactly."

She and Steven hadn't had sex in a while, especially in those last years. Since he'd died, it felt like she'd been dealing with one bureaucratic Gordian knot after the next. She'd been battling the aftereffects of death after several years of dealing with the realities of dying, when she'd been dealing with continual crises that cropped up like Whac-A-Moles.

It was hard to fantasize when you felt so exhausted you didn't dream.

"It's okay," Nat said without pushing any further. Which was why Nat was her best friend. "Maybe you can take some more time with this? Or just pass on the project, give it to someone else?"

Willa snapped out of it. "No! No," she said quickly. She wasn't going to reveal the depth of her desperation here. "It'll be fine. I just, you know, need to push through, find the angle. I'll figure it out."

"You always do this."

"Do what?" Willa asked, confused.

"Decide to brute-force things." There was a note of disapproval in her voice, but again—no pushing. "Well, you are right in one way: somehow, you usually pull it out in the eleventh hour. You're one of the best clutch players I know. Remember that ridiculous pop-up that Steven planned? The one in the graveyard, where we—"

"Cooked with Sterno because the camp stoves and stuff weren't working," Willa said, shaking her head but still chuckling. "That was so last minute. We had *no* prep time. I wanted to kill him!"

"Yeah, but it was amazing," Nat said. "People still talk about that, and you know how hard that is in our industry. Best Halloween ever."

Willa smiled.

"That was you, you know," Nat added. "Steven could dream bigger than anybody I've ever known, but you made things work."

Willa sketched a tartlet, shading it with the pencil. "Now I just have to make this work."

"You will."

With that, they said goodbye and hung up, with Willa promising to check in soon. She looked down at her page.

She'd sketched a bunch of food, some silly cartoon faces, some phrases from what she'd talked about with Nat. One, in particular, stood out to her.

Si tu as peur de merder, tu ne survivras pas dans ma cuisine.

She translated it in her head:

If you're afraid of fucking up, you won't survive in my kitchen.

She wasn't failing. She closed her eyes. *Think sexy, think sexy, think sexy . . .*

Before she gave up and threw the pencil at a wall in frustration, she thought of something.

Hudson, moving the oven. The back muscles flexing beneath his neat black polo shirt. The way his forearms bulged, slightly, with the effort.

The way his blue eyes shone at her.

That half smile.

She took a deep breath, then pulled out more ingredients.

There was not being afraid of fucking up, and outright courting disaster. She'd come up with inspiration somehow. But it was *not* going to be her next-door neighbor.

CHAPTER 13

That Saturday, Willa had earbuds in and was watching Sexy Chef Sam on her phone at her kitchen table. Part of it was because she was trying desperately to connect to the material and get some kind of framework for the cookbook, but part of it, she had to admit, was to avoid Hudson, her handyman/contractor/jack-of-all-trades.

He'd come out on Thursday and given her a quote to fix all the sundry damage that Uncle Harold's adventures in Airbnb-ing had wreaked on the house. All in all, the punch list had included repainting the rooms, tearing out the burned carpet in the second bedroom, patching the wall in the dining room, fixing the curtain rods in the living room, and replacing the built-in cabinets and missing piece of chair rail. Also fixing the banister, which seemed to be missing a few spindles. He had quoted her a reasonable price—honestly, it'd seemed too reasonable, but he assured her that pricing was different "here on the island" compared to California, or even Seattle.

"What kind of time frame did you want, though?" he asked, looking concerned. "Because it's kind of a big job, made up of a bunch of small jobs. Basically, I'm the only handyman on the island, and we've got some elderly people, as well as the local businesses and the schools. So if something goes out that needs an immediate fix . . ."

"Oh! No, I'm not really in any rush," she said quickly, then bit her lip as she thought about selling the house being plan B. "Well, not *really* a rush. Would end of, um . . ." She thought of her deadline. "September be okay?"

His laugh was rich and warm. Seriously, that bass rumble was downright dangerous. "Unless everyone's plumbing and electrical goes out at once, I'm sure I can get you all wrapped up long before then."

She'd almost *swooned*. And promptly agreed, signing the contract.

Now, after buying some supplies yesterday, he was over at her house that afternoon. She'd just decided to stay out of his way as much as possible—both to make sure she wasn't hindering what he had to do and for her own peace of mind, since she still wasn't quite sure what was going on there. She'd figured out she wasn't scared of him. It wasn't a red flag situation. It was just a weird *awareness*, like she was hyperalert and cataloged everything about him . . . like, when he'd walked in that day, she tracked that he was wearing a navy Mariners T-shirt that fit well enough to show off muscles without being obnoxious about it, and a similarly snug pair of jeans, as well as work boots that he'd meticulously wiped before covering them with booties despite her protests. "Don't want to track mud in," he'd reassured her in that fog-deep voice. As he'd walked past with his toolbox and a bucket full of supplies, heading for the living room, she'd taken an inadvertent deep breath in. He smelled like the hardware store, plywood, and paint, plus an overlay of sunshine and maybe hay, something vegetal.

It was like he was in 4K, she realized, and the rest of the world was at low resolution. He stood out, swamped her senses. It was unsettling. It was hard to process.

She decided the best thing was to just ignore it. She had enough on her plate without trying to puzzle out the disorienting response she was having to him.

The kitchen's pine table was the perfect place to work and avoid Hudson. It was too early to experiment with food . . . at least, it was for her. She knew some chefs liked to get food and just start messing with it. Marceline had been constantly on her case, saying that you couldn't *think* a dish, you had to *make* your way to a dish—but Willa was more scientist than artist. She needed a road map, *something* to work with, especially if she had to make a whole cookbook out of nothing.

Not to mention the fact that it was about being *sexy*, for God's sake. She hadn't lied when she'd talked with Nat, about what little she felt she could comfortably discuss. She couldn't remember the last time she'd actually felt turned on, and here she was, trying to create an entire catalog of performative sexiness for a guy whose claim to fame was creating dishes without training and, if she was honest, without a server safety card (especially if that time he made crème brûlée in boxer briefs was any indication).

She tried to ignore the sounds of Hudson in the other room. She was having enough problems focusing, and he did nothing to help with that. He was classically sexy—it was practically an empirical fact. She imagined she could post a photo—*not that she would*—and get thousands of people agreeing. Especially with that gleam in his eyes, that flirty smirk . . .

She shook her head, like Noodle flapping his ears. It was one thing to be attracted to a celebrity or singer or athlete or something, someone who was essentially a fictional construct and someone she'd never interact with on a personal level.

Being drawn to a real-life person? That was something else entirely.

Lusting after someone who was maybe twenty feet away? That felt . . .

Well, she wasn't sure how she felt. But it didn't seem like a good idea.

In her big blank sketchbook, she created four columns: *REPUTATION*, *PREPARATION*, *EATING*, and *COURSE*. Then she tried to think about what the sexiest things for each could be, even stooping low enough to Google it.

Unfortunately, she was coming up blank.

"What are you working on?"

She yelped, her pen leaving a haphazard slash on the paper as she spun to look over her shoulder.

Hudson grinned, looking sheepish. "Sorry, I didn't mean to pry."

"No. No, that's fine," she said.

"Like a menu?" He up-nodded at the notebook. "Couldn't help but notice."

"Oh." Was she blushing? Good God, she might be. Her cheeks felt hot, and she was glad she hadn't written down "sexy," or she'd probably catch fire. "It's, um, a project. I'm working on."

She couldn't tell anyone about it specifically, but he'd be around, so she didn't want to lie either.

"Food, huh?" He sounded amused, but not in a dismissive way. The way he smiled was encouraging, and his gaze was warm. He winked. "You seem like a good cook. Sounds like fun."

She groaned. "You'd think," she muttered, then cleared her throat and said more clearly, "I'm having a little, erm, writer's block. It's been a while since I wrote a cookbook."

"That's what you're doing?" Now he sounded impressed.

She wasn't sure she was supposed to divulge that much. But he might notice, and she doubted it would matter. "Anyway, um, yeah. Just brainstorming, you know."

He glanced at her (very short) list. "Raw oysters?" he asked. His expression didn't change—much—but the clear twinkle in his eyes suggested he was thinking of the usual dirty connotations with the food.

"I can hear a chuckle in there," she pointed out, and his smile grew. "And yeah. They're an aphrodisiac."

She then wanted to crawl into a hole. She'd *just* thought she was glad she hadn't written down even the word "sexy." So why was she volunteering that particular detail?

"I happen to like oysters," he said, continuing the conversation. "You?"

She was nodding before she knew that she was, then cleared her throat again. "But it's an appetizer," she said. "I figure desserts are going to be easy, and I can always create some nibbles, but the mains, the proteins, are going to be the hard part . . ."

Now I'm rambling. Why in the world would he be interested in any of this?

"Sorry," she immediately interrupted herself. "I kind of got lost in planning there. And, um, I want to do stuff that's in season, if at all possible. And come up with unique combinations, not just the usual stuff. This is always the hard part. Figuring stuff out."

"I've been like that on projects," he agreed, leaning against the table . . . in a very distracting, albeit probably unconsciously so, way. His waist was *right there*, for pity's sake.

And what was lower than his waist . . .

NOT THINKING ABOUT THAT.

She shifted her focus to the paper like she'd turn to stone if she looked away. "Did you need something? I've been going on and on."

"Don't worry. I like listening . . . I mean, it was interesting." He then stood up quickly, rubbing the back of his neck. "And no, I don't need anything. I just wanted to grab a glass of water, if that's okay?"

"Oh! Oh." She almost knocked the chair over in her haste. Why hadn't she thought of that? He'd been working for a couple of hours at this point. She looked at the clock. It was nearly three! "I'm so sorry!"

"Why're you sorry?" Again, that bemused expression, like he wasn't sure how to take her but he liked trying. "It's just a glass of water, Willa. You're fine." He gestured to the cupboards. "Do you mind if I . . . ?"

Her cheeks felt like they were on fire at this point. She popped up, opening one door, then another, before getting him a tall glass. When he went to fill it from the tap, she shook her head. "I've got a pitcher. It's nice and cold. And it's got some lemon slices and a bit of mint."

After he nodded, she got the glass rather than the pitcher, which was, in retrospect, foolish. Her fingertips brushed his as she took the glass from him, and she almost dropped it. She turned to the fridge and put the door between them, taking advantage of the cool air and the physical barrier to get some kind of a grip.

What the heck was going on?

She handed him the water, trying to avoid the sensation of their hands touching, but it was unavoidable. She clamped down on a shiver as he took it, then watched, riveted, as his Adam's apple bobbed as he took a long, steady drink.

She swallowed hard too. Sympathy thirst, maybe?

Some kinda thirst.

That thought was like someone goosing her. She moved quickly back to the table. "What are you working on today?" she asked. Her voice sounded squeaky and breathless, and she wanted to kick herself.

He put the now empty glass down on the counter. "Just prep, really. I decided to start in the living room. I'll get the walls cleaned and ready for painting, then rip out the old chair rail and replace it all."

"All today?"

He looked at her like she was adorable. "Not necessarily. Depends on how long I can stay . . . ?"

She bit her lip. Part of her wanted to say that he could stay as long as he wanted, just to get the thing done more quickly. But did she really want him here at night?

Wait. Why should that make a difference?

She was so confused.

It's sleep deprivation. "Whenever. But of course, I don't want you burning out or anything," she tacked on, with emphasis. "I know you've got other work, and the family farm, and all."

"I won't stay too late," he said. "I don't want to interrupt your sleep."

"I'm kind of an insomniac at this point, and I will be until this project's finished," she countered. Then frowned at herself. "But, again, your call."

He smiled. "I'll get back to work, then."

"Oh, right, yeah." She rubbed her arm nervously, looking back to the paper.

He started to walk away, but stopped by her chair for a long beat, not saying anything. Her breathing shallowed, and her pulse started to pick up. She could *feel* the heat coming off him, on the left side of her body, close enough to brush against.

"Uh . . . this isn't . . . I mean, I'm not a chef or anything. Not even all that much of a cook," he rumbled, and she found herself turning to look into his blue eyes. His expression was a little sheepish. "But we do this spicy-shrimp-and-watermelon skewer in the summer, usually at barbecues. It's good. If you're looking for something with protein?"

Spicy and cool, she thought. In season. Something a sexy chef could skewer . . .

Her mind suddenly had a *click* of realization. That would actually be delicious, she thought, scribbling down some ideas on a blank page. "*Perfect*! Thank you!" She beamed at him, so glad that her recalcitrant brain was contributing *something* that she could've hugged him.

"My pleasure." He looked at her . . . she wasn't sure *how* he looked at her. "If I think of anything else, I'll let you know."

He walked away.

Now, she was flooded with ideas. Maybe not all workable, but that didn't matter. All that mattered was she wasn't stuck anymore.

She felt flooded with gratitude as well. She was thrilled, almost drunk with the sensation. Hudson, with his sexy smile and hot body and his . . .

Her brain record-scratched.

His what *now?*

She blinked hard as the thing that had been hovering on the out-skirts of her mind finally walked up and slapped her.

The weird feeling. The hyperawareness. The way her mouth went dry as the frickin' Sahara when all he did was drink some water.

She was attracted to him, more than she'd wanted to acknowledge. Not just that—she was turned on. It just wasn't quite like anything she'd ever felt before. She'd been attracted to people. She'd been dazzled by Steven, who'd romanced her. She'd had boyfriends, in high school and college. They'd been like drinking champagne: effervescent, giving her a ticklish joy. Fun.

This . . . wasn't like that. This was like starving, and he was something she wanted to devour.

If they'd been in their twenties, this would've seemed more understandable. But she was forty-six and a widow. A decade or so of getting worn down had convinced her that sexy fun times probably weren't in the cards, much less finding an attraction that felt like getting slammed with a ten-G force.

She didn't have time to deal with an incendiary crush on someone. But she also couldn't deny the obvious: she needed to write a sexy cookbook, and this guy not only helped loosen up her creativity, he could be the key to making it phenomenal.

This guy is my muse.

That didn't mean she'd make a move of any sort. She wasn't ready for that. But she could maybe let herself fantasize a little, and see what happened.

CHAPTER 14

"Hey, Hudson?"

Hudson looked over from where he'd been working in the living room. He'd managed to get a lot of work done, here and there, at Willa's house. There was the usual emergency work that had interrupted, but he'd managed to see her for at least an hour or two daily for nearly two weeks. He was grateful that she'd been so patient.

It was becoming clear that seeing her was the highlight of his day, and he needed to think about why that was the case—and what to do about it.

She was wearing a pair of loose cargo pants and a T-shirt advertising some kind of food festival in California from a few years before. It had a drawing of vegetables dancing on it, like the snack foods in those old movie-intermission ads. Her short hair was pulled into two low pigtails. The funny thing was, she'd obviously put the pigtails in as a way to keep it out of the way. The fact that it was adorable probably hadn't crossed her mind.

Not in a pick-me way, as his daughter would've pointed out. Willa was this mix of oblivious and no nonsense, he'd realized. She didn't try and tempt him.

She didn't have to.

He'd catch glimpses of her sometimes, when he walked past the kitchen. She'd started fiddling around with food, and the house smelled amazing. She'd hum, and he didn't think she knew, but she danced as she worked, her hips swiveling to an unheard beat as she sliced peppers. She'd do a vague hip pop as she browned meat in a cast-iron skillet.

For a woman in sweats, essentially making a stew, she made the whole thing look outrageously sexy.

His body tightened, and he ignored it, as he'd done since he'd started working here. Just about since he'd *met* her, if he was being honest.

"Need something?" he finally responded, when he was sure his smile was just friendly and not *Hey, let's go have dinner and see what happens.*

"Oh! No, I don't need anything," she said immediately. "It's just . . . you've been working here since nine, and it's been hours."

"Oh?" Did she want him to leave, or something?

"Well . . . I mean, I thought you might be hungry?" She bit the corner of her lip. That slayed him. "So I, ah, thought I'd make you some lunch."

He grinned slowly. She didn't look at him—deliberately, it seemed—and her throat was flushed. Her apple-round cheeks were pink too.

He wasn't sure if she was as aware of him as he was of her, but he was fairly certain she felt something.

He suppressed a chuckle at the two of them. It was kind of ridiculous. He was forty-two, and he was fairly certain she was in her forties. But here they were, acting like teenagers. He certainly couldn't remember feeling like this in ages. He wondered, absently, what her story was.

"I'd love some lunch." He followed her into the kitchen.

"Do you like ham and cheese? Pickles? Mustard?"

"Sure."

He watched as she frowned thoughtfully, that little mouth of hers pursing like a perfect little rosebud as she considered options. "You ever had a Cubano sandwich?"

"Can't say as I have."

She nodded. "Okay. I just made some carnitas, which isn't necessarily standard, but it's close, so that should work," she muttered. She went to the fridge and pulled out an armful of ingredients, then a cutting board. "I'll slice it, instead of the usual shredding it, but it should still work. I don't have a plancha, either, but I think I can fake it."

He had no idea what she was talking about, but he still enjoyed watching her. She hummed softly, and there was a grace to the way she moved. Almost like a dance. He wondered, absently, what kind of music she liked. If she danced.

If she'd like to dance with him.

As he watched her carve slices from the pork, he realized that he was sweating. He'd been wrestling with fixing what turned out to be a problem with one of the HVAC vents, and in the summer heat, it'd been no joke. His face was soaked. Without thinking, he pulled the hem of his T-shirt up, wiping the sweat off.

He heard rather than saw that hiss of pain and quickly dropped his shirt. "Willa?"

She had her finger in her mouth and the knife over the sink. "I didn't get blood on any of the ingredients," she quickly reassured him.

"I don't give a damn about that," he shot back, concerned. "What happened?"

"I . . . um, wasn't paying attention. Knife slipped," she said.

He washed his hands, then took her finger in his hand. It didn't look too deep, but blood welled. "Do you have a first aid kit?"

She nodded. "In the cabinet by the fridge."

"This one?" He guessed correctly, pulling it out. "You washed your hand?"

"I can take care of it," she countered. "I don't . . ."

"I can't tell you how many times I had to do this for the kids," he said, sidetracking her argument and shepherding her against the counter. "I'm a pro, basically."

She looked a cross between confused and amused. "Practically a doctor."

He took a deep breath. She smelled like the soap they made at the farm: sweet floral and honey. He wondered if she'd smell like honey right there, at the juncture of her collarbone and her throat.

He really needed to get it together. This was important.

Frowning at himself, he examined the cut again. He cleaned it with an antiseptic wipe, causing her to hiss again. "Sorry," he said, hating that he'd caused her any hurt, even if it was necessary. Then he daubed the whole thing with some ointment before carefully wrapping it with a bandage. "Not too tight?"

"No," she said, her tone breathless.

They stared at each other for a second, and he felt his heart beating, just that much faster. It was ridiculous, but he was here for it.

"Let me finish the sandwich, then," he said. "Why don't you keep that elevated and sit down—"

That seemed to snap her out of it. "No!" Then she *blushed*. "I mean . . . no, it's fine. I've been cut way worse and still cooked a six-course meal."

"You're a chef?"

"No. It's kind of a long story." She shook her head. "I'll put on a latex glove, and I'll be good." She frowned. "Unless you'd rather I . . ."

"Can we stop this?" he finally asked, with a laugh.

"Stop . . . what?"

"We're falling over each other, trying to be so careful," he said. "I'm a simple guy. I like you, I like talking with you. I would love for you to make me a sandwich if you're offering. I like this house, and I'm glad you're letting me help you with it."

"I hired you!" she said, but there was a laugh there, even if her eyes looked inexplicably wild.

"Whatever. The bottom line is, you don't have to worry about what I'm thinking. I'll probably offend you. I'm not exactly smooth, or suave, or whatever. But I'll tell you if I'm upset about something, or if something's a bother, and I'll definitely want you to do the same, okay?"

"Um . . ." She looked uncomfortable. "I'm glad. That you're going to be honest with me, I mean."

He laughed. "And you're going to . . . ?"

"I think if I was that straightforward," she said ruefully, "my mother would somehow physically transport herself up from Irvine and strangle me."

He couldn't help it. He laughed, because she just made him feel better. Without thinking, he pulled her hand up, giving the bandage a quick kiss.

She stared at him like he'd sucked on her finger. Which . . . well, if it didn't have the bandage on it, would've been really, really tempting.

"Sorry," he lied. "Habit."

She nodded mutely. Then she shook her head, like she was trying to shake off a cobweb. "Right. Lunch." She pointed to a chair. "Sit. You're distracting me," she said with a shy smile.

"Yes, ma'am." He went to the table and sat down, still watching her.

"And quiet," she said.

He considered playing with her, drawing her into conversation, but he didn't want her to cut herself again, or burn herself. She pulled out two pans and put them on burners to heat. He watched as she assembled the sandwich, slathered it in butter, and then put it in one pan while pressing it down with the other. Within a matter of minutes, she had what looked like a restaurant-quality sandwich in front of him. When he took a bite, he moaned, closing his eyes. "This is *so fucking good.*"

When he opened his eyes, she was staring at him. He realized he'd cursed, and winced. Not only was it unprofessional, probably, but it was just . . . not classy.

Willa struck him as really classy. He cursed internally this time.

Not that he realistically had a chance. Not that he was even sure what he'd do if he *had* a chance.

But she looked down at the table, and then smiled. "Thank you," she said. With a fierce, quiet pride. "I like feeding people."

He tilted his head. "I don't get you."

Her gaze popped up. "What do you mean?"

"I don't know," he admitted. "I just . . . you're interesting."

Her laugh was short, and she tucked her hair behind her ear. "I assure you, I'm not."

"Do you like the island?"

She nodded. "I like that the water's so close," she said. "And that it's small. And I'd only been here a few times before, but I always loved the farmhouse."

"Are you considering staying or selling?" he asked, giving her time to answer his question while he continued to eat what was arguably one of the best sandwiches he'd ever had in his life.

"I haven't quite gotten that far," she said quietly, resting her head on her hand, her gaze unfocused, like she was looking at options in her mind. "Selling's plan B, but plan A's really hard, so . . . I don't know. One thing at a time, you know?"

He couldn't remember how many times he'd told himself that as the kids were growing up. When Amanda had left and he was struggling with managing them and feeling the loss of the marriage, the fact that he was living with his parents and toddler twins on island. Seeing his dreams of being a restoration expert vanish.

"Yeah," he finally said, with feeling. "I get you."

They chatted about less loaded subjects as he finished his meal. Finally, he pushed back, feeling full, just this side of food coma. "That," he said, "was awesome. Thank you."

"It's really nothing," she said, and when he quirked an eyebrow at her, she chuckled. "Really. If it were my A game, I'd have made the pan Cubano from scratch, and the pickles. Maybe even the mustard."

He whistled. "Damn. Must be hard to impress you."

"Nah." She smiled at him. "When it's just me, I've been known to eat ramen noodles with a slice of American cheese."

"What the hell?" he couldn't help but blurt out, and she laughed.

"It's when I'm tired, don't worry," she said. "Or when I get a craving."

"You like barbecue?" he found himself asking.

The idea had been brewing for a while, but he hadn't known how to get an opening. Now, he had the opportunity . . . and he was shooting his shot.

"I love barbecue," she said. "There's just something about it, you know? Even backyard barbecue tastes better."

"Great." He smiled. "My family has a barbecue every year. You should come."

Just like that, her smile fell. "Wait, what?"

"It's no big deal, but it's next weekend. It's a little early, but the Fourth lands during the week," he said. "It won't be too crowded, but there will be plenty of islanders there. Good way to meet your neighbors," he coaxed.

"But . . . I mean, they don't know me . . ."

"This way they will."

She bit her lip again. God, he wanted to do that.

He pulled out the big guns. "My parents would love to meet the woman I've been telling them about," he said, gauging her reaction. When she blanched, he backed off, adding, "Because I've been working here. And they knew your great-aunt."

"Oh," she said softly.

"It'd mean a lot to me," he finally said. "Please?"

She stared at him. "Okay."

He wanted to jump up, fist pump. It just *meant a lot*. He wasn't lying.

"Perfect." He loaded the plate in the dishwasher. Then he retreated, hoping he hadn't pressured her too much. He still wasn't sure where he thought today would go—really hadn't planned on admitting as much as he had, probably because he hadn't really admitted it to himself until it was ridiculously obvious that there was *something* there. But just because they had this goofy, magnetic, almost . . . well, he'd describe it as sweet . . . attraction to each other didn't mean that it would go any-where. He just knew that it felt like it was more than physical, different from the things he'd allowed himself to feel in the past. His marriage had been too early and too immature, and the one relationship he'd tried, with Sylvia, had been too stressed and had too many problems on both sides.

Now, at his age and where he was in his life, things could be different. He was willing to try.

Then again, maybe she'd sell . . . and maybe that was the best thing for them. But for now, he'd take this small step forward, even if he wasn't sure what path they were on. Or if they were even on the same path.

CHAPTER 15

Willa was surprised how many cars and motorcycles clogged the farm's driveway and what turned out to be their makeshift farm-stand parking lot. She parked on the road rather than risk getting boxed in. She had one plan: get in, give her contribution to the barbecue without any repeat of the goat incident, and then, after some pleasantries and light mingling, making a clean getaway.

It wasn't that she thought she'd dislike Hudson's family. If they were like Hudson and Kimber, she was sure they were wonderful: fun, friendly, kind. Hudson had made it clear that they were interested in meeting her.

It wasn't meeting the other islanders, either, or the fact that she'd be meeting relative strangers. She couldn't count how many parties, charity functions, and meet-and-greets she'd been to, even hosted, with Steven. Celebrations had been his life's blood, once upon a time.

She closed her eyes, sitting in the still car for a second. She wasn't avoiding the barbecue because of Steven, either, she acknowledged—and that was a bittersweet insight. She'd always miss Steven. The two years that had passed since his death didn't change that. But his passing wasn't dictating her choices, and it wasn't like she was living with his ghost, no matter how she recognized that memories still floated around her like steam . . . sometimes wisps, just a scent, sometimes strong enough to burn.

No, it was all the cookbook: the deadline, the pressure, the sheer necessity. She ought to have said no to the party. She could've made some excuse, made it up by bringing food some other time. *After* the deadline. But Hudson had asked her, with that hint of a dimple and those twinkling eyes and that rakish smile, and she'd heard her traitorous voice agreeing before her brain caught up with what she'd said.

She knew by this point it was attraction, especially after he'd basically called her out on it and admitted the same. She wasn't a fool. But the sensation was so alien and rusty that it was like relearning a language she hadn't spoken in decades. She hardly had the time to focus on anything, and she still wasn't sure what she'd do with the knowledge even if she did have the mental bandwidth for it.

She didn't deny it came in useful for the cookbook, though. At least, that's what she told herself. The sexy chefs in the TikToks made her smile. Hudson, when he lifted his shirt to wipe the sweat from his forehead and revealed that six-pack? Made her *gasp*. Her mouth went dry again, her brain fritzed out, and her heart slammed itself against her rib cage like a prisoner railing against containment.

For the love of God, find some *modicum of chill.*

She pulled it together. She would tentatively let herself feel . . . *whatever this thing was*, in the safe confines of her home, after she got what she needed to done. Otherwise, there was no way she could get the cookbook written. She'd just . . . admire him.

Respectfully.

From a distance.

And not today.

Even if pulling it together was like trying to throttle a rocket—sometimes it got loose and overwhelmed her.

When she finally felt like she'd pulled herself together (and when she realized her food needed to get to a freezer as soon as possible), she headed out. She had a brand-new batch of goat-cheese-and-honey ice cream made with what she'd initially saved for herself from the basket, now contained in an extra-secure plastic tub. She'd also made a burnt caramel sauce for it, and a test run of some chili-watermelon popsicles, taking inspiration from Hudson's original skewer suggestion. They both seemed perfect for summer and great for a picnic.

She glanced at her phone for the time. Half an hour, she told herself, then back to working on the damned cookbook.

There was an eclectic mix of partygoers at the crowded farm. Music played from speakers she couldn't see. Two charcoal grills were going . . . burgers, some kind of ribs maybe, from the smell of it. There was a keg nearby. It was flanked by some men and women in leather vests with patches and things that suggested they belonged to the motorcycles in the lot, but they all seemed friendly, interacting with people in Mariners T-shirts or tank tops. The age range was wide. There were teenagers tucked in corners, laughing and messing around. There were some young kids chasing each other with water guns. Even a few babies dotting the crowd, being handed around and fussed over.

She noticed a little nervously that the goats were running loose, and an assortment of those assembled—bikers, teens, and casual civilians—were trying to corral them back in their barn, with a varying degree of success, as the goats tried desperately to get at the food. When the crowd let out a roar of success at finally capturing the rascals, she couldn't help but smile.

It was idyllic. Fun. She wasn't surprised by Hudson's family having a happy gathering, although she was surprised by how the simple sweetness of the scene hit her. In some ways, it made her miss her friends from their restaurant days in the Bay Area, before the foreclosure and before Steven's condition had gotten bad enough to have them move down to LA. In other ways, it made her wish that she could slide into this community and just *fit*, like slipping into a warm bath.

Maybe when the book's done . . .

She made her way to the front of the house, intent on finding the kitchen. In her experience, the kitchen was the heart of any party, and the frozen desserts wouldn't keep themselves cold.

"You made it!"

She glanced over to see Kimber. She had a drink in hand and had been hanging with a few others that looked her age, with dyed hair, piercings, tattoos. They sent her friendly smiles and nods. Kimber looked thrilled.

"Hi," Willa returned with a warm smile, Kimber's obvious fondness making it impossible to do anything else. "Okay to put these in the freezer? Or do you have an ice chest?"

Kimber's eyes went wide. "Is that more of that ice cream?"

Willa nodded, and Kimber looped an arm through hers. "Come with me. I can't *wait* to try this!"

Willa found herself drawn into the farmhouse. It was bigger than hers, or at least looked that way from the outside. The kitchen was on the ground floor, and as she'd expected, it was crowded with people laughing and talking. Food was laid out on the large square kitchen table as well as the kitchen counters.

"Grandma," Kimber said, interrupting a conversation, then smirked and nodded at Willa.

The woman was wearing a tank top and a pair of jeans. Her gray hair tumbled around her shoulders. She wasn't wearing makeup that Willa could tell, and she had laugh lines from obvious decades of merriment. Her blue eyes twinkled, just like Hudson's.

"It's nice to meet you," Willa said reflexively, then handed over the food with both hands. "Ah, you'll want to get that in the freezer . . . ?"

"Not before I get some!" Kimber protested, and the grandmother shook her head but laughed.

"Greedy. Get us both bowls," she instructed before turning back to Willa. "I'm Marigold, but you can call me Mari. Can I get you a drink? We've got some fresh blackberry-mint margaritas going."

"They sound weird," Kimber added over her shoulder as she scooped out two bowls from the container. "But they're good. Did you want some of this?"

"No, thank you," Willa said, first to Mari, then Kimber. "The small container is the sauce for it, by the way. It's, um, a burnt caramel."

Both Mari and Kimber cooed. The other people in the kitchen, mostly women, looked at her curiously.

Mari's smile widened, almost impossibly. "This is Willa! She's Caroline's great-niece—you remember Caroline, the one who made those baby blankets and had the Swedish meatballs for potlucks? Willa just moved into her house."

There was a chatter of happy, excited acknowledgment, with people saying "hello" and "welcome," and some random offers of "if you need anything," which made her chest warm. She nodded back, feeling shy but grateful.

"Hudson's doing repairs at her house," Mari added, but her expression seemed . . . smug? Maybe not that—she didn't seem the type—but the little sentence seemed to convey more meaning, and Willa wasn't sure why. "He invited her to the barbecue."

The way the kitchen went into a stunned silence made Willa freeze, especially when all of them immediately stared at her.

"*Really*," someone drawled. Mari nodded with satisfaction.

Then, just like that, questions and comments exploded around her.

"Are you moving to the island permanently, then?"

"What do you do for a living?"

"Hudson, really?" a woman said to Kimber, shock clear in her voice. "But . . . he never . . . she's an islander! He's never been with anybody from the island! He just, y'know, goes off island for, erm, fun!"

Mari glared at the woman, who immediately reddened and headed out the back door, mumbling something about checking on her husband, since he was helping to man the grill.

"This ice cream," Kimber said, obviously trying to change the subject, "is amazing, Willa."

"Thanks," Willa said, feeling uncomfortable. Did people think she and Hudson were dating? Or . . . was he so anticommitment that him expressing potential interest in *anyone* was a matter of conversation? It was hard to tell. She wasn't even sure how she felt about it. Small towns were hotbeds of gossip, weren't they? She only had Hallmark and romances she'd read when she was super stressed to go off, so she wasn't entirely sure. "That means a lot, coming from you. Your dad's mentioned some of your farm-stand products, with the berries and such. I'm impressed."

Another person laughed. "You should try her cookies!"

Kimber rolled her eyes.

"You bake?" Willa smiled, feeling a true kindred spirit.

"Sometimes, when I feel like it," Kimber said. "I made chocolate chip cookies."

"Those are my favorites," Willa admitted. "I don't make them that often, and I feel like now, too many people write them off as too basic, but they're classic for a reason. I've got a recipe that's a mix of Smitten Kitchen's and J. Kenji López-Alt's versions. Can I try one?"

For the first time, she saw the self-assured young woman actually look embarrassed. "Right. About that . . ."

The assembled group burst into laughter. Willa wondered if she'd somehow accidentally stumbled into a faux pas but couldn't for the life of her figure out what it was.

"They're, uh, edibles."

Willa didn't put it together. They were cookies. Of course they'd be edible?

The confusion must've been clear on her face because Kimber laughed awkwardly. "That means they've got weed in them."

Kimber seemed so uncomfortable—as if she was expecting Willa to judge her, and that she was going to be found wanting—that Willa immediately felt bad. She liked Kimber, and had since she'd met her. She just had this liveliness, this confidence. It didn't seem right to put her in the position of being judged at all.

Willa had never had weed. For that matter, she'd rarely drunk, really, and in college, she'd been a bit too uptight to do much more than that. Steven hadn't indulged, either, since he'd hated the sensation of smoke in his lungs and felt that weed "ruined the flavor" too much to make it worth his while to consume orally.

What the hell? She could always walk home if she needed to, she reasoned, or get an Uber. Or maybe she could consider letting someone else give her a lift.

She shook her head at herself. By a specific "someone else," if she was honest. She didn't take favors from just anyone, but she felt pretty confident that Hudson could drive her.

She didn't feel as bad asking him to help, for a good cause like this, if she needed to.

"I'd love to have one, if you're offering," she said bravely, and the responding smile on Kimber's face was worth it.

"They're . . . I mean, they're not gourmet or anything," Kimber hedged after retrieving a plastic container from a high shelf in one of the kitchen cabinets. "But they're okay?"

She broke the cookie into fourths, for some reason, putting it all on a napkin.

Willa popped one of the pieces in her mouth. She couldn't help it . . . after years around chefs, after helping Steven open his own restaurant, after hearing shoptalk—hell, after her food science degree—she automatically went into analysis mode.

"I do mean to, um, adjust the recipe," Kimber said when Willa hadn't said anything for a while. "I know it's not quite right, but I don't know what to fix. Maybe more chocolate chips?"

"It's not that," Willa mused. "It's interesting. You really get that grassy flavor . . . very vegetal. Not that it's a bad thing," she rushed to reassure her. "I think if you amped up the other flavors . . . Do you brown the butter?"

Kimber shook her head. "Did you want a glass of milk to go with it?"

"That'd be great," Willa agreed, and Kimber turned away to get her a mug. She ate another quarter.

"That'll give it more of a nutty flavor, stronger," Willa said. "And let the dough sit overnight. Freeze, if possible. That'll make a difference. I like making my own brown sugar, going a bit heavier on the molasses too. Those could all help. I wonder if there's something—not to mask it, exactly, but to use as a counterpoint . . ."

Willa frowned thoughtfully, then ate the other two pieces. In her mind, she could already think of the adjustments, and the challenges. Marijuana was a strong flavor. She wondered if it would work better in something savory, herb heavy, to disguise it.

"Maybe I could have another one?" Willa asked. "I'll be able to pin it down."

Now everyone was staring at her again, and she winced, suddenly feeling self-conscious. She wasn't even sure how much marijuana cost, and she was asking for more. Good grief, had she completely lost her social skills?

"Willa," Mari said carefully, "you *have* had edibles before, right?"

"Actually, no," Willa said. "Why? Is that a problem?"

Kimber went pale. "Shit," she breathed.

"Oh, dear. I think you'll be staying with us tonight, sweetie," Mari added.

Fear suddenly gripped Willa. It literally hadn't occurred to her that it would be a problem—she'd focused on the cookie, not on the special ingredient, at least not past how it tasted. She'd figured it was one cookie. "Is this going to be bad?"

"No," Mari said in a confident tone that was belied by the concerned look she swapped with Kimber. "But we'll be keeping an eye on you. Just in case."

CHAPTER 16

Hudson noticed that Willa had arrived and disappeared into the kitchen, but he'd given her a bit of space, letting her make friends without him hovering. He knew that once they were next to each other, his own expression would show how obviously attracted he was to her, and he wasn't quite ready to hear the peanut gallery of Marre Island weighing in on whether or not it was smart, or grilling her about her future plans (or him about his intentions), or giving him advice. This thing between him and Willa felt delicate, almost private. So he was giving her time and space, although he was making sure of where she was and what she was up to.

He'd seen Kimber taking her around, introducing her to some people, and his mother doing the same. Initially, she had that "polite but cool" expression he'd first seen on her—that wall of, well, classiness that wasn't judgy but wasn't welcoming either. But she'd started to come around. He'd said hi, and she'd waved back, her cheeks going pink.

He'd been standing by his father at one of the grills, nursing a beer, when he'd greeted her. His father must've caught his smile, because when he turned back to him, his father's eyebrows had jumped up.

"What?" he asked, trying not to sound defensive.

"I haven't seen you smile like that in years," his father said. "Maybe ever."

Which was why he'd given her an hour, while he socialized with islanders and his dad's friends and even some of Kimber's crew, before slowly making his way toward the kitchen, where he knew Willa had disappeared to.

He knew that, left to her own devices back at her farmhouse, Willa would still be acting like a mad scientist of cookbookery, muttering to herself, stirring and baking, humming and dancing. Still, if she was going to be on the island, it wouldn't hurt her for her to get to know the people around her, because they sure as hell would want to get to know her. He hadn't been exaggerating: they relied on each other on the island, and they didn't keep score. Sure, there was the usual small-town bullshit—like Mrs. Tennyson *still* trying to get him together with her daughter—but when you couldn't just drive to the nearest grocery store at eleven at night, or you couldn't get a professional to help you out in a storm and your generator ran out of gas, it was good to know you had neighbors and friends who had your back. Even people who annoyed you were part of the island, and they'd learned to have that trust.

Well . . . maybe not with annoying fucking Patrick, the new owner of the Victorian across from Willa—the bougie gentrifier who wouldn't know true architectural style if it fell on him. He could fuck himself, and he hadn't been invited to the barbecue.

He up-nodded a few hellos, giving a bro hug to one of his dad's friends, a quick regular hug to his mom's knitting partner in crime, Libby.

Amanda had hated it, being part of the community, a little part of him remembered. Hated *needing* to be part of the community. He'd sort of written it off as the usual teenage rebellion when they'd been in high school, but he'd figured out soon enough that it went deeper than that. There was no way they could've managed the twins when they were first married without that not-so-invisible network, and while she was grateful, she'd also resented every sympathetic nod, every donated set of clothes, every "don't worry about it" as they'd dropped the kids off for babysitting so one or both of them could grab a few hours' sleep.

She'd practically choked on every casserole.

That was ultimately why they had divorced, other than the obvious reason that she was trapped in a life she did not want. Personally, Hudson didn't have any problem with the island's support system, since he'd needed the help even more once it was just him and two toddlers. He loved his family and was grateful for this community in his bones, and he wouldn't forget it.

Even if sometimes he wanted just a little something different.

"Uncle Bruno, *really.*"

Hudson winced as he opened the back door into the kitchen. It sounded like Kimber and his "uncle"—one of Dad's oldest biker friends—were getting into it. He prayed it wasn't politics. While he liked that Kimber stood up for herself and he loved Bruno, he really did not feel up to playing mediator or watching their antics today, especially when he was, deliberately or not, trying to impress Willa.

"Hey, what's going on?" he interrupted, looking around.

His father and Uncle Bruno were leaning against the center island, one he'd installed a few years ago. Across from them, like an opposing army, were his mother and Kimber, arms crossed, matching frowns, chins tilted up in challenge. More surprisingly, Willa was standing between them, looking a little dazed. Not scared or nervous. Just sort of . . .

Out of it? Not the numb, withdrawn Willa he'd first met, though. More like a floaty, untethered Willa.

That made him seriously nervous.

Before he could really process it, Kimber shouted, "Who I fuck isn't anybody's business!"

His mouth dropped open. He was used to Kimber's tirades, but even for her, this was pretty crass. His mother cleared her throat. "Kimber . . ."

Kimber quickly pointed at Bruno. "*He* said it first!"

Would you believe she's twenty-three years old? My daughter, folks.

Bruno growled and looked imposing. It didn't help that the guy was over six feet and built like a Frigidaire. His shaggy hair was grayer at this point than the dark brown Hudson remembered from when he was a kid, and his thick beard didn't hide his scowl. Not that Kimber seemed to care, and not that Hudson thought he'd hurt her or anything. But it was a party, and for *once*, just once, Hudson wished they could do it without at least one incident.

He wasn't going to pretend to be something he wasn't, and he wanted Willa to accept him for who he was. Furthermore, anybody who had a problem with his family wasn't someone he was going to have anything to do with. But again, just for once, he really, really wished that they could discuss stuff without turning it into a free-for-all worthy of reality TV.

"He's judging my dating life," Kimber accused with a scowl of her own, not backing down.

Bruno scoffed. "Sleeping with a new guy every couple of days isn't *dating*," he pointed out. Kimber responded by rolling her eyes.

"When did you get so conservative, Bruno?" Hudson's mother asked pointedly. "Remember the seventies? We were *plenty* promiscuous back then, right?"

"Yeah, but you settled down with Dan here, and you put that shit aside. You were younger than Kimber."

"Yeah, and Dad was even younger than that when he and Mom had Jeremy and me," Kimber shot out. "I want to go for that why?"

"Hey," Hudson snapped, and at least she winced.

"Sorry, Dad," she mumbled. "But you see what I mean. Dad does *exactly* what I do, and I don't see you getting on him for being a man-whore now."

"*Jesus.*" Hudson glanced at Willa, worried about her reaction to that term and the fact that Kimber had directed it at *him*. They hadn't really discussed much in that area.

He hadn't even kissed her yet, and here his daughter was, acting like he was . . . How had his mother put it? *Nailing and bailing* everybody he could get his hands on.

He literally cringed.

Willa didn't seem to care. She just had a lopsided, amused smile. Then she started giggling.

"It's different," Bruno said with a wave of his hand. "Your dad's a *guy.*"

He might as well have waved a big red flag in front of a pair of bulls. Hudson sighed as his daughter's and mother's feminist lights went from "armed" to "fire."

Shit. Now it's on.

His father must've had the same thought because he looked up to the ceiling like he was praying for strength. "Bruno, Bruno, Bruno . . ."

Kimber's eyes narrowed. "You are *not* going to—"

"I'm just saying," Bruno interrupted, apparently physically incapable of reading the room, "a key that opens up a lot of locks? That's a master key. But a lock that opens up to any old key? That's the definition of a shitty lock."

Kimber's face turned purple, and Hudson's mom's eyes went even wider, her nostrils flaring. His dad groaned.

Hudson knew they were about a second away from an epic shouting match. He was fully ready to defend his daughter . . . not, he knew firsthand, that she needed it. She'd been fighting her own battles since she was six, even some of Jeremy's. And his mom was certainly not somebody to cross, something Bruno knew. Still, Hudson couldn't just stand there.

But to his shock, he didn't need to.

Willa, as the kids would say, had entered the chat.

"Not a combination lock."

He blinked. So did everyone else. Willa had said it with a surprised, just-this-side-of-loud tone of voice.

"What was that?" Bruno said, half challenge, half I-have-no-idea-what-you're-talking-about.

"A combination lock technically opens to anyone who has the knowledge of the numbers," she explained, slowly, like a professor would. "All you need, then, is knowledge that is included with the lock, which can be given to as many or as few people as desired."

She looked so *earnest*. Bruno, on the other hand, just looked confused. She must've thought the same thing, because she continued, looking into his eyes like she was giving a TED talk.

"Theoretically, you could just open those locks through trial and error. There's also the possibility that you're a locksmith who opens locks for a living, or a thief who opens locks with ill intent. Oh! There are also biometric locks, like they have at, like, the Pentagon or highly classified military bases. Or retina locks, although maybe those are mostly in movies. That kind of thing."

She snapped her fingers, like she'd just thought of something. It was almost painfully adorable.

"Then there are things like hotel locks. Those keys are *disposable*. They are recoded constantly, so even the same key can't necessarily open the same door twice." She whistled. "Loooooootta locks. Lotta *keys*."

"What the hell are you talking about?" Bruno finally burst out, disgruntled.

She tilted her head and smiled, so soft and gentle and sweet Hudson felt his stomach jitter and his heart speed up. It was like being at the top of a roller coaster, just before that drop.

That was always his favorite part.

"What I'm saying," she answered, slowly and gently, "is that the analogy of key and lock only works with the assumption that one, a lock is only supposed to have one key, and two, it is the lock's fault if it fails in this capacity."

"I like her," Kimber murmured, and his mom nodded, a small, satisfied smile on her face.

"Also, it makes the assumption that every key is trying to access and open every lock possible," Willa continued. Not in a superior way, but almost like someone who really geeked out about something and wanted you to somehow be just as enthusiastic as she was. Hudson felt that way when he talked about clocks. She was looking at Bruno like she was *begging* him to understand, and he was absolutely flummoxed in light of that attention. "That it's the *purpose* of a key. It also implies that a key that only opens one door is somehow inferior . . . which, I mean, my car key only turns on my car, and I'm pretty okay with that?"

Bruno still stared at her. Actually, they *all* still stared at her.

"But ultimately the key-and-lock analogy—presumably indicating penetrative sex—is impossibly reductive and needlessly judgmental, which I don't think you mean to be. Sex is not Fort Knox. Which I don't even think uses a key. Anyway, a woman can be whatever kind of lock she wants to be. And some men might think that they're master keys when really, they're key cards."

Bruno stared at her in silence for a long second, suspicious. "Are you fucking with me?" he asked, his expression like a storm cloud. "Trying to make me feel stupid? Huh? You think I'm stupid?"

Now every muscle in Hudson's body tensed. He'd seen bigger men cower in front of Bruno, and he'd actually seen Bruno kick somebody's ass at a family cookout once, a long time ago. (Granted, the guy had been drunk and gotten belligerent.) Hudson knew he would never hurt a woman, though, and he certainly wouldn't lay a finger on Willa. But his every protective instinct was going bananas.

Even if Bruno wouldn't hurt her, Hudson wasn't going to let him scare her.

He started to step up to Bruno, ready to go toe to toe, even if, in his sixties, his honorary uncle would still make a fight of it.

But again, Willa surprised him.

She beat him to it and stepped right up to Bruno's chest, looking up at him, since he had over a foot of height on her, her brown eyes intent and earnest. She still smiled, shrugging slightly.

"I know you're not stupid. But for the past twenty minutes, I heard you talk about building Kimber's bike when she was six, and ask about the goats she loves, and even tell her about your kids. I also know that you're saying this stuff because you're worried about Kimber and you don't want her to get hurt, which is *awesome*." She patted Bruno on one of his ridiculously muscular arms, one that had questionable tattoos and more than a few scars. It reminded Hudson of when she petted Noodle on the head. "I could be wrong, but I feel that if you realized that *you* were going to hurt Kimber, you wouldn't want to. So I just . . . thought I'd create a little break. Gave you a second to think about what you were saying, and another way to look at it. Sometimes we just need a little break to process things."

Her eyes widened, like she'd just realized something.

"Holy shit! That's what you do with a salad course. *I am a salad course.*"

Then she smiled. Broadly. Ridiculously.

In that moment, Hudson watched one of the baddest-ass men he'd ever known fucking melt like a marshmallow.

If possible, Hudson fell a little bit harder for this woman as he felt the roller coaster drop in his stomach, and he smiled so wide he thought his face would crack.

"You are a trip, little girl," Bruno said with one of his deep, barrel-chested laughs, chucking her chin like she was fifteen and not in her forties.

"In the name of full transparency," she stage-whispered, leaning a little closer, "I am also apparently baked for the first time in my life, so . . . that's a thing."

Now Bruno almost doubled over laughing.

Hudson, on the other hand, glared at Kimber and his mom as this sank in. It explained a *lot*.

"Kimber? What the hell?" He was at Willa's side before he even realized he was moving. "How much did she have?"

"She asked!" Kimber protested, but she still looked a little guilty. "But . . . yeah. She had a full cookie before I realized and could stop her."

He turned back to Willa, who was staring at Bruno's tattoos like they were Saturday morning cartoons as he painstakingly (and with obvious amusement) explained what each one was. Her eyes were as big as Bambi's but a little unfocused. "This is her first time?" Hudson whispered as nervousness twisted his stomach.

"That's what she said."

Fuck.

"Willa," he said softly a couple of times, until she looked away from Bruno. And by that, he meant she moved her entire head to focus on him. "You okay, baby?"

Baby?

What the hell?

He hoped to God his family hadn't caught that.

She had to think about it, but then she broke out in a smile again. "Oh! Yes. I mean, a little . . . dizzy," she admitted. "Spinny. And hungry. I could absolutely *murder* a fresh-baked sourdough loaf right now. With some French butter. Nobody does butter like the French, let me tell you . . . oh! Or croissants." She sighed. "They're a pain in the ass to make, but fresh croissants are *incredible*. With . . . some fresh lemon curd. Or Kimber's goat cheese! That was *so good*."

"There's some on the cheese board," Kimber said with a grin.

"*Cheese board,*" Willa crooned, like she'd just discovered the Holy Grail. "I forgot about the cheese board! That fresh honeycomb with the goat cheese—that's why I used it in the ice cream—oh, and the toasted baguette, and oh my God the cherry tomatoes, *those tomatoes*! And the raspberries!"

Swear to God, she sounded like she was going to orgasm.

Was he supposed to feel guilty that he started chubbing up hearing that? He shifted a little, forcing himself to focus.

"I'm keeping an eye on her," he said pointedly to his family and Bruno. "She can't just ride this out on her own."

"Can I have more cheese board?" she asked him, her full lips curving into a smile.

"Yes, I'll get you a plate," he said. At her wistful look, he grabbed a cracker and loaded it with some cheese and raspberries. She took it and stuffed it in her mouth like a hungry squirrel, moaning happily.

He shifted again. At this rate, this was gonna be a long night.

"Yup. You take care of her," his dad said, and the laugh was *right there*.

"Sorry, Dad," Kimber said again, genuinely apologetic, although her eyes were bright. She was going to text Jeremy about this, he could just *tell*.

Only his mom seemed able to keep it together, looking between them with a serious expression. "She did have some good ideas for the cookies, though."

Willa tried to respond, but cracker crumbs started to fly out of her mouth. She swallowed hard, then started over. "All about browning the butter. And letting the dough cool twenty-four hours. Kenji's a genius, and you really can't go wrong."

Then she shot him another soulful look.

"Gimme a second," he said, setting her up with another cracker to tide her over while he quickly loaded up a plate. She had all the signs of the munchies settling in. He grabbed her a lemonade, too, and handed her the plate. "C'mon. We'll go sit outside."

"Okay!" She'd already snagged a handful of nuts and was chewing before taking another step.

He guided her, a hand on the small of her back, toward the back door, only to hear Bruno say, "You be real careful with that lock, son!"

He blindly flipped him off as they headed out the door, ignoring the laughter that followed them.

CHAPTER 17

So this is being high.

Noodle had decided that High Willa was his very best friend and had curled up companionably against her stomach, snoring with soft little wooshes, and it was the cutest thing she had ever seen in her life. Also, how had she not noticed how insanely soft his fur was? She could pet it for hours.

She actually may have petted it for hours. Time was feeling a little squishy at this point.

Honestly, being high wasn't that different from being drunk, in her opinion. Of course, it had been a long time since she'd actually been drunk, now that she thought about it. She'd never felt comfortable losing control, definitely not with people she didn't trust. Steven had been the bon vivant of the two of them, and he'd been the one who liked alcohol—wine, whisky, you name it. Not to excess, he'd point out, and she'd agree. But . . . perhaps more than the average guy.

His drinking was like everything else about him: extra.

Still, she remembered being drunk with friends, so long ago. She and her friends from college had partied after they'd passed finals. She'd also gotten tipsy with them during Saturday mimosa brunches now and then, when Steven was out of town and she was going to stay at somebody's house. She remembered the feeling of warmth, of easy laughter about the smallest, silliest things. The cocoon of *I'm with my people.*

She also remembered waking up puking on the rare occasion in college, and the headache that followed. She really hoped that wasn't going to happen here, especially since she could *not* seem to stop eating. But she wasn't sure if weed involved a hangover.

Hudson walked over with yet another plate of food for her. She was fairly certain it was her third helping, but she didn't care. She made grabby hands at him, and he laughed as he handed it over and then took his place next to her. After they rebuked Noodle, he moved to pout for a second before trotting after Kimber, who was eating a burger with Bruno.

"I have literally never had goat cheese Brie before," Willa said happily as she smeared it on fresh bread. "And this is your own blackberry jam, with homegrown jalapeño? Are you kidding?" She took a bite, groaning before he could even answer. "If you aren't selling these things at your farm stand, I am going to cry."

"Kimber's working on it," Hudson replied. He was looking at her with an amused smile.

They were sitting under a maple tree, on a spread-out blanket in a corner of the backyard. She sighed, leaning against the trunk.

"Kimber's smart. And a good cook. Your mom too," she added.

"Thanks. I'll tell them." His smile widened. "It'll mean a lot coming from a chef like you."

"Oh! I'm not a chef," she protested, like muscle memory.

"You went to culinary school and stuff, right?"

"No," she said, then cleared her throat. "I did get a degree in food science, though. Also, I did work in restaurants. Sort of. It's a little complicated, and it was a long time ago."

He tilted his head. "But . . . you're writing a cookbook?"

How to explain? Especially to someone not from her weird world? "That's not being a chef, trust me. That's more like . . . I don't know. Being a technical writer or something."

He still looked puzzled. "I'm sorry. You can tell me to, y'know, fuck off if this is too personal, but . . . do you *like* to cook? Because it seems like you do."

120

She stuffed a bacon-wrapped fig in her mouth to buy herself some time. It was filled with feta and an almond, and she wanted to cry over how good it was.

"It's been a long time since I really enjoyed cooking," she admitted finally. "Honestly, it's been a long time since I even cared about eating."

She registered the concern on his face, but the effects of the cookie were enveloping her. It was like watching herself from a long way away, dispassionately. She sensed that she might regret some of her actions later, but she couldn't seem to register enough motivation to stop herself, or even care.

That's Future Me's problem.

"Does that make the cookbook thing, um, difficult?" he asked, then nudged the plate at her.

"Ooh, olives." She hummed happily and popped one in her mouth. Then she ate some nuts and spread honey on another round of baguette. "Yes. The cookbook thing has been really, really hard. It would've been hard even if I wasn't writing for a ding-dong whose claim to culinary fame is posing shirtless as he licks whisks."

Hudson let out a surprised snort of laughter. "And he makes money that way?"

"Yup. Millions of followers," she confided. Although she sensed her voice might be a bit loud, sharing this little detail. *Is it a secret if you're yelling?* her clear internal voice asked, almost bored. "Now, I have to come up with a bunch of recipes for him. And they have to make sense together. They have to be stuff he can flex around and presumably cook safely without a shirt—"

"No bacon, then," Hudson joked.

"I *know*, right?" she agreed. "And the theme's *sexy*. Everything's got to basically scream sex. And he's got to be able to be sexy *making* it. Whipping, yes. Skinning a chicken? Probably not so much."

Hudson started laughing, rolling on his side. She grinned helplessly at him.

He really was a good man. Her rational, silent internal voice pointed out that she trusted him. She wouldn't be in this position if she didn't somehow trust him and his family.

A little, tiny tug of worry occurred, but it wasn't strong enough to pierce her current feeling of disassociation, which was so much more . . .

Familiar.

She pushed the thought aside. It was so much better to just eat cheese and avoid reality for a while. She'd probably print that on a T-shirt if she remembered this tomorrow morning.

Of course, part of her really hoped she wouldn't remember any of this tomorrow morning. "But what do I know?" she said, reaching for more food. She was going to make herself sick at this rate, but she couldn't seem to stop herself: it tasted so good, and she just wanted to keep *consuming*. It was about experiencing the tastes more than it was an actual hunger. Everything was just . . . *enhanced*, so outrageously *extra*. "I can't even remember the last time I enjoyed sex, or knew what was sexy. I am probably the worst possible person for this project, but here we are."

She closed her eyes and sighed around a fresh raspberry, savoring the taste as the fragile fruit disappeared on her tongue. When she opened them, she blearily saw that Hudson was sitting up and staring at her. Not with judgment or disgust. A bit of surprise, and a sort of should-we-talk-about-this expression. She was very familiar with it, having seen about a million variations since Steven's death.

"It's not a big deal," she quickly reassured him. "I mean, finishing this is going to be difficult, but as to actually having sex in my life, it's not a huge component. It's like . . . like being . . ." Her cloudy mind struggled for an analogy. "It's like being a vegetarian. It's not like I'm going to die without it, and I can come up with plenty to work around it."

He chuckled again, shaking his head. "Darlin', you've obviously been eating the wrong meat," he said in that rumbly voice of his, eyes bright.

"I don't suppose you can, though," she added.

The chuckle stopped abruptly, and he swung his eyes to hers, flashing with . . . hurt? Irritation?

"Because I'm a guy," he asked carefully, "or because I'm me?"

She sighed, reaching over and patting his shoulder in what she hoped was a comforting gesture. He glanced at her hand, and she wondered if it was perhaps too hard, so she stopped, opting to rub his bicep—*Wow, bicep. That* is *a bicep, right? The upper arm thing,* her impaired brain rambled happily—and try to explain herself.

"Bit of both?" she finally said. "This lady in the kitchen hinted that you didn't get involved with women from the island. She wasn't being, like, bitchy or possessive about it," Willa quickly interjected when Hudson winced. "And there was Kimber's, um, manwhore comment."

Hudson groaned, face-planting into his crossed arms on the blanket.

"I am not judging at all," she added. "I know plenty of people who have plenty of sex, with all sorts of partners. As long as it's safe and consensual, I figure to each their own."

He finally emerged, propping himself up on his arms to look at her. "I guess you haven't really dated since your husband died."

She felt that, piercing even the haze of the weed cushion. "Too much to deal with," she admitted. "We . . . there were debts, even before he was sick, and him being sick just made it worse. Then he . . ."

She swallowed hard. She didn't say it.

She didn't need to.

"It was sooner than we thought," she finally continued. "Then my great-aunt died, and she'd made me executor, which was unexpected. But I'd also just gone through executing an estate, and I guess it was all fresh? I had that skill set, right there. No time or interest in dating. Or sex."

She let out a long sigh, lying on her back, looking at the stars. There were so many, even with the slight orange haze of light pollution from the mainland. It was beautiful, she thought.

"But things are calming down a little, right?" That note of concern, again, in his voice.

She glanced over. He was stretched out next to her, not too close, but still, close enough for her to catch the scent of his soap. Like her sense of taste, her sense of smell seemed heightened too. The air around him was redolent of almonds and honey and an underlying spice that she knew, from him working in the house, was just *him*.

"Have you ever been a caretaker?" she found herself saying, almost dreamily. It was like there was only her and Hudson, and he actually cared what she thought, what she was going through. Not that he necessarily did. But for once in her life, she just wanted to not give a shit. Just tell someone what she *really* felt, without worrying about how they'd feel, or what they'd tell her to do. Just be *free*, and not feel beholden or worried, or plan her next step.

"I'm a parent," he said, his eyes glowing with warmth, his smile self-deprecating. "I was a parent of twins, unexpectedly, at nineteen. Just out of high school."

She whistled low, or at least, she tried. His smirk suggested she might've screwed that up. "That's a lot," she pointed out. "Twins at any age would've been tough, but if you weren't expecting it, and you were barely grown yourself . . ."

"It was challenging," he agreed, and she saw his expression harden. "Harder when my ex-wife left."

She gaped. "When was that?"

"When the twins were about three."

"Shiiiit." She hadn't meant to respond that way and quickly facepalmed, a little too fast, a little too hard, with no sense of proportion. "Sorry, sorry," she quickly said as he scooted closer and made sure she was okay.

"It's okay. I said that a lot in the beginning," he said, with a shrug and that dimple-flashing smile, even if his eyes weren't as bright as they usually were. "But I love them more than anything, and it was worth it. Besides, my parents helped so much—I don't know what I would've done without them. Even then, though, there were days when I just wanted to punch holes in the walls. Or I'd get in my car and just yell my ass off with the windows up. Or even cry," he tacked on, in a low voice. "It's easier now, obviously, but for a while there, I was just . . ."

He petered out, just kind of gesturing. But Willa felt like a bell had rung inside her, a resonant, glorious *yes*.

"You *get* it," she breathed reverently. "Sometimes, it was just like treading water in the open ocean. I wasn't really enjoying anything. I was just trying to stay afloat."

"Yeah," he said, his voice a little ragged. "I get that."

She propped her head up on her arm, mirroring him, staring into his eyes as he stared into hers. It was this crystalline moment. Magical.

So, of course, she had to crash through it.

"Once," she said, with no transition, "Steven cheated on me."

His eyes went wide, and his eyebrows went up.

"It was after we lost the restaurant. He regretted it immediately, and he never did again. But you know what my response was?" she asked, but didn't wait for a response. "I mean, not out loud. But my first gut reaction was: *Good. Thank God.*"

"What?" he croaked. "*Why?*"

"Because I was so, so tired," she said around a yawn, "and it was one less thing I had to do."

Which seemed to remind her body that she was still running at a sleep deficit. Even though the blanket was a bit scratchy and the ground a teeny bit hard, she sighed, cradling her head in the crook of his arm.

"Whoa, no, no," he quickly said, tugging her up. "You're getting couch lock, sweetheart. You do *not* want to sleep out here."

"What's couch lock?" she mumbled. Tiredness hit her like a hammer.

"It's . . . shit, I keep forgetting you've never had weed," he muttered. "It's slang. After you smoke, or whatever, you hit a point where you're super tired and don't want to move."

"So tired," she murmured in agreement as sleepiness started engulfing her like a tsunami.

She didn't know where he guided her. Barely heard him talking to his mother and Kimber and his father. She remembered petting Noodle again, and protesting (or trying to) when they told Noodle he couldn't sleep with her. She followed where he tugged her, making little grunts of discomfort when he insisted that she use the bathroom (by herself) and then put on a T-shirt that billowed on her.

Finally, she was able to stretch out on a very soft mattress. She felt a blanket being tucked around her. Then she sighed herself into sleep.

CHAPTER 18

At nine o'clock, Hudson was up and in the kitchen. His parents were down at their cabin, sleeping in, and Kimber had already been up to take care of the animals. According to her note, she'd headed over to Seattle to have lunch with a friend. After making sure that Willa was tucked in and that he could hear her if need be, he'd crashed in Jeremy's room. She was still snoozing, which didn't surprise him, given last night's whole thing.

He was glad that he had the house to himself, except for Willa. He'd found himself digging through some of the closets until he found a tray that his mother had used when any of the kids were sick and that they'd used to give her breakfast in bed on Mother's Day. He'd cleaned it up and now had the beginnings of breakfast ready.

His phone rang as he started to make a fresh pot of coffee. When he saw it was Jeremy, he answered. "Hey. You missed a helluva party."

He heard Jeremy sigh. "Wish I'd been there."

Hudson knew what was coming before he even asked the question: "Something wrong?"

"Wendy and I broke up," Jeremy said. "For real, this time."

Since Hudson had heard that twice before, he wisely bit his tongue. "I'm sorry. You okay?"

"Other than I need to move out? Sort of."

"You know, if you need anything—to talk, or a rental deposit, or whatever—you can ask, right?" Hudson couldn't help himself. Hearing either of his kids in pain made his chest hurt. "Seriously. Anything I can do."

There was a moment's hesitation. "Um . . . actually . . ."

Hudson started the coffee machine, waiting.

"Can I move home?"

That, he hadn't been expecting. Much like his mother, Jeremy hadn't been able to wait until he could move off island. "Are you sure? I mean, it's fine. We'd love to have you, but I'm just surprised."

The sadness he'd heard in Jeremy's voice when he'd first spoken was even heavier now. "Things just aren't working out the way I'd hoped," he said slowly. "I mean, I know that I had trouble pinning down what I wanted, but . . . I don't know. I'm not a music producer, I'm not a video producer. I'm just spinning my wheels, working at an electronics store and trying to show people how to work their phones or why they fried their tablets, or why they should've gotten Malwarebytes before they downloaded all that porn."

Hudson snickered.

"I just didn't think this would be my life." Jeremy sounded both baffled and upset.

Now Hudson took a deep breath. "I'm saying this with love, okay?" he said slowly. "You're only twenty-three."

"Yeah, but I've been out of school for two years," Jeremy said. "I've been working. I've been living on my own . . ."

"With your girlfriend," Hudson interjected, stopping himself from pointing out that she'd taken up a lot of Jeremy's time and mental bandwidth over those years. "You've been figuring out what you want to do, that's all. Nobody's expected to know what they want to do right out of the gate."

"I dunno. Those K-pop idols that Kimber loves know what they want to do from the time they're, like, fourteen or something," Jeremy argued. "I thought I was going to make movies, but then I got sidetracked. Then I thought I was going to be a YouTuber, and I couldn't get traction, so that just fizzled. Then I wanted to just be a video editor, but nobody wants to take a chance on me because I don't have the best portfolio . . ."

He trailed off. Hudson waited to make sure he was finished before giving his opinion. "You're looking at somebody else's highlight reel and comparing it to your behind-the-scenes bloopers, Jem." Hudson smiled, using Jeremy's childhood nickname just to hopefully make him smile too. He watched the coffee drip into the empty carafe as he chose his words carefully. "You've got time. So fucking much time, like an ocean of it. Just because you're twenty-three and you don't quite have it together doesn't mean that you won't ever, okay? You're just figuring it out."

"I don't know," Jeremy said, but with less conviction and hopefully less despair than he had before. "I just feel lost."

Hudson's heart ached for his kid. "C'mon home," he said. "We'll figure out the logistics of getting you moved. And we've got leftovers from the barbecue."

"That does sound good," Jeremy said. "I've been living on ramen the last week. I didn't feel like cooking, and shit's just too expensive to eat out all the time."

"I could probably convince Grandma to make you your favorite dinner, fried chicken," Hudson said, as a final incentive. "The good biscuits, even."

"I'll be there this afternoon."

Hudson laughed. "Thought that'd do it. Love you, see you later." They hung up. Then he went about his initial goal: getting breakfast for Willa. He set up a plate with toast and small mounds of goat cheese, butter, and jam. He added a bowl of clean berries from the garden. Then he poured a mug of coffee and found the small pitcher of creamer and the sugar bowl his mother used for visitors. Finally, he added a cloth napkin and silverware. It looked nice. Then he decided to just be "completely extra," as Kimber would say, and added a small juice glass with water and some of the marigolds from the garden.

Did it look like he was trying too hard? Maybe. But if nothing else, it was an apology. His family had, accidentally, gotten her high as a fucking kite, after all.

He brought it to his room. He'd left the door cracked open so he could hear her if anything was wrong the previous night. She was in one of his T-shirts, just under his light blanket, so he'd hoped that it wasn't an issue. He held the tray in one arm and then tapped the door. "Willa?"

He heard her gasp. "Yes?" Her voice was bell-clear, no trace of sleep, which was more than he could say about himself when he woke up.

"Okay if I come in?"

"Hudson?" There was a pause. "Um, yes . . . ?"

He opened the door, then grinned. Her hair, normally so perfect, was mussed. Her cheeks were flushed, and her eyes were wide. "Good morning," he said, then nodded down to the food. "The bathroom's down the hall, but I thought I'd bring you some breakfast."

"I slept here?" she asked.

"Yup."

She glanced around the room, then down at the bed . . . then at him. "Did I . . . did we . . . ?"

It took him a second. Then he couldn't help chuckling. "No, sweetheart. I slept in my son's old room. Although I guess he's moving back in . . . never mind, it doesn't matter. I considered bringing you home to your house, but your car's here and all, and you really weren't in any state. We wanted to make sure you were okay, anyway. Even though it wasn't that big a dose, edibles are unpredictable, and we should have been more careful."

She groaned loudly, then burrowed under his cover, dragging it up over her head. "I am *so embarrassed*," she said, her voice muffled by the blanket.

"Why are you embarrassed? None of this is your fault." Now he sighed. "In fact, I have to apologize. That never should've happened. I am so sorry that you were put in that position."

Now her head emerged, her hair even more haywire than before, although the look of determination and sternness still gave that no-nonsense, ridiculously *precise* impression, even if she looked rumpled as hell. "No! It wasn't Kimber's fault. That was all me. I didn't know what I was doing."

"It's exactly *because* you didn't know what you were doing that we should've been more careful." Something he'd spoken about to Kimber at length.

"I don't think it'll ever become a regular thing for me," she admitted, "but it was kind of nice. To just let go for a while."

He could imagine. So often she seemed to have the weight of the world on her shoulders, and for those few hours, talking and looking at the stars, crooning along to music, she'd seemed so light. He could've stared for hours. "Anytime you like," he said. "I'm happy to help."

She stared back for a second, her cheeks and her ears going pink. Then her eyes narrowed.

"I . . . talked to you, didn't I? About my project, stuff like that."

He couldn't lie to her. "Yeah, you did."

He watched her throat work as she swallowed, her mind seemingly going back to what she'd talked about. He could even tell the moment she processed exactly what she'd revealed to him.

"Shit," she breathed, and then dove under the blanket again.

He couldn't help himself. He chuckled, sitting on the edge of the bed. "It's okay, Willa," he reassured her. "I'm not going to tell anyone."

She wriggled. "I am a humiliation burrito."

"You don't need to be," he said around a laugh. "But your coffee's getting cold. You want to use the bathroom first?"

She popped her head out again, just the top, up to her eyes. She was beginning to look like a ground squirrel. "You didn't have to make me breakfast," she protested, her words muffled.

"No, I didn't," he said.

She took it in. Then she nodded and retreated to the bathroom. When she came back, she sat on the bed, against the headboard. "You're

131

so nice to me." She sounded . . . not confused, exactly, but almost reproachful. "I'm sure you had other things you have to do today."

"Not a thing," he said. "I was thinking of stopping by and working, actually."

"No!" she shot out, then looked down at the plate like buttering her toast was the most important thing she could do in the world. "I mean . . . it's Sunday. You should rest. You've been working at my house for weeks."

He nodded. He didn't want to push her. He liked her, of course, and he'd said as much, but he didn't want to be that guy. If she needed space, he'd give it to her. He watched as she nibbled at the toast and drank the coffee, feeling happier in that quiet moment than he'd felt in a long, long time. Finally, she smiled at him shyly.

"Thanks, Hudson," she said.

He took the tray. "My pleasure."

"No, not just for the breakfast," she pointed out. "Last night. Inviting me here. Making sure I was okay. I just . . . thank you."

Now his chest heated. He wanted so badly to put the damned tray down and scoop her up against him—not just for sex, although that would've been . . .

You've never brought a woman to the house.

He nodded. "Really. My pleasure."

She smiled. "I'm going to get going, then."

He brought the tray to the kitchen, then walked with her to the door, where her shoes were lined up next to Kimber's shoes and his mother's moccasins. "Let me know if you need anything," he said, then walked her to her car.

She smiled at him as she got to the driver's side door. "See you Monday?"

Her hair was still a mess, one wisp hovering in front of her face. He reached out almost unconsciously, tugging it out of the way and smoothing it down behind her ear like he'd seen her do countless times . . . before trailing his fingertips along her cheek, right to the edge of her chin. "See you Monday," he repeated, moving his hand away.

She stared at him for a long second, and it seemed like they were just frozen there.

Then she nodded, got in the car, and drove away.

He trudged back to the farmhouse. He was so, so fucked when it came to this woman, and he had no idea what to do about it.

So instead, he did some laundry, cleaning the bedding in his room and in Jeremy's, before falling into a rabbit hole of clock-fixing videos. That usually soothed him. When his phone rang, he thought for a second it was Jeremy again, but instead saw Willa's number and smiled.

"Just can't get enough of me, huh?" he teased, then wondered if he'd gone too far.

He was gratified when he heard her giggle. "More to the point," she countered, "guess who can't get enough of *me?*"

He blinked.

It's me. I can't.

But he didn't say it.

"Noodle," she said. "The little Houdini broke into my garage again. I'd drive him over, but I don't know how he'd do in my car."

"Don't worry about it," Hudson said quickly, keys in hand before she'd even finished the sentence, his heartbeat already picking up. "I'll be right over." Then he waited a beat. "And I might as well do a little work, right?"

"Up to you." But there was a grin in her voice, he thought.

Oh yeah, he was in trouble here. But he was already out the door before he let himself dwell on it.

CHAPTER 19

Honestly, she probably didn't *need* to call Hudson.

She was currently snuggled up with Noodle on her couch, looking at a messy sprawl of sticky notes that she'd scattered over the surface of her coffee table, still unable to figure out how to write the stuff that wasn't just ingredients and instructions, much less in Sexy Chef Sam's voice. It really would help for her to talk to the guy, even for an hour, to figure out the personal touch that separated a recipe from what readers expected these days. While so many people were trained to "jump to recipe" on a blog post, she knew that if readers or home cooks were shelling out money for big glossy cookbooks, they needed more than . . . well, any recipe they could jump to in a blog, quite frankly. They were buying the personality.

Of course, she'd been out of the game. For all she knew, she could make it like a calendar, just having sexy photos of him holding up "two eggs" or "a half cup of milk" with his tongue out, and it'd sell. She giggled at the thought, even as she internally hoped it was a joke.

She'd kind of figured out some possible recipes, some adapted from Sam's videos, some she'd played with herself in the past or worked with at various pop-ups. She knew that Vanessa technically just wanted a finished product and that—hopefully—they weren't expecting a whole lot out of this. But this was still her entry point, and she had too much pride in her work to make just a collection of clichéd Valentine's Day recipes. She needed to create food that was sensual—and, yes, sexual—as well as appealing.

So despite having the recipes, she had to, essentially, sexy up her current potential list. She was so very, very tired—and, for the most part, still felt unsexy.

Unless you're around Hudson.

Yesterday's barbecue, with her brief but memorable foray into the world of marijuana, was the first time she'd felt relaxed in longer than she could remember, and she didn't regret it. She'd eaten the whole cookie because she'd been intrigued: the grassy taste wasn't entirely unpleasant, but it was hardly nuanced, and she felt like she could adjust it. When was the last time she'd felt like playing with food just for the hell of it? Just experimenting out of sheer joy?

It was like when your arm fell asleep and you worked on waking it up—it felt great to get the sensation back, but it also stung like crazy. What she *did* regret: letting Hudson see her so vulnerable, and worse, blurting out things that really, really did not need to be said. Not that she didn't trust him, although she didn't know exactly why she *did* trust him. But she'd let things spill with him that she hadn't even told Nat, and Nat was one of her best friends.

She couldn't believe she'd told him about Steven.

She couldn't believe she'd told him the details about the cookbook project.

And she really, *really* couldn't believe she'd told him about her hopelessness, her numbness.

She rubbed her eyes with the heels of her hands. Rather than withdrawing from her, being judgy or critical . . . he'd kept an eye on her while she slept (or rather, given up his own bed to sleep in his kid's room, while still making sure she was all right) and then brought her breakfast in bed.

Yet another thing on her "I can't remember the last time . . ." list. Much as she'd loved Steven, the guy had never, ever brought her breakfast in bed. It wasn't their relationship dynamic. She had no doubt that he'd loved her as well. But she'd also known that he loved the spotlight, loved living life in the biggest, brightest, most exuberant way possible.

She also knew, deep down, that Steven lived like that because his doctors had told him at a young age that there wasn't a cure and that as he got older, it would only get harder. That he'd die too soon, and that his life, by necessity, had to be limited, or it'd be even shorter.

Steven, being Steven, had said *Fuck that.* He'd chosen the path with no limits every chance that he got, and she'd been his willing companion.

Hudson wasn't like that.

She wasn't sure what that meant, or why she noticed. Or why she really liked spending time with him . . . or what to do with that knowledge.

In a repeat of their first meeting, she startled when he knocked as Noodle leaped for the door, barking his head off. She shushed him as she opened it, watching with a smile she couldn't stop as Noodle cavorted around Hudson.

She didn't stop smiling when Hudson looked at her with a warm, affectionate expression either.

"I'm not sure how he keeps getting in," she said with a note of apology, even though she was glad that he was there.

She followed Hudson as he went out to the garage, checking out where Noodle's point of entry might be. There was so much stuff, haphazardly stacked and completely unsorted, that she didn't even park her car in there . . . which, she imagined, might be a problem come winter, if there was any kind of snow.

"Does it snow here?" she asked, as Hudson rummaged around.

"Sometimes. More, lately, and worse than it used to. But don't worry: I've got a plow attachment on my truck. I'll make sure that you aren't stuck. And if the power goes out, we've got a good generator, the wood-burning stove in the main house kicks ass, and we have a bank of batteries with the solar panels from the barn." He looked over his shoulder at her and winked. "You can always crash with us if you need to."

Again, that consideration was making her melt. Among other things. She cleared her throat. "Thanks. I've got a fireplace, but . . ."

She stopped abruptly as he moved some boxes out of the way and then crouched, his head going out of sight—but his ass suddenly presented in front of her, a perfect bubble butt. And she wouldn't even have considered herself a butt person.

She swallowed hard. *Respectfully, that thing is a work of art. God. Damn.*

She coughed, mentally slapping herself. Seriously, she was almost fifty, for God's sake. Not a teenager!

". . . um, but I didn't, ah, know how to light it," she finished. "Since it's summer, it's not like there's a need. I'll figure it out in the fall, I guess."

"I'll make sure that the flue's clear and that you know how before winter," he promised, his words dampened by the detritus around him. "Okay, I think I see where the guy's getting in."

"Oh?" She walked over, craning her head to look. While the stuff obscuring her view meant the light was dim, she saw it: rotten boards that had somehow been torn out.

"He's lucky he didn't get cut or scratch himself," Hudson said, and she immediately felt concerned. "I'm going to board this up."

"Yes," she agreed, worried. She loved Noodle, and the last thing she wanted was for him to get hurt, even if she would miss his visits.

"I'm going to see if there's anything in here I can use, if that's okay?" he asked. "Otherwise, I've got some plywood scraps in the truck."

"Whatever you need," she said. She stood there for a second, watching as he looked around, until he glanced over at her and she realized she was just literally watching him. She wasn't helping. If anything, she was just sort of hanging out like, again, an attention-starved teen. "I'll just go back to the living room!"

She sounded like a hamster squeaking, so she rushed back into the house before she could humiliate herself further.

Back to work, back to work. Even the punch of stress was worth it . . . almost comforting in its familiarity. Of course, then it was just trading in one set of problems for another as she felt the clench of despair and fear.

She decided to test a few recipes, even if she wasn't sure quite how to organize things. A list of recipes and a shitty framing mechanism was better than nothing at all. Desserts were the easiest, if the most overt. She decided chocolate with chili powder—sweet and heat. A truffle. Was it basic? Yeah. But she wasn't exactly a font of inspiration right now.

She had just finished the ganache and was playing with the chili ratio when Hudson walked back in.

"I've been thinking about your problem," he said without preamble.

"Which one?" she joked, but it came out a little brittle.

"Your cookbook."

If her hands weren't covered in chocolate, she'd have hidden her face. "I really wasn't supposed to tell *anybody* about that," she said.

"I promise, I'm not going to say a word," he said, and she believed him. Then again, who was he going to tell? Nobody who would get back to her publisher. But she appreciated that he took her seriously. "But you were saying that you weren't feeling, um, sexy. Remember?"

She knew she was blushing. You could toast a marshmallow from the heat of her face, from the feel of it. "Oh, God," she whispered, looking at the floor.

He nudged her chin up, his eyes looking into hers. He wasn't making fun of her. If anything, he was looking at her carefully. "I'm not saying this to make you feel bad, because you shouldn't." It wasn't stern, but it was, well, *firm*. "I just wanted to say that maybe you're approaching this wrong."

"I'm having problems approaching it at all!" Her voice sounded like a wail, and she bit her lip.

His smile was warm. "The thing is, you're thinking of it like . . . well, like the guy you were talking about. All flashy, over the top, that kinda thing."

"The man cooks without a shirt," she pointed out. "And the bottom line is, he's the client and I'm the ghost. I need to match his approach and his . . . well, his voice, basically."

"Yeah, but I think you might be focusing on the wrong thing," Hudson continued.

She waited, a hair's breadth away from irritation. Was he trying to mansplain ghostwriting cookbooks to her? If that was the case, she was going to be very, very peeved.

"Don't laugh, but I watched a few of the guy's videos," he said, and her eyes widened. "I mean, he's not my type or anything, but I saw what he was doing."

Like you need any help being sexy! He could probably teach a master class. Of course he saw what Sexy Chef was doing!

She bit back a giggle, and his grin turned sheepish, even as his eyes twinkled with amusement. She couldn't help but ask, "What was he doing, then?"

"Yeah, he stripped off the shirt, but that wasn't . . . look, I'm a flirt," he said. "Not even going to pretend I'm not."

"I have suspected," she answered, deadpan.

"I'm not the best-looking guy, but . . . okay, this sounds terrible, but I have not, erm, had difficulty . . ."

"You hook up a lot." He squirmed, and she knew she shouldn't, but somehow she sadistically enjoyed his discomfort.

He rubbed the back of his neck, which was slowly turning red. "'A lot' is kind of . . ."

"Just cut to the chase," she teased. "Be my flirt guru. What's he doing?"

The fact that even his cheeks were turning pink was so unexpectedly cute she could die. "It's not his chest. It's the smile, the wink, and the way he looks into the camera," he finally revealed. "A guy could be a bodybuilder or look like a movie star, but if he doesn't turn it on, boost the charm, then it's not gonna matter."

She frowned, momentarily distracted, then shook her head. "But that's just going to be the photos," she said. "What's that got to do with my recipes?"

"You're thinking of the sex itself," he said, no longer embarrassed. He seemed frustrated that he couldn't get his point across and obviously blamed himself. He took a deep breath and tried again. "It's . . . look, I have nothing against strippers."

"Neither do I," she agreed. "Sex work is work."

"But it's like hitting you with a sledgehammer," he said. "That's the whole point. It's zero to sixty, then she steps off the stage. You're trying to make these in-your-face, sledgehammer, slam-you-against-a-wall dishes, right? And you're not feeling it, so it makes it even harder on you."

She walked to the sink and washed her hands, mostly to hide her face as she processed what he said. He was right, of course. She was trying to write sexy and channel a kid who exuded pheromones like a fire hose blast, and it was coming out *awful*. Clumsy and disconnected and just . . . *wrong*.

"So what do you think I should do?" she asked quietly, turning back to him when her hands were dried.

"I think you should go slower," he said.

"I don't have *time* to go slower," she protested. "The book's due by the end of summer!"

He shook his head. Then she saw him take a deep breath. "I didn't mean . . . Can I show you?"

She nodded, confused.

He then bracketed her, putting his hands on either side of her on the sink. She could feel the heat from his body, smell the spicy, woodsy scent of him. His eyes were blazing, but he was right . . . it was that small, lopsided smile that mesmerized her.

"You okay?" he checked in.

She barely let out a squeak. She could hardly breathe.

He then traced his nose up the side of her throat, from her collarbone to her earlobe, before whispering in the filthiest, sexiest voice she'd ever heard in her life. "See? You don't have to be naked to be sexy as hell."

She held her breath, her body vibrating like a tuning fork. She didn't know what was going to happen next, and she both feared what it might be—and *craved* it.

To her shock, he took a step back, nodding.

"See you tomorrow."

Then the man had the audacity to *wink* before turning, whistling to Noodle, and then strolling out the door, like he hadn't just turned her to a puddle on her kitchen floor.

CHAPTER 20

The man was trying to kill her.

He hadn't pressured, hadn't nudged her about doing anything. Hadn't even brought up his little object lesson from the other day. In fact, she'd wondered if she'd just conjured the thing up in some weed-induced hallucination.

Instead, he'd slowly been showing her just how sexy little things could be.

He'd brought her things from the farm, things she hadn't asked for. He'd given his usual excuses—"We had too many strawberries" or "I know how much you like the goat cheese," as if they didn't have an actual farm-stand business where these things could be sold—but his offerings had been small and thoughtful, and *somehow*, every time he handed her something, their hands wound up brushing just the tiniest bit. Just enough for her to be aware of it. As he gave her these gifts, he'd send her that lopsided half smile, and his gaze would be hot and lazy, and she'd feel it like a physical thing.

Somehow, they managed to keep passing each other in the hallway or the narrow space between the kitchen island and the counters. He'd brush behind her or in front of her, the barest of touches, before moving away again. She'd get a breath of his scent, a second experiencing the firmness of his muscles, and then . . . gone.

Finally, she'd been experimenting with some rose-cut poached apples (which wound up being too finicky and not at all suitable for the cookbook), and he'd stood behind her, close enough for her to feel the heat of his body without actually making contact. He sniffed at the dish over her shoulder.

"Smells delicious," he'd said.

No. He'd *purred*.

She swore, every time he was near her, her system was bordering on overload. Whatever he was doing, if he was even doing it deliberately, was working. She'd found herself sneaking glances at him whenever he was nearby, and when they were actually talking, she'd find his gaze lowering to her lips as she talked, raising her temperature by a good ten degrees.

She knew that she was attracted to him just as much as he appeared to be to her. She was just seriously, seriously out of practice and wasn't sure what to do next.

With that in mind, she made an excuse and told him to stay home or do other work or whatever for the next few days. She couldn't even remember what she'd said, just that he'd agreed, and now it was two Hudson-free days later. Basically, she needed space because if she didn't get it, she'd probably say *Screw the cookbook* . . . and then screw him, instead, however that went.

I do miss him, though. How had that happened so quickly?

Maybe after the cookbook, she'd see what happened.

She didn't feel guilty about that decision, per se. She wasn't sure how Steven would feel about her dating, or even being attracted to someone, after he died. It wasn't ever something they discussed. She got the feeling he wouldn't mind, given his approach to life in general. She was pretty sure if she'd died, he would have moved on, and she would've wanted him to.

They'd always lived a big life until his diabetes had caught up with him. He'd never lived ideally for that illness. He'd simply tried to balance out his wildly extravagant lifestyle with more insulin, kicking the can down the street, making it Future Steven's problem—and, occasionally, Present Willa's.

She knew, on some level, that Steven had been spoiled. He was the only son of an LA lawyer and semifamous painter, and his diagnosis had hit his parents hard, showing that even their money could not protect them from genetics. He'd been gorgeous, charming, utterly vivacious. Mischievous, with a naughty smile and a fuck-it-let's-go attitude that somehow helped him get away with murder.

She'd struggled so hard to help him keep that smile. It was the sort of thing that made you feel like you were standing in the sun on a tropical beach. She'd fallen, hard and quickly, when she'd met him at twenty-three. She'd had a high school boyfriend, but they'd broken up when they went to different colleges. In college, she'd had a few little fling-type things, but she hadn't really been adept at the whole dating scene. If she hadn't met Steven when on an internship, she had no idea what would've happened.

Instead, she was married at twenty-three and widowed at forty-four. And in that time, she'd lived with one sole purpose: keeping Steven happy and healthy, not necessarily in that order.

Now, she was alone, which she should have expected but somehow hadn't. She was struggling, which wasn't unusual . . . but that wasn't comforting, either, especially as she saw ahead of her a lifetime of somehow figuring out how to function when her sole purpose was gone.

She felt the tears before she registered what they were. Grimacing, she wiped at them with irritation. She had a slate of recipes, or at least contenders. She needed to get them tested, get them written, then piece together all the connective tissue that would make this an actual cookbook. Then they could do what they wanted with it, as long as she got paid.

The last thing she needed was a distraction.

But what happens when the cookbook's done?

She bit her lip. She'd take a page out of Steven's book for now . . . that was Future Willa's problem. With any luck, and from what she'd inadvertently heard at the barbecue, Hudson might've moved on by then, for all she knew. He seemed to like sex, and from what she'd experienced, she'd bet he was unbelievably good at it.

If he moved on, it would suck, but she had to admit it would solve her problem.

Men came and went—sometimes literally—but mortgages were seemingly forever. That was the issue at hand, and she had to focus.

She was making chai-poached pears this time, with cinnamon whipped cream. It'd photograph well, it wasn't too hard, and it tasted fantastic. A bit autumn-y, but she was pretty sure she could push the sexy element.

The pears were cooling and she was working on whipping the cream when she heard a scratching at her back door. Since she was blasting music, she wasn't sure initially. After turning it down, though, the scratching sound was unmistakable.

"You have got to be kidding me," she muttered, opening the door carefully.

Sure enough, there was a cheerful Noodle, who strode in like he owned the place.

"Why? Why are you here?" she wailed as he wagged his tail at her and gave her a doggy smile. "It's because I gave you chicken, isn't it? I did that *once!*"

Okay, technically twice. Because she'd had some boiled chicken for her gỏi gà, a Vietnamese salad that was perfect for summer. He'd looked at her with literal puppy eyes, and it would take a stronger woman than her to turn that fuzzy little face down.

After sniffing the air to gauge if there was anything he could possibly beg for, he strutted over to the braided rag rug her aunt had in front of the fireplace, curling up with a happy huff.

She tugged at her hair. "You," she said with no venom, "are a menace to my plans."

The whole reason she'd told Hudson to stay home was because she thought she'd get a break. Apparently Noodle had other ideas.

At least she knew what to do this time. She pulled out her phone and texted Hudson.

WILLA: Guess who's back at my house? 🐶

His response was immediate.

HUDSON: Sorry! We're used to coming in and out and he's a bullet. That, and I'm pretty sure he's figured out how to open the screen door.

Willa couldn't help but grin. "You're too smart, Noodle," she said, and he thumped his tail against the floor.

WILLA: Don't worry, you know I love Noodle. How about I just keep him overnight?

There. That sounded casual, right?
His response, however, wasn't.

HUDSON: If it's okay, I'll just swing by. Jeremy's home, and it's his dog.

Her heart started pounding, and her stomach fluttered. She didn't have any real reason to tell him not to come. If she said "No, I'm keeping your dog" or "Why doesn't your son grab him?" it would be even more obvious that she was dodging him, and she didn't want to hurt his feelings at all.

Of course, she could also just be an adult and communicate clearly. But how did you say "I think I'd like to bang you like a screen door in a hurricane, but I haven't had sex in almost half a decade, and I'm conflicted, and I'm not sure what we're doing, and I have this whole work thing that is affecting the rest of my life" without sounding . . . well, unhinged?

She didn't know what she'd do if someone dumped all that on her. It was probably unfair for her to consider tossing Hudson in the deep end of that kind of mess.

So she sucked it up and waited for him to stop by.

He was there in minutes. He walked in through her unlocked front door, since he'd been here so often working, and she'd felt ridiculous insisting that he knock every morning when he showed up for work or when he came back from the hardware store or whatever. "Smells good in here," he said.

"Pears aren't in season quite yet," she said critically, studying the plate she was assembling before piping some whipped cream and garnishing it with some grated cinnamon. "But it should taste pretty good." She took a few pictures with her phone.

"Looks like you're making progress." He sounded approving.

She smiled back at him, and the warmth and encouragement in his expression made her heart stutter. "Slower than I'd like," she downplayed.

"Thank you for hanging on to this little escape artist," he said, nodding at Noodle, who was snoozing in a sunbeam, happy in the autumn-scented kitchen.

"It's really my pleasure," she said. "I'm sure he's used to being here because he's been here with you, and I'm glad he likes it here."

"He scratched at your door?" Hudson asked. When she nodded, he shook his head. "That's not going to be a problem, is it? I really will get on Jeremy to make sure that he stays put, if you want. Maybe we could . . . I don't know, get an electric fence or something."

She let out a yelp. "Those zapper things? Absolutely not!"

The look on his face said he was glad that's how she'd answered. "I don't like them either."

"I don't mind if Noodle scratches the door," she said slowly, her brain whirring as she worked on a solution. "But I listen to music loud sometimes. It helps me think. If it was raining again, I'd hate to not hear him."

"I could put in a doggy door," he said.

She thought about how much she'd budgeted for the renovations, minor though they were, for potentially flipping the house. Even with Hudson's discounts, which she felt bad about, it was the number of things that needed to be fixed that added up. It'd be tight, but . . . "How much would that cost?"

"It's on the house."

"No, I couldn't!" she protested. "You're already doing so much . . ."

"You're looking out for my family's dog. It's the least I could do."

"No," she said, stubborn this time. He just . . . he just kept *giving* to her. Her parents would be appalled that she was essentially freeloading this way, and while he didn't seem to be expecting anything, she still felt weird. "Let me pay for it."

"All right." He smiled. "Dinner, and we'll call it square."

"I know you like my cooking," she said with a weak laugh, "but that's not anywhere near even."

"We can go to dinner to this new restaurant on the island," he said. "It's kind of bougie, but it's supposed to be really good."

"All right, I'll buy you dinner," she agreed, thinking she'd insist on him ordering, like, lobster or something.

"No, I'd be buying *you* dinner."

"That's not—"

He tilted his head, then held out his hand, surprising her into stopping her sentence. Slowly, unsure, she took his hand. It was calloused and hard, much bigger than hers. His fingers exerted gentle pressure, then stroked the back of her hand.

"I'm asking you out, Willa."

His words cut across like a laser, and she froze.

"Unless I'm making you uncomfortable," he said, his deep voice careful. "Listen, I don't want to be that guy. I know I work here, and I'm in your space all the time. I think that there's something between us. Like I said, I'm definitely attracted to you, and I thought you were attracted to me. But if I'm crowding you or making you feel scared . . . I won't bring it up again, period. I respect you, and the last thing I want you to feel is anxious around me."

That. It was things like that, the thoughtfulness, the carefulness. There was really no protection against it.

"Willa?" he asked slowly. "I guess I should . . ."

"You can put in the dog door," she said slowly. "Then . . . we can . . . go out to dinner."

She swallowed hard. That was one of the hardest sentences she'd ever said.

"But I can't promise more than dinner," she added softly.

His expression was *so* gentle.

"Well, I can promise," he said, in that deep, rough-but-soft voice of his, "that I'm never going to ask for more than you're willing to give."

CHAPTER 21

This was a bad idea. It'd been a bad idea when he asked her out, but now it was a *really* bad idea. It was way more expensive than he'd thought, for one thing. Not that he couldn't afford it. Again, that was the blessing of living with his family and combining his income, the farm-stand proceeds, and his father's wages to cover costs—what little was left on the mortgage and their relatively simple bills. But still. The ambiance was good, he'd give it that, but the food had better be outstanding for those kinds of prices.

Who the hell can afford this on the island?

That was the thing, though. It wasn't for the local islanders, at least not the ones here now. It was for the tourists and the soon-to-come gentrifiers.

Hudson gritted his teeth. He was in his best pair of jeans and a pair of midnight blue suede sneakers, and a navy button-up shirt that Kimber insisted he wear. Both Kimber and his parents had given him the thumbs-up.

As much as he liked Willa, he didn't want to change, for her or anyone. But he did want to show that he could fit into her fancy food world, if he needed to. He wanted to show her that he listened. He wanted to show her, in her language, just how special she was.

Now, he was on this very tentative date with the skittish Willa, who looked . . .

Unimpressed?

Fuck.

But it only got worse.

"Hey. Handyman Hudson, right?" Patrick, the asshole from the Victorian, said, walking up to the hostess's stand with a broad grin before turning to Willa. "Good to see you, man! Sorry I couldn't go with you on the bid, but you know how it goes."

Hudson grimaced and shook his hand, avoiding the guy's attempt at a bro hug by simply making the shake harder. Patrick winced a little and let go, but his smile didn't waver. "Who's this?" Patrick asked, staring at Willa.

Why are you here? Why do you care who she is? What, did the guy work here or something?

"This is Willa," Hudson said, wanting to add *my date* but not sure how she'd react to that. He didn't want her to think he had expectations. Or, you know, that he was pissing a circle around her.

"Willa," Patrick repeated, looking back and forth between the two of them, like they were an equation that didn't make sense. Then he narrowed his eyes, zeroing in on her. "Don't you live across the street from me? You seem familiar. I live in the Victorian off Maple Lane."

"Yes," she agreed. Her voice was demure, her smile polite and friendly. "I'm your neighbor."

Patrick's smile widened a little. "Been on the island long?"

Seriously, dude? Right in front of me? Hudson's jaw clenched.

"Just a few weeks." The smile stayed, though her brown eyes warmed. "It's nice. I like it here."

"We were just going to have dinner . . . ," Hudson said, hoping the guy would finally get the message.

Patrick's smile seemed both amused and, when he looked at Willa, predatory. It occurred to Hudson that her simple sundress was probably on the expensive side, not that he knew much about that kind of thing. She was wearing jewelry, and her hair was pulled back somehow with little wisps framing her face. She looked impeccable. Untouchable.

Patrick just looked like an asshole, but an asshole who was wearing a suit that probably cost more than every article of clothing Hudson owned put together. He refused to back down, though. Not out of some caveman this-is-my-woman bullshit (even though, okay, he really wanted to be with Willa, and the thought of this douchebag waltzing in and trying to impress her with some superficial crap made him want to howl). He wasn't embarrassed about who he was, what he did for a living, or how much money he had.

He was pretty sure that Willa didn't care, either, and wouldn't be embarrassed. But he realized they'd been existing in a bubble since they'd met. Sure, she might find him hot. Would she be like some of the women at the bar, though? The kind that thought he was fine to fuck but not to keep?

"Welcome to my restaurant, then," Patrick said, shaking him out of his thoughts. "I can't wait to hear what you think of it."

"*Your* restaurant?" Hudson repeated, aghast.

He smirked at Hudson in surprise. "What did you think I did?"

"I thought you said you were one of those tech bros who retired here," Hudson replied, unable to keep the sourness out of his voice. He seemed to remember something like that from their first contact, anyway. He knew that if he'd ever had a chance at remodeling the Victorian, as a backup at this point, he was probably fucking it up—but let's face it, it would've been a long shot anyway. And working with Patrick as a client would've sucked.

"Retired?" Patrick laughed. "I'm not old enough for that. I *was* in a start-up, we sold for a killing, and after that, I just wanted a change of pace." That was said for Willa's benefit, Hudson could tell. Patrick accepted two menus from the silent hostess. "Here—I've got a special table. I'd be happy for you two to use it."

"That'd be lovely," Willa said smoothly.

Hudson felt anger burning in him like coals. This wasn't the guy trying to do them a solid. This was a guy trying to show Willa who the better bet was.

Motherfucker.

"I've always wanted to open my own restaurant," Patrick humble-bragged, glancing over his shoulder at Willa as Hudson brought up the rear, feeling like a third wheel. "And honestly, Marre Island is perfect. It could be another Whidbey, with the right direction and growth."

"Fantastic," Hudson muttered. Just what they needed. He didn't mind tourists: they were a necessary evil, and the islanders relied on them. But he did mind investors coming in, making everything a goddamned Airbnb, raising property taxes and rents until the locals had to move out.

Surely Willa saw that? She'd hated what her uncle had done to the house. She wouldn't buy this guy's line, would she?

He hated feeling this unsure.

"Have you experienced a true farm-to-table restaurant?" Patrick continued, again acting like Hudson wasn't even there.

His molars were going to crack if Patrick kept this shit up.

Her smile was small. Secretive. Almost catlike. He remembered her talking about her restaurant experiences. "A while ago."

"You haven't had anything like *this*," Patrick promised, with a car-selling smile.

Hudson regretted everything. He should've just worn a clean T-shirt and his work boots and had his mother make some of her killer veggie sandwiches, and said the hell with it. Taken her on a picnic on the beach or something, mosquitos be damned.

The table was by the window and had a view of the sound and a fancy, newly built dock. Patrick was definitely showing off: that he had money, that Hudson was just some handyman jackoff, trying to punch above his weight class. Hudson's chest burned like acid as he took the menu Patrick offered with a smile.

Before Hudson could read a word of it, a waiter brought two small plates to the table and set them in front of the two of them with a flourish.

"Are either of you vegetarian?" Patrick asked. "Lactose intolerant? Any allergies?"

Hudson almost lied, just to screw the guy's attempt to impress. But a quick glance showed a pretty good menu, and he didn't want to get stuck eating fancy cardboard just because Patrick was being a dick. They both shook their heads.

"Fantastic." Patrick really did sound enthused—Hudson would give him that. "Then these appetizers should appeal to you."

Hudson glanced at the small plate.

What am I looking at?

It was like he'd fed Noodle a bunch of small Rice Krispies, and the dog had eaten some grass and then shit these two rolls out on a stylish black plate.

That said, he'd eat the plate itself before asking.

"This is a Dungeness-crab-and-goat-cheese salad with grapefruit and shallot, in a savory cannoli shell." Patrick did a little gesture, muted jazz hands. "Enjoy. And I want to let you know: the meal is on me tonight."

"No," Hudson growled, truly pissed now.

"I must insist," Patrick said smoothly, his eyes lighting with triumph. "Please. Consider yourself my guests for the evening."

Hudson could see he was trapped: couldn't make a stink about it without looking like an asshole. Patrick had, essentially, boxed him in.

Willa studied Patrick for a second, then smiled—that small smile again. Was she impressed by this dickbag? With Hudson, she'd been almost panicked by accepting any sort of favor and pushed back against anything she thought was uneven. This was not going to be a cheap meal.

Why the hell wasn't she putting up a fight?

Was it that she just didn't want to feel in debt to *him*? Connected to *him*?

Hudson's stomach knotted at the thought. No matter how it tasted, this meal was going to *suck*.

She took a bite of the roll thing in front of her. "Delicious," she assured Patrick.

Patrick beamed back. At this rate, Hudson wouldn't be surprised if he pulled up a seat. "Thanks. You know, it was inspired by Chef Marceline Dumonde, over at the Cloisters in San Francisco. It's a famous restaurant," he added.

"Oh?" she murmured, finishing the appetizer.

"The play of acid, sweetness, creaminess . . . Chef Dumonde calls it the trifecta. Said it was the perfect play of flavors. And if anyone understands the pursuit and creation of perfection in cuisine, it'd be her. She—"

"She believes in *natural* perfection," Willa corrected.

Hudson blinked. So did Patrick. Willa didn't raise her voice. She didn't need to. It was like when she'd stopped Bruno in his tracks when he was irate at the barbecue, only this time she wasn't high. Her quiet voice was just effective, probably because it was unexpected, and it had that cool, precise edge to it that, for whatever reason, turned Hudson on.

Patrick, on the other hand, just looked confused. "Like I said," he tried to continue, getting back on track, "Chef Dumonde believes in pursuing, ah, natural perfection . . ."

"No, she believes that nature holds perfection. Not chefs." Willa shook her head. "Man-made attempts at perfection weren't just pale facsimiles to her, they were downright frauds. So you either abandoned perfection or you pushed as close to nature as you could. And got used to failing."

Now Patrick looked amused, almost indulgent. "Trust me. I've studied her menus for years. I even had one of my chefs stage in her kitchen. I've seen every documentary. I'd have read her cookbooks, if she had any, but all we have are her occasional recipes in magazines and some notes from people who worked under her . . . and I've read every single one I could get my hands on." He acted like he'd just made the winning argument in a court case. "Her nuage des pétoncles is hailed as perfection, just as she'd designed it."

"She's said publicly that she'll never do that dish again, though," Willa pointed out. "Ultimately, she thought it was unworkable and pretentious."

Now Patrick was starting to look irritated. Hudson, on the other hand, had no idea what the hell was going on . . . although, he had to say, it was starting to get entertaining.

"She *never* said that." Patrick sounded scandalized, almost insulted. "Because it was perfect! She just doesn't like repetition."

Willa sighed. "It certainly sounds like you're certain."

Patrick's smile was back, smugger than ever. Hudson didn't even know how he could pull that off. "I am. I've known restaurateurs for ages. I'm friends with plenty of top chefs. I *know* this world."

She looked torn . . . then strangely determined. Then, to Hudson's surprise, she pulled out her phone. "Forgive me," she said. He wasn't sure if she was apologizing to him or to Patrick. "One second."

It was a video call, and sound erupted from it: clangs, someone yelling numbers and food names and weird commands: "fire two," "two corn," "three crab," "three duck."

"Willa?" A woman's face filled the screen. She had short steel-gray hair pulled back in a yellow bandanna and wore chef's whites. Her voice had the silky tone of a native French speaker. "Non, is it really you?"

"Bonjour, Marceline," Willa said, and damn, her saying the word in that fluid accent made her about a million times sexier somehow. Hudson shifted in his chair. "I'm sorry to be calling you during service, especially for such a trivial thing, but I promise it's brief."

Patrick's jaw dropped. The guy literally gaped like a fish on the bottom of a boat.

It was fucking *awesome*.

"Amie, you can call me any time. What do you need?"

"A quick question: How did you feel about your scallop cloud? The nuage des pétoncles?"

The woman let out a sharp crack of laughter. "That was such merde," she said. "Overconstructed pretentious critic whore bullshit. You know that was a disaster."

"I thought so, but it'd been a while," Willa said, with a small, bittersweet smile.

"What in the world brought that on?"

"Bit of a bar bet," Willa said, and Marceline let out that boisterous laugh again.

"I can imagine. Restaurateur, eh?"

Patrick's cheeks went flame red, like he'd been standing in front of a pizza oven. Hudson rubbed his stubble to cover his smile at the guy's discomfort.

"Something like that." Willa shot a quick glance at Patrick. "I appreciate you taking the call, and I'm sorry if I bothered you. I know how busy you are . . ."

"Non, I don't think so." Now Marceline's voice was stern. "I can't talk now, but now that I know you're actually talking to people, don't think you can escape a call from me. We *will* catch up."

Willa nodded, looking both rueful and embarrassed. "Of course."

"A bientôt, Willa." With that, they hung up.

"You know *Marceline Dumonde*." Patrick looked like embarrassment and anger were warring with envy and desire—not necessarily for her but for her contacts, what she could do for him. Although yeah, Hudson was sure just wanting to bone her was in the mix.

Willa nodded back, then smiled at the busboy who filled their waters, thanking him in a soft voice.

"You have her *on speed dial*," Patrick added.

Willa tilted her head. "I have several old friends in the industry," she said with a small shrug. Not humblebragging like Patrick had. Just . . . being humble.

His conflicted expression finally settled into greed. "I had no idea," he admitted. "You must've thought I was such an ass!"

Now Hudson's eyes narrowed. He wasn't going to . . .

"I'm definitely glad that you're here," he said, and Hudson could've sworn that he really *was* going to pull up a chair. "I'd love to—"

"It's been years," Willa said, with a soft, sad finality. "That's not really my life anymore. I've been out of the scene. I think you're doing something lovely here, though, and I'm sure we'll enjoy it." She took a shaky breath. "It's going to be the perfect date. Thank you so much for your generosity."

She emphasized the word. "Date." Even self-absorbed Patrick couldn't miss it.

Hudson grinned. He couldn't help himself. He could see the moment that Patrick realized he'd been put in his place, despite all his efforts. Not only had he been shown up as a blowhard, he was stuck picking up the tab.

"I'm sorry about that," she said in a low voice, after Patrick walked away, as she looked over the menu.

"About what?" Hudson looked at the menu, too, wondering if he should just pick the most expensive thing on it. Petty? Sure. Did he feel guilty? Nope.

"About saying this was a date," she said, and he stiffened, and not in the good way. "He just seemed like he was hitting on me—"

"He was," Hudson agreed, and she blushed, biting her lip. Which was cute as fuck and made his brain pause for a second, wondering what that felt like.

"I could've handled it a different way. Told him I wasn't interested, but I know guys like him especially, and that takes *forever*. He wanted a pissing contest, he wanted to prove something, and he'd be over for every course, bragging or trying to 'persuade' me, and it would've really ruined the meal."

"Yeah, he would've." He looked at her. "And it *is* a date. Right?"

Her smile was just this side of shy, but also happy. "I didn't know if you wanted other people to know, though."

At this point, he'd have gotten a billboard, an ad in the *Marre Weekly*, and maybe even a skywriter. "I don't mind at all," he said, his voice going husky.

He slid his hand over the tabletop. She looked unsure . . . then, slowly, she scooted her hand over and took it. She had a few cooking calluses, and he saw the remnants of old cuts and burns, no doubt from her times cooking. But comparatively, her hand was impossibly soft and fit perfectly in his.

He liked the look of them together.

"I probably shouldn't have bothered Marceline either," she said with a sheepish grin. "But I remember so many restaurateurs like that. Steven used to make fun of them, and I'd make fun of *him* when he started acting like an ass. He said I was his conscience."

There it was again: that bittersweet smile.

"I guess this Marceline's kind of a big deal?"

Willa bit the corner of her lip. Not like she was laughing at him or amused at his expense . . . at least he didn't feel that way. "Her tasting menu is booked at least a year out and, last I checked, costs five hundred dollars. Per person."

He choked. "Holy shit."

"Not including alcohol." She sipped her water.

He liked food as much as the next guy. But . . . what the fuck? "Is it gold plated or something?" he muttered.

"It's strange if you're not from that world," she admitted, then grimaced. "Actually, it's weird even when you are. But then, it's *your* weird. You just . . . fit in, I guess?"

The sinking feeling returned. "Guess that's your world, then?"

Where people could drop five hundred bucks on a single dinner with no booze. Where they made clouds out of shellfish and had fancy words for what was essentially a taquito.

Now a look of incredible sadness crossed her face. "Not exactly," she said. "Not anymore, anyway. Not for a long time."

Unsure of what to do, he broke into the cannoli-thing with his fork. "The cookbook," he said. "That's going to get you back in there."

"The cookbook's a paycheck," she said with a shrug. "Once I figure out how to write a seductive cookbook for Mr. Sexy Chef, I'll figure out my next step."

"Well, I'm here to help."

She smiled, and it was real this time, a little warmer, even as her cheeks blushed. He loved that blush.

"You are," she said, almost under her breath.

Grinning, he took a bite, then grimaced, letting out a small groan.

"You okay?" she said, immediately concerned.

"It's just . . ." He scowled at the plate. "It's really good. Goddammit."

She let out a surprised laugh, and he smiled back at her. He hoped whatever she wanted worked for her.

But selfishly, he also wanted her to stay on the island.

He really wasn't sure what to do with that knowledge.

CHAPTER 22

Hudson had everything he needed to install the doggy door. He'd left Noodle at home with Jeremy, who was still nursing his wounds from the breakup and quitting his job.

He let himself into Willa's house like he lived there—he'd only been coming for about a month, but it was becoming one of his favorite things, to the point where he resented being called out on emergency jobs.

He heard music playing. Willa had moved on from simply humming, and now she was always surrounded by music. It was an indicator of her mood. She was constantly surprising him with the wide, wild range of stuff she was into. Movie scores and classical when she was trying to puzzle something out. EDM and angry alternative when she was *really* stuck on something. And poppy, happy music when she was actually in the kitchen cooking—often from the eighties and nineties, which was fun. He'd seen the way she swayed, sometimes punching out a lyric under her breath when it was a song she really liked, and when she was doing something natural that she didn't need to concentrate on.

Today was a cooking day, he thought with a smile as he headed down the hallway. It was salsa music, some of his favorite. He didn't recognize the song—or rather, he kind of recognized the song, but didn't know why.

He froze when he hit the archway to the dining area and saw her bopping around. She was singing along in Spanish, he realized. And then realized the reason he recognized it was because it was one of her favorite songs, from a Japanese animated show. Only it had been "salsa-fied."

Never thought I'd get turned on by a salsa version of the theme song to Chainsaw Man.

He would've laughed out loud if he hadn't caught sight of her, basically taking any conscious thought offline.

The way she was moving her hips? *Holy shit.* It was a far cry from much younger women. Obviously, she knew what she was doing, and he was hypnotized as she sang along, her slipper-clad feet moving to the complex steps. She was so immersed, she didn't notice him until she turned around.

"*Eeeeep!*" she shrieked, dropping the wooden spoon she'd been singing into.

"Sorry," he said, although he kind of wasn't. He grinned, ignoring the way his heart was pounding. "You're good. I didn't know you were into salsa."

"I'm kind of . . . it's been a while."

"Same." He grinned. "I'm all right at it, basic stuff, but I don't have any fancy moves or anything."

"Oh, I'll bet you have some fancy moves." Then she slapped her hand over her mouth, and he burst out laughing. The shock was clear on her face. She finally grinned back a little as she tucked her hair behind her ear, one of his favorite nervous gestures of hers.

"You look like a pro."

"I took a class ages ago, in college, and I've always liked the music," she said, picking up the spoon, tossing it into the sink, and cleaning the spot on the floor. "My friend Nat and I sometimes hit a club when I'm in the Bay Area, but that's been a long time, too."

They'd been slowly circling around their growing attraction, teasing . . . getting closer, moving away. It was like foreplay. Hell, it was like *edging*. It had been more fun than he realized it'd be.

He liked sex, without question, and he liked flirting. He liked kissing, he liked making out, even cuddling. But at this point, with dating off the table for so long, he didn't play games, didn't make promises of any sort, and was clear up front with the women he had sex with. As a result, he did tend to get to the point a little faster. It was a dick move to take a woman to a fancy dinner, kiss and cuddle and tease her, and then insist that there wasn't anything emotional going on.

This was a mix of hot and just so sweet, so soft, he felt like he was going to crawl out of his own skin. There was obviously more going on here.

He liked that they talked. He liked her blushing, her teasing . . . the way her eyes roved over him, sometimes when she didn't think he was looking, sometimes when he was, like she couldn't help herself as she bit her lip. Or even better, when her eyes went unfocused and he swore he could practically see her desire for him reflected there.

Especially then.

The song was still going, so he held out his hand. She stared at it with wide eyes for a second.

"We're in the kitchen," she stammered, looking flustered.

"We've got the joint to ourselves," he said, in his smoothest voice, and as he'd hoped, she laughed . . . but took his hand.

He was a little rusty, but it was like riding a bike. He started on the right beat, and she followed like they'd been dancing together for years, even though she looked shy. There was space between them, but they moved in rhythm.

Like he'd thought at the bar: you could tell a lot about someone by the way they danced. It was clear Willa loved it—and was good at it, no matter how she tried to downplay it. Once the self-consciousness melted away, she got into it with his encouragement and the fact that he obviously enjoyed it too. He held both of her hands, her movements mirroring his.

He took a chance and twirled her, then attempted a lock-twirl hand switch. Her clear, rough-silk laugh made him happier than he'd felt in a long time.

Then she surprised him as her expression turned slightly naughty. She danced a little closer.

"Oh, it's like that, huh?" he said, but his voice went rough. He saw her dimples pop out in response, and her eyes gleamed. "All right, let's do this."

He remembered the moves. He stepped closer still, one foot between both of hers. He saw her eyes widen, but she didn't step back. So he shifted even lower, holding her waist as they matched their rhythm, going from two people dancing to one hot-as-hell couple, fused together.

And god *damn*, she actually rolled her hips in response.

His body immediately went into oh-my-God-it's-happening mode, but he didn't slow down. He stepped between her jeans-clad legs, show-ing her that he, too, knew what to do with his hips.

Before he knew it, they were grinding. And they were doing it *well*.

She was getting breathless, but he didn't think it was from the exertion of the dancing. He stared into her eyes, his own temperature going up like a skyrocket. Her hands smoothed up his chest, resting on his biceps and clenching lightly.

The song stopped abruptly, with a flourish. They stopped, in each other's arms, bodies still plastered to each other. He looked into her dark-brown eyes, watched the way her pulse still danced wildly in her throat.

He leaned in, giving her plenty of time to pull away. She just kept staring, her head angling upward. Her tongue darted out quickly, a fast pass against her lower lip.

Another salsa song turned on, but he barely registered it. He wasn't interested in dancing now.

His mouth met hers, and for a split second, it was like . . . like when he fixed a clock, and all the pieces finally *clicked*, and everything moved smoothly. She had the softest lips he'd ever kissed, and she moved against him like she had when they were dancing, in sync, anticipating his moves, countering with her own. It was indescribably satisfying. It felt perfect.

Then she made a soft moan that was clear, even over the music, and things went from gentle to hard in a blink.

He groaned in response, moving his hands from her hips, one cradling her jawline, the other weaving into her hair to keep her in place. His tongue moved ahead, tangling with hers as her fingers moved to grip his shoulder, digging in and dragging him closer.

Things got a little blurry after that.

He knew that she'd basically started to climb him, hands linking around his neck, pulling him lower and bringing her higher. He solved part of that problem by walking them backward until his hands met the wall . . . then pressing her against it and hooking her knee over his hip in a way that made his current physical state unmistakable. He thought—or at least, insofar as his brain was capable of thinking—that this would be the breaking point, that she'd pull away. But when he went to pause, to check, she *growled* at him, nipping at his lower lip and . . .

Sweet Jesus. If he'd been impressed by the hip roll during dancing, it had *nothing* on when she was pressing herself against his rock-hard cock.

Part of him wanted to just lift her up, wrap her legs around his waist, and then carry her koala-style to her bedroom, where he would proceed to absolutely *wreck* her for the next twenty-four hours. Sure, he was forty-two, but he still had stamina, and he'd been thinking of her for over a month. And if she kept tugging at his hair, he was definitely leaning in that direction.

But another part of him—a part he hated at the moment—didn't want to fuck this up. She was worked up enough past the point of no return, from the feel of it (and a *fantastic* feel it was), but he couldn't bear the thought of them finally having sex and then her immediately regretting it.

And then, even worse—cutting him off.

As much as he hated it, communication was probably the best plan here. After they talked it through, and when his dick wasn't in the driver's seat, then they could go ahead and tear up the sheets. For days straight, if she'd let him.

With more internal strength than he'd ever used before, he pulled away. The two of them were gulping breaths like they'd been running a marathon, and she looked at him, confused and irritated.

"You sure about this?" he asked. He was concerned, but he wasn't a saint. He also wasn't going to make the decision for her. "Because I am if you are. You have no idea. But I don't want just one night, Willa, and I don't want you to regret this or push me away. If you're in, you need to make sure you're willing to at least try being all in, whatever that looks like."

He saw the minute she registered what was happening—when the lust slid away into shock. She lowered her leg, and he stepped back, as difficult as it was.

"I . . . I'm not ready," she said. "I'm so sor—"

"*Don't* apologize," he said, with a little more snap than he probably should have, but his body was pissed at him, and it bled into his tone. He was glad he'd said something, since this was exactly what he'd been worried about.

He'd made the right decision. His dick could get over it.

He gentled his voice, and he stroked her cheek. "I know you're still getting used to all of this, and I don't want you to go faster than you're ready, no matter how I'm feeling."

Her look of gratitude made the current ache he was feeling worth it. He could tell she still wanted to apologize, but she didn't, so that was a step forward.

"I'm gonna put in the door," he said. "Then you can tell me how the cookbook's going, maybe?"

She nodded, her eyes huge, her hair mussed. She looked sexy as hell.

"Then, when you're done with the cookbook," he said, his voice dark with promise, "maybe we'll dance some more."

He saw the second it registered. Her cheeks flushed.

And she nodded.

With a smile, he went back out to the truck and grabbed the supplies. He wasn't looking for a one-night stand from Willa, not just because she was his neighbor but because for the first time in a long time, he could see something maybe, *maybe* long term. And he was going to build this right.

CHAPTER 23

I'm running out of time.

It was late, but she wanted to believe, had to believe, that in the past week she'd made some progress. She'd come up with four appetizers, three salads, and five desserts, and she had sketched out recipe ideas for the entrées. Now she was testing, as fast as she could. She had notebooks strewn around the central countertop, their pages smudged with chocolate and stained with beet juice and berries. She had rudimentary sketches of how the finished dishes should look. The kitchen looked like a demilitarized zone, but at least she was moving forward.

She was listening to music, as usual. Just not any Latin music. Since her scorching-hot and completely unexpected "dance session" with Hudson, they'd still been in the same general area. He was getting to the bottom of his punch list, and she was still working, or trying to work, diligently. But they had enough sexual tension between them to be seen from frickin' space, and it was taking a toll . . . even if it was fueling some of the ideas, which was a when-life-gives-you-lemons situation if she'd ever seen one. She still didn't have any of the written body copy to connect the recipes, but she had notes detailing what could happen.

She'd also had some sweaty, formless, confusing, *sexy* dreams that left her waking up breathless. Flashes of that kiss with Hudson would ambush her at various points during the day and night: in the shower, when she was going to sleep, and always when she was trying to work. She'd almost cut herself again by not paying attention while dicing the boiled beets for her goat-cheese-and-beet salad, which was ridiculous, especially if it meant Hudson would patch her up again.

Just pull it together, she scolded herself as she worked on her salmon mousse. She was in her late forties, and this was her *living*. If she didn't figure out a way to stay afloat and pay the mortgage, she was going to have to sell the house and move off island—which, let's face it, would be a temporary save anyway. Even if she didn't buy another house and just rented, unless she moved somewhere like Iowa that had drastically lower rents than anywhere on the West Coast, she was going to run out of any profit she made from selling. It wasn't retirement money, as her parents continually pointed out.

Fear, it turned out, was a great motivator. Between the anxiety and Hudson going home, she was able to shift into a hyperfocused panic mode.

She took a picture of the completed mousse, piped into artistic rosettes on baguette rounds and garnished with dill and lemon zest, shaped into a heart. It was a little cheesy, but it ought to get the point across.

She tucked the phone back into her pocket. Three photos done, five to go, if she could manage it. Her eyes felt sandy, and her body felt drawn with exhaustion, but she kept moving forward.

At nearly three in the morning, she was ready to fall over, but the last of the recipes she'd wanted to show Sam was written up and tested. She'd managed to even make some chicken, although that wasn't going to make the final cut. The kitchen was a tangled mess of confusing sounds, the whole place a disaster, despite her trying to clean as she went. It reminded her of times at Steven's restaurant when they'd been shorthanded and she'd had to work the line. She smiled a little. She missed the companionship there, though—working with the chefs, joking with them. Yes, they'd had focus, but they'd also been family. More than that: people who'd been in the trenches of a war they were more passionate about than anyone she'd ever met. She still didn't consider herself a chef necessarily, but she'd loved seeing these people who were so devoted, so bonkers about pursuing a career in something they loved that "wasn't necessary" and "didn't make sense." She'd loved feeling like a part of that.

She loved their passion.

She missed their presence.

That said, she hadn't missed the pressure, and this was like all the negatives of being on the line and none of the camaraderie. She took the last picture, then tucked the phone into her back pocket.

She'd made sticky toffee pudding ice cream, a recipe she'd altered from a special edition of Häagen-Dazs years ago that she'd fallen in love with. After packing it into the freezer, she went to start cleaning up, when she heard a noise outside her back door.

"You have got to be kidding me," she said, with fondness, despite her exhaustion. "Tell me you didn't smell me poaching chicken all the way from Marigold Farm!"

There was a tentative push against the doggy door. They'd trained Noodle—or tried—to use the door itself. It wasn't a big door, so she wasn't worried that a full-size person could get in. It was Noodle size. She thought about opening the door but instead decided to let him make it in himself. It would encourage him to come over when he wanted, and if she kept opening up the door for him, he'd never learn.

She cleaned up as she heard the plastic flap of the door rustle. She was just putting the last dish in the dishwasher and reaching for her cleaning cloth as she finally heard the tapping of claws on the wood floor. "Good job, Noo—"

The word lodged in her throat as she focused in on what had entered her house.

The only thing that made sense initially was that it was obviously *not* Noodle. It was bigger than a house cat but smaller than Noodle. It was also black and bushy, almost like a hedgehog. It had a longish tail that was also bushy, like a bottle brush, straight and spiny.

It also had a thick white stripe running from its head to said bottle brush tail.

She was so surprised, so tired and so baffled, that it took her way longer than it should have to realize that this was a skunk.

The scream started slowly, more like a startled "AaaaaaaaaIIIIIGH!" And then she tossed her cleaning cloth at it.

This, it turned out, was the absolute *worst* course of action, as the bushy little creature was immediately (and understandably) pissed. It must've been drawn to the food, or maybe it had just gotten lost. She wasn't a nature expert. But it was *in* now, and it didn't know how to get out, and it had just had projectiles lobbed at it.

It started stomping its little feet, jumping up and down on its fore-paws as if to say *Oh really? You want to start something?* Then it bared what looked like needle-sharp pointy teeth, making a chattering sound. By that point, she'd backed out toward the hallway, and it advanced on her.

Then it slowly started to raise its tail, turning it toward her.

Some memory of a documentary, or maybe just instinctive common sense, finally kicked in. She spun on her heel and sprinted for the front door, grateful that she hadn't locked it after Hudson left that afternoon. She threw it open just as she heard it make a warning chitter . . . and the foulest smell she could imagine suddenly trailed after her.

She turned back, accidentally taking a breath through her nose. Her eyes watered, and she gagged. It was like tear gas, if tear gas could go rancid somehow. She slammed the door behind her.

She didn't smell like skunk, at least—or rather, she hadn't been directly sprayed. But the kitchen. All her notes. The food in the fridge . . .

She'd heard about what happened when skunks sprayed dogs. It took a month for the smell to wash out, she seemed to remember. She'd heard stories about people washing their dogs with tomato juice to try and cancel it out, only to have them then smell like skunk and V8. It was *not* encouraging.

Not to mention that her house was now going to smell like skunk. How was she supposed to work like that? Or, God forbid, how far out would this put selling the house? Surely no one was going to want to buy a house that smelled like skunk.

I do not need this.

It was as if everything caught up to her, all at once. She let out a yell that was a cross between a shriek and a cry.

"Why?" she shouted. "*Why?* What kind of a net do I need to buy to *catch a fucking break?*"

She didn't know if she was yelling to God or to the void. Or even to Steven, although she doubted it. But she finally broke down weeping, plopping down in the damp grass in front of her porch and hugging her knees, rocking herself as the tears poured out like a broken pipe.

She didn't know what to do. All she knew was she was tired of being alone. She was tired of shouldering all of this herself. She knew she could call Nat, but she hadn't talked to her in too long and had glossed over the realities of her finances and her work state. She sure as hell wasn't waking her elderly parents at three o'clock at night and detailing her latest in a series of what she knew they'd see as failures.

She shouldn't call, she knew. But she just felt so broken. So she pulled her phone out of her pocket, grateful it had some charge left, low though it was.

And after a moment's debate, she hit Hudson's number.

CHAPTER 24

Hudson woke out of a deep sleep to his phone buzzing on the nightstand. He reached for it blindly. "Mrphello?" he slurred, trying to get his bearings. He hoped it wasn't a plumbing emergency—a busted pipe or, God, a flooded house. Both kids were at home, so at least *they* were okay.

"Hudson?"

He shook the sleep off as his brain registered: it was Willa, and she sounded like she was crying. "Willa? Are you okay? What's wrong?"

"There . . . there . . ." She hiccuped, and he was already out of bed, pulling on a shirt and a pair of jeans as he wedged the phone between his ear and his shoulder. He wasn't even consciously thinking about his actions. "There was a *skunk* and it's *in the house* and I think it sprayed everything!"

Ah, shit. While he was sure the skunk couldn't physically hurt her, they were never good things to run into. "Did it get you? Are you sprayed?" he asked. Not that it would've changed anything other than what he'd bring over. He pulled on socks and shoved his feet into his work boots.

"No." A loud sniffle and another hiccup. "But . . . it ruined all my notes. I'm sure they smell horrible. And all my food's in there. And the house, oh my God, the house smells so bad, I had no idea it could . . . and I *need* that stuff. I'm supposed to have all this stuff ready for the chef, and it all smells rancid, and I don't know what to *do* . . ."

She started crying, gulping sobs that broke his heart.

"You hang tight, okay? I will be there in a few minutes."

He waited for her to make a garbled noise that he was assuming was at least "okay" or "yes." Then he grabbed his keys and headed over there.

She was sitting on the front lawn, hugging her knees to her chest and rocking slightly. He shut off his truck and rushed to her. Her tearstained face, lit by the dim light of the moon, looked up at him in anguish.

"I'm so sorry," she half whispered. "I just . . . I didn't know who else to call."

"Oh, sweetheart," he murmured, before hunkering down on the ground next to her, crossing his legs, and pulling her onto his lap. She snuggled against him, and he felt hot tears through the thin material of the T-shirt he'd pulled on. He smoothed her hair and nuzzled the crown of her head as he made soothing noises. "It'll be all right, baby, I promise."

She clutched him harder, like a baby koala bear tightening its grip, and snuffled.

He wasn't sure how long they sat there, him rocking her and nuzzling her, her holding him like he was a life preserver. But finally, eventually, she pulled back a little, rubbing at her eyes and nose.

"Oh my God, I made you a mess," she said, sounding appalled and starting to pull away, but he looped his arms gently around her, rubbing her back in calming circles.

"I genuinely don't care," he said.

"I soaked your shirt!"

"Really don't care," he echoed, smoothing some tears from her cheeks. Her eyes looked puffy, and her expression was one of exhausted pain. "I'm glad that you thought of me. I'm going to help, okay?"

She blinked. *"How?"*

"First, I'm going to see if the skunk is still there," he said, which brought another round of tears. "I'm going to assess the damage, okay? Then, tomorrow, I'm going to look at getting some special fans and filters—the kind that the big damage-repair places use for, like, mold mitigation and things. Don't worry. We'll get you back to normal in no time."

She sighed, and it sounded like a child who had stayed up too late and was fighting sleep. "But . . . I can't sleep in there now," she said, sounding confused.

"I know." He hugged her. "It's late. I'm going to take you home with me, okay?"

She still stared at him, like he'd suddenly started speaking in pig latin for no reason. "Home?"

"My home. My house," he clarified. "You can crash with me until we get your house stuff figured out."

"This is going to be expensive, isn't it?" She sounded a little nervous, and also defeated.

"It doesn't have to be." He'd make sure of that.

She knuckled at the last of the tears in her eyes. "You can't keep doing favors for me, Hud."

"Why?" He nudged her chin up so that she was looking at him. "Why can't I? I'm not expecting anything. You need help, and I can give it. Why won't you let me?"

She swallowed hard enough for him to see her throat working. "I'm not used to this."

"Don't know what to tell you there, other than get used to it. Because I like helping you feel better, and I'm going to do it every chance I get." He nudged her off his lap, then tugged her to her feet. Even though it was summer, there was still a cool breeze coming off the sound, and she was just in a T-shirt and jeans and bare feet. She was shivering. "I'm going to have you get in the truck, okay? I'll be there in a minute."

She didn't respond, just had a blank expression, not aloof this time but lost, exhausted, and possibly near her breaking point. So he walked her over to the truck, putting her into the passenger seat of the cab. She went with him without a word, seeming so tired that she was as pliant as Play-Doh.

Once he got her belted in (just for his own peace of mind, since by that point it really seemed like she'd checked out for the night), he did a quick survey of the kitchen. The skunk must've made it out the door, and yeah, the smell was bad. Eye-wateringly bad. Her kitchen was toast for the short term, and the rest of the house wasn't going to be much better. He'd figure out how to save things from there. In the meantime, he grabbed her key, locked the doors, and then headed back out to the cab, hoping the scent didn't cling to his clothes.

It apparently did a little, if the way her nose wrinkled when he climbed behind the steering wheel was any indication. "God, I did *not* need this," she moaned. "I'm supposed to show photos and recipe stuff to the guy this week, in Seattle!"

"I mean it, I've got this."

He turned on the car, then cranked up the heater. When he noticed she was still shivering, he pulled a blanket from behind the seat and covered her with it. In the darkness, he heard her say, "I'm used to going to the ER at this time of night."

He stilled. "Your husband?"

"We used to joke that his shit never happened during daylight hours," she said, even though there was no humor evident in her voice. "At least the really dramatic stuff. He had tons of doctors' appointments—neurologist, endocrinologist, and the usual garden-variety stuff. But when it looked like he was going to die, or when things just jumped the rails, it was always at like three in the morning."

His heart wrenched. He'd had moments of worry as a parent, but this—he couldn't imagine. "That must've been really hard." Which was an understatement, but what else could he say?

"It was." Her voice was soft, just loud enough to be heard over the engine. "There were days when I was so scared and so tired that I thought I'd just collapse. And . . ."

There was a hitch, a small one, before she continued, her voice only a little thready as she continued.

"I didn't have anyone to call. My parents were older, and while they didn't *hate* Steven, they'd disagreed with our marriage. The fact that I was ten years younger than him, and that we'd gotten married just a little over a year after I graduated from college. They thought that I was being foolish, and they told me that if I was going to make that decision, they couldn't support it . . . and that was *before* they found out he had a chronic illness."

He put the truck in drive and headed for the house. He didn't say a word, just listened to her as the story poured out, her voice watery.

"And if I called his parents—they would've dropped everything, but they also couldn't necessarily *help*," she said. "His father's default was just getting angry. Once, I called them, and they showed up at the ER, and his dad got kicked out for being belligerent. He was a big fancy business lawyer of some sort, and used to getting his way—and used to getting louder when he didn't, until he *did* get his way. So they said he was verbally aggressive, which, let me tell you, only made what I was trying to do harder. His mother was trying to placate her husband and basically wringing her hands over her son."

"That sounds so fucking hard."

She sighed softly. "You wind up doing what you have to. I got used to checking his blood sugar on my phone in the middle of the night, keeping track of his meds and all the side effects—neuropathy, depression, pain control, the whole smash. Making sure his pump wasn't acting up. After a while, it just became routine. Like, your-disaster-is-my-Tuesday kind of thing."

He wanted *so badly* to hold her. He pulled into his driveway, parking in his spot near the farmhouse. When he killed the engine, he turned to her, stroking her cheek.

"I am so very, very sorry," he finally said. "That you lost your husband, and that you had to go through all of that, all by yourself."

"I'm not telling you that to make you feel bad for me," she countered, her eyes shining, not with tears but with gratitude. "I'm telling you because tonight was the first time I've ever felt like I could call somebody and they'd make it better."

He got out of the truck and went to her side of the cab. He opened the door. She stepped out . . . then gave him a hug.

He tucked her against his ribs and nuzzled her hair, faint skunk smell or not. He held her tightly but carefully, wanting to be able to help her for as long as he could.

Maybe forever, he realized. If she'd let him.

He forced himself to focus on practicalities. "I can give you some clothes you can use as pajamas. You'll probably want to take a shower—not that you really smell of skunk," he reassured her, "but just to feel better. Then you can—"

He froze, realizing.

Jeremy was home, sleeping in his room.

Kimber was *also* home, sleeping in *her* room.

"—take my bed," he said.

Apparently she, too, had done the bed math in this situation. "Where are you going to sleep, though?"

"Our couch is pretty comfortable." Which it was. Well, comfortable enough to sit on. Maybe not the best for actually sleeping, but he wasn't planning on sleeping that long anyway. Between thinking of her and getting up and getting a move on fixing her problem, he didn't think he'd crash for more than a few hours.

She bit her lip, distracting him. "I don't want to put you out of your bed, Hudson."

He tucked her hair behind her ear. "Kimber gets up early, and I think you need to get as much sleep as possible," he insisted. "I don't mind, really."

"You already got up at three in the morning to bail me out," she countered, digging her heels in and crossing her arms. "I can't make you have a bad night's sleep too."

He was tired, and he was about to make his case, when she surprised him.

"Why don't we just share?"

CHAPTER 25

After the roller coaster of tonight, Willa should've been exhausted. Between the late hour and all the work she'd been putting in, then the shock of the skunk and her crying jag, by rights she should have been completely unconscious, in a fetal ball in Hudson's bed. But since she'd gotten out of the shower and swum into his oversize T-shirt and sweatpants, she'd felt wired. Stretched out in Hudson's bed, under a thin blanket and cool sheets, she felt like there were currents of static electricity dancing over her skin.

Hudson was in the hall bathroom, the one she'd just left steamy, having his own shower to eradicate any lingering skunk smell. She hunkered down, and his usual scent surrounded her, like a combination of sexy-as-hell satin and reassuring weighted blanket. It still didn't make her sleepy. If anything, it did the opposite.

What, exactly, are you planning to do here?

They'd already both admitted they were attracted to each other. She knew that he was being careful with her, like she was the thinnest, most delicate crystal, and she didn't think she wanted that. Then again, he'd also implied that he wanted more than sex with her . . . and she wasn't sure how she felt about that either.

The thought of sex itself was already daunting, after all this time. Trying to dust off that old knowledge and somehow get retrained as a sexual being at nearly fifty was daunting, especially with a guy four years younger who seemed more practiced.

She knew one thing: she might be rusty at sex and she wasn't sure about relationships, but there was something magic about being with him in the witching hour, when the island was so quiet that it seemed unreal.

She might not be sure what, but *something* was going to happen tonight.

The man in question stepped in, giving his hair a quick rub with a small towel. He wasn't wearing a shirt, just a pair of what looked like basketball shorts. Her mouth actually *watered*. He was the most delectable thing she'd ever seen. Her heart somehow, impossibly, sped up, like she'd increased the incline on an already fast treadmill.

"Sorry," he said, catching her staring at his chest. "Did you want me to put on a shirt?"

It wasn't like the cover of *Men's Health* or anything, or any of those TikTok thirst traps, but his chest was nicely defined, with a smattering of hair. There were random and sundry scars and a few bruises. She got a better look at the tattoos she'd never let herself linger on: tools, some kind of plants. They probably meant something. She wondered what. Maybe he'd tell her.

She'd ask him later, she thought, as her body heated and she felt herself go greedy.

Much later.

She realized he was still looking at her expectantly, and she still hadn't answered. "Whatever—" Her voice cracked, and she cleared her throat. "Whatever makes you feel comfortable."

His grin was downright devilish.

Oh, God. She was *not* going to survive this, she thought as he slowly climbed into bed. "You have to get up at any particular time?" he asked.

She shook her head. Then he set an alarm on his phone and shut off the light.

"Tell me if you need anything else—blanket, pillows, whatever," he added, his voice like velvet in the darkness. "Or if you change your mind about me being in here, I'll understand."

"I think we'll be fine."

She was going to spontaneously combust. She could smell his shower soap now, mixed with the underlying smell of *him*. She wanted to bury her nose in the crook of his neck and just *breathe*, inhale him. Then consume him, either slowly, with lapping licks, or in big gulping bites.

The thing was, she was horribly inexperienced, even at her age. Maybe *especially* at her age. How the hell was she supposed to make a move? She had no frame of reference here. Should she . . . ask? She was very much a proponent of consent, and he'd been the one to say they needed to talk. At the same time, asking felt so awkwardly formal, almost professional.

Pardon me, my good sir. I am interested in doing physical things to you, starting with kissing and moving on to potential penetration. Would you be interested in discussing the parameters of such an endeavor?

Giggles escaped, and she slapped her hands over her mouth, but they didn't stop. If anything, it made them worse. Before she knew it, she was shaking the bed as she turned her face into the pillow to try and quiet herself.

"What *are* you snickering about over there?" Hudson said, amusement clear in his voice.

"I . . . it . . . I . . . ," she tried, but the laughs only spilled out at that point. She was laughing hard enough to cry, and he was chuckling, too—obviously at her, but not in a mean way. When she was finally breathless, she held her stomach, which was sore from laughing, and got a grip. "Sorry. Weird train of thought, and I needed the stress outlet," she said, feeling better. "Besides, sometimes I laugh when I'm nervous."

And of course he latched on to the last bit of what she'd said. "You're nervous?" His voice was coated with concern. "Do you want me to . . ."

She stroked a hand up his bare chest, slowly, finding his throat in the dark and feeling his pulse pound beneath her fingertips. "I don't know how to ask, but . . . I kinda want to kiss you," she whispered, every ounce of courage she had forcing the words out like parajumpers from a plane. "Is that okay?"

A pause, the barest of ones, then a sigh. "That's very, very okay," he rumbled. "Do anything you like. We'll go at your pace."

She swallowed, then caught herself licking her lips. If the last time they'd kissed was any indication, he was really good at it. She, on the other hand, was rusty as hell. She slid toward him, and he moved his arm and tilted his body toward her, making access easier. She was nestled against him, feeling his breath, minty like toothpaste, fanning across her face.

For a split second, she had a moment of panic. She'd kissed men before. Silly, sloppy kisses in high school. Rushed kisses in college, with a few boyfriends. Then Steven, the romantic, the showman. He'd actually dipped her when she'd picked him up from the airport after they'd been separated for a month. It had been a movie kiss, right out of a romantic comedy, and she'd almost literally swooned. But those kisses had gone away, transforming to the perfunctory hello-goodbye kisses that married couples shared in between errands and jobs.

This was different. She was different, and she was tired of being stressed and struggling and denying herself what it was clear she wanted. She was going to kiss Hudson like she was going to fucking war tomorrow. She was going to kiss him like he was keeping her alive.

She was going to do everything she could to try to make him feel even a fraction of the way he made her feel.

As a warm-up, she kissed Hudson's collarbone, tracing the shallow bowl with her tongue and tasting the clean, warm skin there, gratified by his barely perceptible intake of breath. She moved her lips up his throat, feeling the roughness of his stubble against her lips. Even the scratchiness was exciting against her skin. She took a page out of his book, nuzzling along his jawline until she got to his earlobe. Feeling fizzy like champagne, she playfully nipped at it.

He let out a laugh, and she responded with one of her own, feeling a pulse of joy. "Oh, it's like that, huh?" he challenged, gathering her closer.

She felt the laughter fall away and stretched, her mouth feeling against his face blindly until she found what she was looking for.

His lips were firm, just as they'd been the first time they'd kissed . . . warm, insistent. She parted her lips easily this time, and he teased her with his tongue, an action that made her body shiver and her thighs start rubbing against each other of their own accord, restless heat building between them.

She shouldn't have worried. She wouldn't say it was like riding a bike—although *that* brought some delicious pictures to mind—but as soon as he kissed back, as soon as they connected, it was purely instinctive.

And hotter than hell.

Before she knew it, she was in the same state she'd been in after they'd salsa danced in her kitchen. She wasn't thinking, just feeling. Everything was either sensation or emotion: the taste of him, the scent of him. At some point, she tugged him until he crushed her into the bed, her legs spreading to give him space to notch between them. She felt his hardness against her pussy, and her hips rolled, and he groaned into her mouth. They were breathing harsh, choppy breaths.

She wove her hands into his hair, pulling him harder against her mouth. Her legs wrapped around his thighs, her heels digging in, encouraging him.

He pulled back just for a second. Her eyes had adjusted, but she could still only make out the barest details in the dark. "We have to be quiet," he said.

Some sanity came back, like a dip in cool water. His kids were here, and he probably didn't want to advertise what was happening.

"Oh," she said, immediately dropping her hands to the sides of her face. "I'm sorry, I . . ."

"No," he growled, and then—*oh my Lord*—he grasped both her hands in one large palm, pinning them above her head as he propped himself up with the other. "You have nothing to be sorry about, and I'm not trying to stop. Not unless you want to."

Then the traitor actually *rolled his hips*. His dancing was no lie, and anybody who could move his body so sinfully ought to be registered as a lethal weapon. She whimpered, biting her lip to at least try to keep the sound inside.

"What's it going to be?" His voice was rough as hell, and he felt like a furnace.

She felt on fire as a result.

"I don't want to stop," she breathed. "I want *more*."

When he kissed her, she swore she could feel that sharp, mischievous smile against her lips.

"Whatever the lady wants," he said, and she braced herself for what was going to come next.

CHAPTER 26

Hudson thought he was burning alive.

He liked sex, and frankly, he'd had plenty of it in his life. All sorts of women. Fun sex, athletic sex, slow sex. He'd made sure that they all had a great time, as best he could, and he had enough practice to make good on that promise.

But this . . .

Holy fuck.

Now, she was underneath him, her breathing choppy, her body writhing against his as her cloud-soft voice begged him for more. He wanted all of her, all at once. He didn't even know where to start.

When she whimpered, he kissed her, hard, feasting on that small, plush mouth of hers. He was gratified when she sucked his lower lip into her mouth, her hips moving restlessly.

First things first, his brain frantically thought. Clothes. He was wearing a pair of shorts, and she was in a T-shirt and sweatpants.

He pulled away for a second, releasing her hands and gulping in a breath against her throat. "I want to feel your skin," he rasped. "Clothes. Off. I want to taste you."

God. That wasn't smooth. But he was too hungry for her to be smooth.

"Yes, please, yes," she chanted, wiggling. Even his smallest sweats had been way too big for her, so they slid off easily—and she hadn't had underwear. He reluctantly rolled off and shucked his own shorts like he was trying to beat a world record, still clumsy in his desperation. He wanted to laugh about it—it was pretty funny, if he'd had enough mental power to think about it—but before he could, she'd peeled his shirt off from over her head and pressed herself to him.

It was like being branded, impossibly hot skin to skin. He breathed her in, the sweet smell of her mixed with his soap. She clung onto him like she wanted to devour him, and he felt the same, their mouths moving almost frantically. His rough hands moved over her soft skin, and for a second he felt remorse, like a devil somehow getting his hands on an angel.

The tension between them had been building for weeks, and now that they were finally giving in to it, he thought he'd explode. At the same time, he didn't know if he'd get another shot at this, and if this was going to be his only night with Willa, even if it was good filthy fun, he didn't want it to be something quick and forgettable.

He wanted her to remember this, because he knew, deep down, that this was changing everything for him, and it was going to imprint on his brain like staring at the sun.

God, I don't want this to be only one night.

He pulled back, somehow, ignoring her soft sounds of desperation. He'd be hearing those sounds in his dreams for years, he thought. He moved his mouth lower, sucking circles against her throat, her collarbone, her shoulders. Nipping at her skin, gently enough not to hurt, but serious enough to heighten what she was feeling until she was panting and thrashing a little against the pillow, one hand covering her mouth.

He wanted to smile. Actually, he wanted to fucking *howl* triumphantly at how she was responding, but he'd told her to be quiet, and he had to at least try to do the same. He traced a circling loop around her chest, seeing how she responded. When she arched her back, he got the answer he was looking for . . . then sucked in her nipple, gratified when a gasp punched through her attempts at silencing herself.

He pulled back enough to tease her. "Shhhh," he whispered, knowing his breath was going to brush against her now damp skin. Then he put his mouth to her opposite nipple, his tongue swirling around like she was ice cream, her creamy skin just as delicious.

She moaned, bucking slightly against him, encouraging him. Pleading with him, silently. Or at least quietly.

He moved lower, heading for her belly button, holding her hips. If she wanted it, he wanted to have sex with her, tonight. But he wanted her to be nice and wet for him first. They weren't kids, and he knew sometimes that, turned on or not, women needed a little help in that area. He'd be happy to use the lube in his drawer, a bottle he'd only used for getting off on his own, to ease the way if she needed it. Still, he'd rather at least try to get her wet—and get her off—first.

Besides, it'd be fun for both of them.

He kept going, pushing the thin blanket and sheet off and fitting himself more solidly between her legs, putting her thighs over his shoulders. He could hear her breathing, choppy, and saw that she was frantically grabbing handfuls of his sheet. He kissed her inner thighs as his fingers parted the curls between them. She shuddered reflexively as he started to stroke the folds they were hiding.

"Tell me," he said. "Tell me if there's anything you don't want . . . or anything you want."

"But . . ."

He chuckled softly against her skin. "Whisper it, baby."

She shivered.

"Please," she murmured. "I . . . I don't . . . I can't say it."

"You want me to taste this pretty pussy of yours?" he said, taking pity on her.

"*Please*, Hudson." She said it like the words were torn from her.

"Since you asked nicely," he said. Then he licked her, over her entrance, tasting her just like he'd said. Exploring her, taking his time, and enjoying the way she wriggled, struggling to push her pelvis up to his searching mouth. He finally stiffened his tongue, pushing it hard—a preview of things to come. He replaced it with two of his fingers, feeling the grooved muscles inside. He stroked, gently but firmly, until she made a soft squeal of shock and pleasure.

There it is.

He started stroking it, keeping a steady pressure and tempo, until she was breathing like she'd been running a marathon. He could feel her clit, hard and pronounced, and he put it into his mouth, matching the rhythm of his fingers with his mouth.

She pulled a pillow over her head, but it didn't matter—she still let out a rippling cry that he felt sure anybody awake, and probably anybody asleep, heard. Her whole body trembled, and he could taste her tangy flavor on his tongue as she flooded with wetness. He let her ride out the aftershocks, slowing his motions when she pressed at his head, nudging him away.

His body was now screaming at him. He wanted her so fucking badly. "What do you want to do now, Willa?" he asked, his voice harsh with desire. Because he knew what he wanted—but more than sex, more than fucking, he wanted her to feel all right. Actually, he wanted her to feel amazing. Safe. Cherished. Adored.

He wanted her to feel like the center of the world. And if that meant he didn't get off tonight, he'd live with it, because tonight was about taking care of Willa.

"Hudson," she breathed. "Can you . . . can we . . . ?"

"I'm gonna need you to use your words this time, sweetheart. This one's too important, and I don't want you to wake up tomorrow and regret anything."

"I won't, I promise," she said, her low whisper fervent. "I want you to fuck me, Hudson. Like you mean it."

The words made his already hard dick even harder, somehow, although her choice of words somehow also made him smile. "Trust me, I mean it."

He reached into his nightstand, getting a condom out of the open box. He rolled it on with shaking hands and internally scolded himself, but his heart was beating out of control. He wanted to make sure this was good for both of them, not just him.

"Hurry, hurry, hurry," she pleaded, and he let out a rough laugh.

"I don't want to be *that* fast."

"I don't care!" she said in an equally rough whisper. "I want you inside me, *now*."

"Demanding," he said, surprised. "I like it."

She wrapped her legs around his waist, pulling him in, barely giving him enough time to position himself at her entrance. "I want it hard, and fast," she rasped. "This once. We can do it slow later, and you can impress me with your stamina and your skills and whatever. But right now, I want to feel your cock stretching me out until I can't breathe. I want those salsa-dancing hips ramming me until I can't see. I want you to fuck me through the goddamned *floor*."

Oh, *fuck*.

He hadn't known what to expect from her. He'd been intrigued by cool and precise Willa. He'd been charmed by shy, sweet Willa. But dirty-talking Willa shocked him in the best way, and he felt his body say *Yes, ma'am* and just get to work.

He slid home inside her, bottoming out and barely registering the tight hot grip of her before his hips did, indeed, start ramming inside her, starting slow and building up in speed and intensity until they were both sweating.

All sense of finesse left the building. She clawed at his back and tugged at his hair as his hips moved like a jackhammer.

The two of them tussled with desperation. He sucked marks on her. She bit him. All thought of being quiet? Gone.

He felt the pressure building, and there was no way he could stop it. "Willa, I'm gonna . . ."

"Yes yes *YES!*" she whisper-shouted, biting his shoulder, and he felt her tighten around him like a fist.

His body went haywire. He slammed into her as she held on for dear life, before his vision basically blacked out and his brain shut down. With a muted shout, he collapsed on top of her.

It took him a long second to get his bearings back. He propped himself up in a plank. "Are you all right?" he asked. Because no matter what she'd asked for, he'd essentially gone wild there. "Did I hurt you?"

She let out a long, contented sigh, her hips moving against him. "Mmmmm, no. I feel great."

He chuckled softly, withdrawing carefully and taking care of the condom before . . . well, flopping next to her. Then she laughed in response, and before he knew it, the two of them were giggling like kids at a sleepover.

"I don't think we were quiet," she said, and the two of them pressed their faces into the pillows, trying to stifle their laughter.

"Yeah, we screwed that up," he agreed. He reached out, pushing sweat-damp hair out of her eyes. "Worth it, though."

"Totally." She was quiet for a second. "Thank you, Hudson. For everything."

"You never need to thank me," he said back. He heard her yawn, and he stroked her hair. "Get some sleep, sweetheart. It's been a long day, and everything can wait until tomorrow."

He could tell from her even breathing that she'd fallen asleep. He hoped she'd sleep in, but he'd get up and make sure that things were handled before she woke, as best he could.

He wasn't sure what it was, or if it was too fast, or anything. For all he knew, this was going to be either the start of the most important relationship in his life or a romantic disaster of apocalyptic proportions.

Fuck it, he thought, cuddling her close. It was too late. No matter how she felt about it or what she decided, he was already all in, and no amount of thinking it through would change that.

CHAPTER 27

Willa stretched out, waking slowly in Hudson's bed, feeling like a cat in a sunbeam. Until she realized that it was eleven thirty. Granted, maybe that wasn't really late, considering she hadn't gotten to sleep until about five in the morning, after an emotionally exhausting evening *and* some rigorous physical activity. She hadn't had any kind of workout in a while, and that particular kind was . . .

Thorough.

She blushed hard enough to see it on her chest and stomach when she tossed the sheet aside, showing that she had, indeed, fallen asleep naked with Hudson. Which brought up a point. Where was Hudson?

He probably wouldn't have stayed in bed until almost noon, she reasoned. Maybe someone had called needing something urgently fixed. It sounded like that happened a lot. She also didn't know what his schedule of work was, or what he'd be juggling now that her place was currently unable to be worked on—not unless he had a gas mask and was willing to smell rank.

She could feel anxiety start to creep up on her, and she shook it aside. She'd already wasted the morning. Last night had been amazing—and, on the other hand, a setback. She didn't have time to moon over whether or not Hudson regretted what they'd done. Or how she felt about what they'd done, come to that. But right now, she had to figure out how she was going to deal with her house and the meeting with the sexy chef.

She pulled on the big T-shirt and sweats he'd given her the night before, then went to the bathroom and got herself cleaned up as best she could. He'd tossed her clothes in the washer, she seemed to remember, which was just off the kitchen.

As she got closer to the kitchen, she heard voices—friendly, amused chatter. She rounded the corner, peeking in nervously.

Noodle saw her first. He jumped up from under the kitchen table, scampering over to her with his wide doggy smile and ridiculously fast wagging whip tail. She petted him, stroking his sleek sides before patting his head. He licked her wrist, love in his eyes.

"There she is!" Mari said. "Come on, sit. We eat lunch early because of farm hours." She nodded at the counter, where there were sandwich makings spread out.

Kimber was sitting at the table, squabbling with a young man who looked like a younger version of Hudson, except with honey-blond hair. He looked over at her curiously even as Kimber bounced out of her seat like Tigger, giving her a hug.

"Hey, lady!" Kimber said with a squeeze. "Heard you got skunked!"

Willa winced at the memory. "Unfortunately, yes. Your dad was kind enough to, um, rescue me."

She saw a quick glance dart between Kimber and Jeremy, and she wondered if they'd already been aware of that. He'd probably told them, right?

Would he have told them . . . anything else?

She didn't think he would, to protect her privacy. Still, she thought back to last night's activities. The way that, despite her best intentions, he'd managed to draw sounds out of her that she hadn't made in years. Possibly ever.

I swear, I tried to be quiet! The heat of a blush came back. She wasn't sure if this was better than someone's parents hearing you have sex, or worse.

She didn't really want to think about either alternative, so she cleared her throat. "Can I help you with anything?"

"Nah, it's just ham-and-cheese sandwiches," Mari said. "If that's okay? I mean, it's nothing fancy."

"I'm fine with not fancy," Willa reassured her. "Not that I'm a chef, but ask any chef what they cook for themselves, and it's always simple stuff."

She sat at the table, aware that she looked scruffy, her hair uncombed, no makeup . . . in their father's clothes. It was ten times worse than a shame walk.

"So are you and Dad dating, or what?" Jeremy said.

"Jeez, Jem, you can't just *ask* if they're dating," Kimber squawked as Mari, efficiently making sandwiches, rolled her eyes at the two of them.

"Why not? Dad hasn't brought anybody home in forever," Jeremy protested. "I mean, not since we were little, and that was just . . . What was her name?"

"Sylvia, maybe?" Kimber mused, then shook her head. "I don't remember. I think we were like five or six."

"Eh. I remember she made really good tamales one Christmas," Jeremy said. "Like *really* good. But then one day she just wasn't there."

"Yeah, what happened to her?" Kimber asked Mari.

Mari looked pointedly at Kimber, then looked over at Willa, frowning.

"Oh, come *on*, it was forever ago, I'm sure that Willa doesn't mind."

Mari sighed, then went back to making sandwiches, speaking with her back to them. "They just didn't work out, and they broke up."

"That was, like, his last actual girlfriend, though, right?" Jeremy asked.

Willa heard Mari mutter something like *these damned kids* before she answered, "Yes, I suppose she was."

Jeremy looked back at Willa with curiosity. She decided to turn the situation, much as she had in conversations with investors who had asked uncomfortable questions. "You must be Jeremy, then," she said.

"Oh, right! I forgot you two hadn't met," Kimber said. "You didn't make it to the barbecue."

"Wish I had," Jeremy said, wiping the condensation off what looked like a glass of iced tea. "Wait, you were at the barbecue?"

"She wasn't dating Dad then," Kimber supplied helpfully. "She came over because she'd rescued Noodle."

"Oh! You're the lady on the phone!" Jeremy's smile was wide and happy, and the dimples pitting his cheeks reminded her so much of Hudson that she couldn't help but smile back. "Thank you for taking care of Noodle, by the way."

The dog in question suddenly pressed his cold nose against her bare knee, causing her to squeak in surprise. He gave her a doggy smile, and she shook her head at him, although she couldn't keep herself from smiling and was pretty sure that her weak attempts at trying to get him to stop begging weren't going to work. "It was my pleasure. Noodle is an awesome dog."

"It's actually because of Noodle she got skunked," Kimber added. "Dad said that she had a doggy door put in because she was afraid Noodle would get out again and get caught in a storm or something— he does seem to like her house. But the skunk got through the door instead."

"Shit, I'm sorry about that," Jeremy said.

"It's not your fault," Willa said. "I didn't even think that there were skunks on this island, honestly. There aren't a ton where I'm from."

"Where are you from, Willa?" Mari interjected.

"Um . . . California. Born in Irvine, went to college at UC Davis. I lived in the Bay Area for a long time, then in the LA area for a while," Willa rambled nervously before clamping down on her mouth. They hardly needed to know all of that.

Mari put sandwiches in front of all of them before retrieving her own plate and a glass of iced tea. "This your first time in Washington? I admit, I don't remember you visiting Caroline."

"I was closer to her when I was younger, and when she traveled more." Willa smiled, remembering the feisty older woman. "When I was a kid, I used to spend a week or two at her house during summers, and we just always kept in touch. I'd only been out to her house here once or twice, and just for a few days." When Steven had been ill, and she'd hated leaving him alone that long. He'd resented his mother looking after him, feeling like it was babysitting, so she'd avoided that too. "It's so beautiful here."

"We love it," Mari said with pride. "We even had Hudson here—well, in the cabin. We built that first. But we raised him here in the farmhouse, and then we all raised the twins here too."

"It's wonderful here," Willa said, and she meant it. She'd loved San Mateo and San Francisco, but there was something about this little island that just soothed her, even with all the stress she was currently under.

She took a tentative bite of her sandwich, since the thought of stress reminded her of the cookbook and the house and everything she was going to have to do. She needed to figure that out. Hudson had mentioned something about special fans or damage remediation or something?

Which also reminded her: Where *was* Hudson?

The back door opened, and she heard Hudson's voice from the mudroom. "Hey, gang." She could hear him wiping off his boots before walking into the kitchen, where the rest of his family was all smiles. He gave everyone smacking kisses on top of their heads—until he got to her. Instead, he stroked her cheek, then nudged her chin up so he could look into her eyes.

"Hey, you," he murmured, his voice low and rumbly, his eyes heated.

"Hey back," she half whispered.

He seemed to remember that they had an audience, because he cleared his throat and grabbed his phone. "I called the damage place, my friend over in Everett—they deal with skunk stuff all the time, he says, and he's giving me a deal on an ozone generator that ought to get the smell right out. I sealed the kitchen with some plastic until it gets here, though. Jeremy, can you help me do some cleaning?"

Jeremy wrinkled his nose, but Hudson's expression must've made him change his mind, because he quickly nodded.

"If we get the surfaces the skunk hit, it'll make it easier and quicker," he continued. "And I grabbed your notes and notebooks, and put 'em in a big plastic bin I have . . . spritzed them with Febreze, carefully enough that the ink didn't smudge, and then covered them with baking soda after they dried. So they'll be a mess, but they won't stink too badly, and you can maybe rewrite them?"

Willa felt relief hit her, and she stood up, hugging him. She wasn't generally a hugger, but she was just so grateful, and it seemed the right thing to do.

"Thank you," she whispered to him.

He hugged her back, almost lifting her off her feet. "I didn't want you to worry," he said against her ear, and she shivered. "My friend did say that their ozone stuff is out on a job, though, so it'll be a few days. I know you need to do stuff before you meet that chef guy, right?" She let him go, her heart sinking a little, but before she could tailspin, he quickly added, "You don't have to worry. You can stay here as long as you need to. And . . . do you need to use the kitchen?"

She looked at Mari. "I do. I still need to test some recipes." Then she was struck with an idea, one that would help reduce some of the guilt. "If you all don't mind—would you be interested in being guinea pigs? I still have to do the entrées, and I could make some meals?"

"I'm not saying no to that," Mari said enthusiastically, while Kimber's eyes shone. Jeremy looked curious.

"Can you do it without the notes for now?"

"I'm still tinkering with stuff, so it should be fine," Willa said.

"Okay. Then I'm gonna grab Jeremy here and get cleaning."

He leaned in for a second, like he was going to kiss her. Instead, he just smiled at her, that bone-melting smile that made her feel like a meringue dissolving on someone's tongue.

His tongue, her mind supplied, and she felt her cheeks heat. He winked, grabbed some lunch meat and cheese, rolled it up, and stuffed it in his face as he headed for the back door.

"At least have a real lunch!" his mother called after him.

"In a hurry," he said, his words garbled from his full mouth. "Let's move out, Jeremy!"

Jeremy stood up, stuffing the rest of his sandwich in his mouth and downing the iced tea in one go. Then he headed for the door, but paused, looking over his shoulder, his expression puzzled.

"He likes you a lot," he said, and even though it wasn't a question, she could sense the unasked ones anyway. *Why you? Why now?*

She was pretty curious about that, herself.

CHAPTER 28

"God, I forgot how bad skunk stinks," Hudson said from behind his mold mask. He was lucky he had a few from a small mold job he'd tackled for the Garcias, who ran the boat launch. "Good thing he made it out of the kitchen and back out the doggy door, or this whole house would be saturated."

He'd figured that the skunk had started down the hallway but then turned around and fled the way he came in. So they used heavy-duty clear plastic and taped off the dining area, kitchen, and hallway so the scent wouldn't travel any farther into the living room or, hopefully, upstairs. Armed with vinegar solution, they started wiping down all the surfaces.

Jeremy had been strangely quiet for the first few minutes. It could've been because he didn't want to open his mouth or breathe in any more of the skunk scent than necessary, but Hudson knew his son well enough to guess that wasn't it. Sure enough, after a few minutes, Jeremy just dove in.

"So what's the deal with you and this Willa?"

Hudson sighed. He was wondering that himself.

The sex had been fantastic, even if they'd had to be quiet. Maybe on some level *because* they had to be quiet, honestly. Not that they'd succeeded in that. Willa was incredibly responsive and enthusiastic. She seemed almost surprised by her own responses. Every emotion was clear across her face: if she liked something, he knew it.

He fucking loved that.

He'd like to explore that more, when they had more time, more privacy. When she could really let loose and be as loud as she wanted, and when it wasn't three in the morning after a long day. Maybe sometime soon, he could have that chance.

"We're still figuring things out," Hudson hedged finally, when Jeremy stopped cleaning to stare at him.

"Are you dating?"

"We haven't really talked about it." He couldn't tell what Jeremy's expression was behind the mask. Was he upset? Encouraging? "Are you okay with that?"

"Does it matter if I am?"

That didn't sound promising. "It's not going to stop me, necessarily," Hudson said. "But I'm not going to ignore it if you and Kimber hate somebody. You know that."

"Yeah, but we're not dating her, are we?" Jeremy said, more insistently.

"Do you *not* like her?" Frankly, he hadn't seen that coming. Willa might be a little withdrawn and might come off as aloof or shy. But she was also sweet, and thoughtful, with a core of steel that most people probably didn't know about. He couldn't imagine anyone actively disliking her, much less one of his kids.

"I literally just met her a few hours ago," Jeremy said, and at least he sounded amused this time. "I don't know her well enough to say one way or another. But I could tell in under five minutes that *you* like her a hell of a lot. More than anybody I've seen in a long time."

Hudson scrubbed the center counter with a little more force than it needed, while Jeremy squatted down, washing off the lower cabinet fronts. "Again: is this a problem?"

"It's just weird," Jeremy said, not looking at him. "Kimber mentioned it. You haven't had a girlfriend that we know of since Sylvia or whatever, back when we were little."

"You remember her?" That felt like a punch in the gut. He'd hoped they'd forgotten his poor decision.

He'd started dating Sylvia three years after the divorce, when the twins were barely six. She'd been awesome: fun, about his age, great with the kids. But she had an ex who was in the military, and when he came back from his tour of duty, they'd decided to give it another try. Hudson'd been disappointed, and hurt—but more important, one night Jeremy had crawled into his lap, asking why he hadn't seen Sylvia.

"I don't think Sylvia's going to be around much anymore," Hudson had told him, unsure of what to say. He was pretty sure she was moving somewhere back east, like North Carolina . . . and even if she wasn't, he got the sense that her ex-now-boyfriend wasn't going to love her visiting the kids of the guy she'd been with while he was deployed. "I know you like her, and I'm sure she'll miss you."

Jeremy had stayed very still before his little body let out a very big sigh. "Why don't they stay, Daddy?" he'd asked.

That hadn't been a punch in the gut. That had been a stab right in his heart.

The funny thing was, as tough as Jeremy liked to act sometimes—the way he'd played sports in school, smack-talking with his college friends, all that—Kimber was the hard one, the more practical of the twins. Jeremy was the romantic. It was, Hudson suspected, part of the reason why Jeremy'd held on so long to his relationship with Wendy when it was so obvious, to the rest of the family anyway, that it wasn't going to work.

In a lot of ways, Jeremy took after him, if his marriage was any example.

"So is it serious?" Jeremy prodded, shaking him out of his memory. "Or is it . . . y'know, just sex?"

"I didn't have her over for sex. I gave her a place to stay because she needed one," Hudson started defensively, only to stop short when Jeremy's arched eyebrow called bullshit.

Cathy Yardley

"Come on, now. I was just getting to sleep when you got in," Jeremy said, and Hudson could hear the grin in his voice. "Trust me, by the time I figured out what was going on, I had those noise-canceling headphones on and death metal blasting *so* damned fast."

Hudson felt his cheeks and ears heat. "Shit," he muttered, which made Jeremy laugh, at least. "We didn't wake up Kimber, did we?"

"You know her. She's slept through cannon fire."

Thank God for that. Although with his luck, Kimber wouldn't care, or worse, would somehow try to give him helpful tips. He shuddered.

"Still, sex hadn't been the point," Hudson continued. "I haven't known her that long, but . . . I don't know. She's special. There was something about her that just hit me from the minute I met her. And the more I got to know her, the more I liked her. I've only known her for a month or so, but we just click."

"Sounds like Grandma and Grandpa," Jeremy teased with a laugh, moving on to the next bank of cabinets.

Hudson scoffed, wiping down walls. "Let's not go overboard. I just . . . her husband died two years ago."

Jeremy's laughter stopped. "Shit. Sorry. That sucks."

"Sounds like she's had a tough time," Hudson said. "Like, really hard. And she's determined to be independent, doesn't want to take anything from anybody."

"Like Mom?" There was an edge to his words.

Hudson wasn't going to open that can of worms. "No. More like she worries if she doesn't do everything herself, she's weak, somehow. So she pushes herself until she's ready to snap. She hasn't had anyone to lean on, really, so this is all she knows."

Hudson finished one wall, and by the time he turned to the other, he noticed Jeremy staring at him thoughtfully. "You want to be that," Jeremy said. "You want to be someone for her to lean on."

That was it, exactly. He wanted to take care of her, or at least he wanted the opportunity for them to take care of each other. He sure as hell wanted to make sure that she wasn't hurt, or stretched too thin,

202

or burned out, or worried and anxious. He didn't want her to feel exhausted and alone. Not ever again.

"Yeah."

"Then it doesn't matter if it's only been a month, does it?" Jeremy said.

Hudson shook his head. "I'm definitely open to it," he said. "I've put it out there. But she's . . . careful. I don't want to crowd her, in case she decides to just bail because she doesn't want to deal with it."

"Run? From a relationship with you?" Jeremy sounded both amused and shocked. "I thought every woman over the age of twenty wanted to bag the island's most eligible bachelor, even if you are old."

"Like I said," Hudson replied, refusing to take the bait, "Willa's different."

"She gonna stick around, at least?"

"God," Hudson said, "I hope so. Because I really like this one."

CHAPTER 29

After Willa had explained that she'd need to go to the city to meet with the sexy chef guy, Hudson volunteered to drive her there. He'd seen she was a little nervous about driving in the city, and he had his own stuff to do, so he figured it made more sense for them to both go together. Now, it was a few days later, and they'd taken his truck onto the ferry and were now cruising across the sound toward Seattle. It was an hour-long trip, so they had time to kill. They were standing on the deck, looking out at the water. It was July, so it wasn't cold, but it was overcast, and the breeze coming off the choppy water wasn't exactly warm.

"You okay?" he said, checking in with her.

She nodded, but he noticed her shivering a little. She was wearing a T-shirt with a thin jacket over it, and while that'd been fine for the island and in the truck, it wasn't holding up to the bracing wind coming off the sound.

"We can go inside—"

"No, really," she interrupted with an apologetic half smile. "I get seasick. Sorry, I know that's gross."

"Hey, no. It's good to know." That probably scratched any idea of him getting her a snack from the ferry's dining area.

"Besides, the view's gorgeous." She sighed happily, leaning her elbows on the railing. "I always liked looking at the ocean when I lived in California."

"Did you grow up by it?" He leaned his back on the railing, close enough to hear her over the sounds of the ferry and the water.

"No. Irvine's inland, and I didn't trek out to the beach much. I didn't like it enough to put up with the drive," she said, turning her head a bit to meet his gaze. "And college was inland too. But I interned in San Francisco. Then I met Steven, and we lived in the Bay Area. I spent a lot of time in San Francisco, and San Mateo, which is kind of south of it."

"Did you like it?"

She nodded. "It was a fun time in my life. I was in my twenties and thirties, and I was doing all this fun stuff. Learning things." Her eyes went unfocused, and she turned back to the water. He strained to hear her. "Steven was really into the foodie scene, and we were always going to new restaurants or hanging out with restaurateurs or chefs."

"Is that how you got into writing cookbooks?" he asked.

"Eventually, yes," she said. Then she bit her lip. "Steven had a trust fund from his grandparents. I don't remember how they made it. But he tried a bunch of different things. Like worldwide food tours—that was before we got together, although he did take me to Europe, and we led a foodie tour of Florence, which was awesome. Really off-the-beaten-path stuff."

Hudson squirmed uncomfortably. He'd never been to Europe, although at one time he'd wanted to, because it was so rich in history that they actually tried to preserve. He'd actually never been out of the country. He'd done a road trip with Kimber when she was deciding what college to go to, so he'd been to UC Davis, and later, all the states between Colorado State and University of Nebraska and back. It had been exhausting but worth it, even though she'd eventually decided she couldn't bear being so far from home.

Still, there was a big difference between Steven seeing the Eiffel Tower and him seeing the world's largest covered wagon. He felt his stomach clench a little as he mentally yelled at himself. He didn't have to prove himself to anyone, and he wasn't going to let her previous husband's memory make him feel bad about a life he was proud of.

"But we had some bad decisions and had a run of bad luck," she said. "We bet big and lost. *Big.*"

He wondered what that meant but wasn't sure if they were at the point where he could pry.

"Like, lost-our-house big," she admitted.

He winced.

"By that point, Steven was getting sick," she said, and though her voice was steady and her outer appearance that calm, porcelain surface, the pain in her eyes was almost hard to look at. "When we started to get behind on mortgage payments and bills, I was scrambling for work that I could do easily and that paid fast. I sold myself short, but we got money in the door. Just wasn't enough."

He whistled low. "I'm sorry," he said. "That sounds hard."

What was Steven doing?

"We moved down to Southern California, by his parents," she said in a low voice. "Steven took the loss really hard. Like, super depressed. Then it kind of kicked his health problems into high gear."

He saw that she was still shivering and immediately took his leather jacket off and draped it over her shoulders, ignoring the cool air on the bare skin below his T-shirt sleeves. "Listen, I don't mind hearing about this at all," he said, tugging her to face him and pulling the jacket snugly around her. "But you don't have to tell me anything either. You don't owe me any explanations, and I don't want you to hurt."

She smiled, even if it was sad. "It's funny. I don't really talk about it much. Everybody I would've talked to about it either already knew him or I lost touch with when we moved."

"Do you still talk to them now?"

She looked surprised, then shrugged. "There hasn't been much reason to," she said slowly.

He quirked an eyebrow at her. According to his kids, it was his that's-bullshit look, one he inherited from his father.

Her cheeks reddened, and he didn't think it had anything to do with the wind. "It's hard, you know?"

"What is?"

"The widow part."

The wind picked up, and he had to lean closer to hear her words over it. It was definitely getting colder too. He glanced up, hoping it wasn't going to rain.

"The thing is," she continued, "everyone says they're sorry, and I can just say thank you, because I was sorry too. But a lot of them don't know what to say *beyond* that, and it just makes it worse. Some people said things like it'd pass with time, or I just needed to grieve, which . . . well, I knew that. Some even said things like it was part of God's plan, and considering how long he'd been suffering, maybe it was for the best."

"What the fuck?" he blurted out in shock. "Who says that?"

"At the memorial service too," she said darkly. "There were some people who made some veiled references to his behavior catching up with him, that he should've . . . I don't know, eaten healthier, or quit drinking, or done whatever holistic treatment they'd read about on Facebook. It was *so* frustrating. Some of these people had been my friends."

He made a strangled noise, but hopefully, she hadn't heard it over the noise of their surroundings. She'd already been hurting. How in the world did they think that would help?

"Some people in his family asked me about what my plans were, or asked really personal questions about my finances. I can deal with those kind of questions from, like, my parents, but not Steven's cousin twice removed or my uncle."

He grimaced. *Why do people have to be such assholes?*

"People offered all kinds of help too. They weren't all bad," she rushed to assure him. "But . . ."

"But you don't like taking favors," he said with a gentle smile, so she'd know he wasn't criticizing her. "I might not know you that well, but I know that much."

She smiled back softly. "Yeah. That's a rough one."

They were quiet for a minute.

It really was colder, he realized.

"Speaking of favors," she said, "thanks for taking me. I could've driven myself, but it is nice to have the company."

"My pleasure," he said. "Like I said, I needed to go into the city anyway."

"Something for the island?"

"Having lunch with the twins' mom."

She blinked, slowly enough for him to realize that it was surprise. "Everything all right?" she asked slowly, before quickly tacking on, "Like you said, I'm happy to listen, but if you don't want to talk about it, that's fine too."

They were so careful around each other, he realized. It was like building something very delicate. He found himself hoping that one day it'd be really strong.

He shook his head. *Think about that later.* "Not a big deal. I think she's worried about Jeremy. She might want a progress report on Kimber too."

"She doesn't talk to them?"

"They don't really talk to her."

"That's hard," she said, compassion plain on her face. "For all of them, I imagine."

"I was angry for a while. Tried to keep it from the kids, but you know . . ." Then he stopped. "Well, actually, I guess you might not know how they are."

"I haven't had them," she said, her lips pursed in an amused grin, "but I've been one, so yeah. I know. They're smarter than most adults give them credit for."

He frowned. "Mind if I ask you a personal question?"

Her peal of laughter surprised him. "At this point? I feel like I've unloaded most of my personal history. You could probably ask me what color my underwear is."

His brain stuttered for a second as that processed. They hadn't repeated the activities of that first night, mostly because knowing his kids were in the house had made both of them a little hesitant. They hadn't been saints or anything—he'd made out with her until his balls ached, and he got little to no sleep as a result. But he wasn't going to exactly fix that situation here on the ferry, either, so he forced himself to stay the course.

"Why didn't you have kids?" he asked. "I mean . . . did you not want them, or were you not able to have them?"

Her expression snapped into that polite, polished, aloof one—the one she used when she retreated behind her wall.

"I'm not judging either way," he added.

Her mask slipped enough to show her skepticism. "Were you angry with your ex-wife for not wanting kids?"

He huffed out a sigh. "I'm not going to lie. At the time, I was," he said. "But that was because I was twenty-two years old, mostly scared, and I had no idea what I was doing."

She relaxed a little.

"I'm not angry with her anymore, and honestly, I didn't have the right to be angry about her choices. Not about that. We both made some serious mistakes, and we probably should have made better choices when she found out she was pregnant. Do I wish she had a better relationship with the twins? Sure. But I can't do anything about that now, and besides, it's between the kids and their mother. I can just love them and support them as best I can and hope things work out."

"That sounds really healthy," Willa said. "Steven didn't want kids. Even though it's not technically hereditary, I think he was afraid any kids he had would be at risk to have diabetes too. Besides, I hate to say it, but kids would've interfered with all the things he wanted to do. We didn't have pets because of it. Honestly, we didn't even have houseplants." She looked at the water for a second. "It broke his parents' hearts, but ultimately, I think it was the best decision."

"Did you want them, though?"

She shrugged. "I don't know. I didn't feel strongly one way or the other. I'd like to think if I had some, I'd be a good mother, but I don't . . . feel like I'm missing anything. And I hate to think what it would've been like if I had to take care of them with everything else that wound up happening."

He nodded, thinking of how unsupported she'd felt, how alone. Then, without meaning to, he shuddered.

"Oh!" She touched her bare hand to his forearm, and winced. "Oh, you're cold. Here, take your jacket back."

"No," he said firmly. "You need it more than me."

"I know I need to buy warmer clothes," she said. "If I'm still here in the fall, that's first thing on my list."

He tried not think about how those words stung. It was way too early, and he was way too attached, but there they were. He looked at her, swamped in his slightly oversize jacket.

Then he snapped his fingers. "I've got an idea."

He took the jacket from her, smiling at her puzzled expression. He put it on, then opened the front in invitation, like a circus tent.

She laughed, stepping into his chest and leaning her cheek against his T-shirt as he bundled them both. He kissed the top of her head before tucking it under his chin. "Better?"

"Better," he heard her say, only slightly muffled against his chest.

He waited a beat.

"So. What color is your underwear?"

Her bright laughter was warmer than his jacket, and he loved it.

CHAPTER 30

Willa took a few calming breaths as she made her way through the bland hallways of the nice boutique hotel in Seattle. She had finally been able to get a meeting with the chef, Sam, a.k.a. Sexy Chef Sam, to discuss the recipe ideas she'd come up with, get his opinions on them, and figure out what kind of content she could add to imbue the nonrecipe copy with his persona and flavor. She felt a little weird about meeting him in a hotel, but his manager had expressed, via Instagram message of all things, that Sam was already overbooked and that it was apparently a big deal for them to meet at all. She'd gritted her teeth, agreed to keep it to no more than half an hour.

Now, she was outside the door. She knocked, tentatively at first, then with a bit more force.

The door opened to reveal a medium-height white man in a pair of overlarge jeans and a white-and-navy striped shirt. He didn't look that much younger than her—she'd say late thirties at best, but more likely forties. She supposed he looked stylish, but there was an element of deliberate "I'm totally not trying" that she remembered from her restaurant days. He looked her up and down, not in a sexual way, although there was definitely a sense of assessment.

"Cookbook lady?" he asked without preamble, and when she nodded, he ushered her in impatiently.

"And you are . . . ?"

"Thorn, Sam's manager," he responded, looking back at his phone.

She nodded again. He'd been the one who'd messaged her about the meeting, then.

"Sam!" Thorn barked. "Out here!"

She waited for a second, surveying her surroundings. A suite, she noted. Two bedrooms, from the look of it. The living area, with a small conference or dining table, as well as a wet bar with a minifridge and microwave, and the usual flat-screen TV with a couch in front of it. She went to the table, quickly getting out her sketchbook and the photos she'd printed to save time and give a better idea of her work so far.

Sam came out of one of the bedrooms. He was wearing a white T-shirt so highly reflective it was almost blinding over a pair of baggy jeans that slipped down just enough to show the band of what she had to assume was designer underwear. It seemed like she'd seen him without his shirt more than with, so the difference was jarring. That said, he didn't have that try-hard impression, which she appreciated.

He was horsing around with two other men, who were laughing and joking. One was a very tall Black man, and one was a shorter, pudgier blond man. They all seemed to be friends.

"Dude, you need to come to Seattle more," the short one wheedled.

"You guys are always working, though," Sam replied with a smile. "And Dave, aren't you working on a new project or something? Going to Japan?"

The Black man smiled. "Company's sending me to talk about designing some displays for one of their advertising partners. Week in Tokyo, you should come with. Billy is even taking time off."

The shorter guy nudged him. "In *Tokyo*! I have *always* wanted to go to Tokyo!"

Thorn's eyes lit up. "Now there's a good idea, Sam. Japan. I want to schedule you for that, by the way. A few parties, some collabs, and there are some content ideas I think we could work on."

Sam looked startled, like he'd forgotten the man was there. "Um . . . yeah. That sounds good!"

Dave and Billy exchanged glances. "C'mon. I'm hungry, let's get lunch," Dave said.

Sam grinned, ready to head out.

"Sorry," Thorn interrupted again, looking stern and not at all sorry. "But I need Sam to do this thing. Then this afternoon, he's got a few influencers to meet up with, and there's a party tonight."

"Ooh, a party?" Billy's grin was wide. "I totally want to go to a party!"

"It's very exclusive, I'm afraid." Door guy's whole expression said *hell no*.

Unfortunately, she knew Thorn's type. He was the money guy, the dealmaker, the fixer. Every project seemed to either have one or need one, and while he was going about it like a cudgel, she could only imagine what it was like to work with something so lightning-in-a-bottle ephemeral as a video-content creator's career. They seemed to have shorter potential longevity than restaurants, and those could have the life span of mayflies.

Sam looked chastised, and he turned apologetically to the other two. "We'll definitely catch up tomorrow, if nothing else," he promised.

They bro-hugged it out and then went out the door. Thorn glared at her.

"Thirty minutes," he warned her. "We've got a full schedule."

"Of course," she said in her best placating-the-demanding-customer voice.

After a second of staring, he harrumphed. "I'm going to make some calls," he said to Sam, then disappeared into the second room, the door closing. She heard his gruff voice rattling away.

"Hi. I'm Sam. I guess we haven't been properly introduced." He held out his hand, an almost shy smile on his face, a far cry from the I-am-going-to-seduce-the-fuck-out-of-you mischievous expression he constantly wore in his videos.

Thank God. She didn't know what she'd do if he was that *overt* in real life. Probably lose the battle against laughter. The guy was good looking but way too young. Besides, she still couldn't get over watching him slap that pork belly.

"I'm Willa," she said, sitting at the table and gesturing for him to do the same as she pulled out her notebook. "Thanks for taking the time. I will try to be brief. I've watched your videos, and while it would've been easier to have more of a sit-down to discuss the recipes and whatnot prior to this, I understand that you've been very busy."

"Yeah." He sat, rubbing the back of his neck and grimacing. "Sorry about that."

Her smile was easier. Somehow, it reminded her of Kimber or Jeremy. "Really, it's fine," she said. "Let's talk about what I've come up with, all right? This way you can give your insights—anything you like, anything you hate. And I'm going to ask you some questions about yourself and the kind of personal content you want to include around the recipes. Once we come up with a complete list, I may email you for some additional little details I can include and a writing sample so I can mimic your voice."

She walked him through what she'd come up with. Thankfully, he was a perfect collaborator. He was impressed, maybe even a little intimidated, by her knowledge, and he made notes on his phone for things he'd want to try later. He even asked her tentatively if he could email her after the book was done for test ideas and questions. While it was outside the scope of her work, she agreed because, again, he reminded her of the twins. He was sweet and earnest, and she appreciated that.

The half hour was coming up fast. "I'll see what I can work with here," she said, gathering up her notes. She felt more confident, even though that deadline was heading at her like an oncoming train. She noticed him looking hesitant. "What? Is something the matter?"

"Do you think this cookbook's going to work?" he asked quietly.

She felt her stomach drop. This was a hell of a time for him to think about backing out. "Do you not want a cookbook?" she asked.

"No! It's not that." He glanced at the closed door where Thorn had disappeared. "I wasn't even supposed to be doing all this, you know?"

She blinked. "What are you talking about?"

"I was working as a barista at a café in San Francisco," he said. "I'd just graduated from the arts college with a degree in graphic design. The photography and video editing were just for fun, stuff I goofed around with. I started these videos as a *joke*, for a girl I was dating."

"Wow."

"They were public, but I really . . . I mean, how was I supposed to know the algorithm was going to pick it up like that?" He laughed nervously, running a hand through his dark wavy hair. Rather than looking frazzled, it did that perfect tousle. *Good lord, the man truly* does *wake up like this.* "Anyway, I did a few more for laughs, just to see. The whole thing kinda snowballed. Girlfriend dumped me because she didn't like all the attention I was getting. Especially the comments women were making, like they wanted me to eat *them*, stuff like that."

She cringed on his behalf. The internet had created anonymous animals out of people, and the fact that they saw these fictionalized versions of real humans made them think that they could say anything, do anything, and have no regret for it. "Sorry."

He waved a hand. "I mean, it hurt, but it was like a year ago, and . . . well. Thorn came up to me and said he could work with me and I could make a lot of money, and the dude *was not kidding*." Sam sighed. "But . . . I need to be 'on brand' more. He's really pushing the sexy thing. So I've got to get this right."

She felt a little ache in her chest at just how close that sentiment hit.

"The audience is easily bored too," he said. "Thorn's always saying that."

"He's not wrong." She hesitated, then nodded firmly. "Don't worry. This will be plenty sexy, fit right in with your brand. It may not seem that way, but I am confident it will come off that way."

He snickered, and she rolled her eyes.

"Grow up," she warned, "or I will throw a slipper at you."

He laughed. "A slipper? Why?"

"It's an Asian thing . . . never mind." She smiled at him, shaking her head a little, feeling both amused and protective. "Your whole vibe is sexy to near absurdity. There's a playful quality."

"Thorn thinks that subtlety is overrated," Sam said, sounding defeated.

"Well, you can be overt but still fun." She started sketching possible dishes after doing a quick sketch of his smirk, his hair, those twinkling eyes in the corner. The cartoony Sam held out a dish. "We can do some things in the main, maybe, that are funny, almost silly, like your videos. You're trying for seductive, but you're also not taking yourself too seriously. Hmm. Big meat. Um . . . big heat?" She frowned. "Feel like we need a third thing to complete that. Something else big."

Sam laughed again, wiggling his eyebrows. "Well . . ."

"Eh! Think of me as your auntie who has known you since you were little and who will *not* put up with your silliness," she scolded playfully, making him crack up some more. "I sincerely doubt your publisher's going to want a picture of your hot dog. Besides, it'd technically go under meat, anyway."

By the time they were done, she had a complete recipe list, and he promised he'd answer her email with more personal details. It was more than she could've hoped for. They'd even talked about how he could film some of the recipes. Not in their entirety, obviously—he'd want to keep the bulk for the book itself—but as teasers and trailers.

"That would be great," he said. "You should come to LA and film with me sometime—"

"Are you kidding?" Thorn yelped. They both flinched as the man came out, phone in hand but obviously shut off. He looked fierce. "Honestly, I didn't want you two meeting at all. It's just not necessary."

Sam glared at Thorn. "Man, you're being kind of a dick."

"What do I keep telling you?" Thorn didn't seem to mind the accusation. "This crowd is fickle, and all of them have a parasocial relationship with you. They want to believe you're real . . . and in a lot of ways, they don't care if you *are*, as long as you don't burst the bubble.

Same reason why I've told you it's better to either stay single or keep a relationship hidden."

"Like a K-pop idol," she mused. Thorn finally looked at her.

"You get it," he said, although it was grudging. "The thing here? They want to believe that he's totally self-taught—"

"But I am!" Sam protested.

"But also a kick-ass gourmet chef. With a six-pack and a fuck-me grin," Thorn said. "If they find out a middle-aged woman wrote your cookbook for you, they're going to feel betrayed." He paused, then glanced at her. "No offense," he muttered.

She shrugged. "None taken. It's the business."

Sam, on the other hand, looked horrified.

"You have what you need?" Thorn said. "Because I've got to get this guy to a photo shoot with a few partying influencers on a boat in the sound, on one of the few days we *don't* have shitty overcast skies. Then you've got that party tonight at the Space Needle."

Sam looked defiant for a second, then deflated, nodding. "All right."

"Don't worry," she said to Thorn but also to Sam. "I've worked with top culinary chefs before, completely anonymously. I know how to stick to an NDA."

"You better hope so," Thorn said . . . again, both to her *and* to Sam. "Because this whole thing hinges on him being the real deal, so we can't fuck this up."

She closed her sketchbook and headed out the door. She liked Sam more than she would've thought, given the sheer goofy aspect of his videos and what she was expected to do. Now, she just hoped they'd get through the project without a hitch.

The sooner she got this done, the sooner she got paid. She got the feeling Sam would understand that perfectly.

CHAPTER 31

The little Thai place was nice, walking distance from the parking garage where he'd stowed the truck and also near the Space Needle and stuff. Most importantly, it was close to Amanda's law office.

"Thanks for meeting me," she said. She was wearing a suit-type thing—a deep-purple jacket and skinny skirt with a pale-gray top. Her hair was pulled up, making her expression tight, and she was wearing glasses. Those were new. "I know you don't come over to Seattle if you don't have to, and I'm sure you've got plenty to do."

"No problem, I was going off island anyway," he said with a shrug.

She sighed, poking at her green curry. He looked at the remains of the dish in front of him: khao soi. He'd never tried it before, usually sticking to pad thai on his few forays into the cuisine (usually when eating lunch with Amanda). But Willa's passion for food had made him curious, and he had to admit, the coconut-rich broth, with the fried crispy noodles on top, made the whole thing pretty tasty.

She sighed again, deeper this time, then pushed her bowl away. "It's about the kids."

He suppressed his own sigh. Of course it was about the kids. He braced himself.

"What's the problem?" he said, then winced. "Sorry," he tacked on. "That came out harsher than I meant it to."

She still grimaced in response before drinking the last of her iced tea. "Jeremy quit his job," she said. "Or at least, that's what he said on Instagram."

"I know."

"And you were okay with it?"

Hudson shrugged. "He's twenty-three. Doesn't matter if I'm okay with it or not, does it?"

She pursed her lips. "Do you know why?"

"He wasn't happy, from what he's said," Hudson said. "The job sucked, and he wasn't going to go anywhere with it, so I don't blame him."

"Did the last two jobs suck too?" she pressed, her eyes filled with worry. "He was only at the big electronics store for, what, a few months? And the ones before that . . . that dinky little computer repair place in Shoreline, I think. Or working for the college's video tech department."

"Where are we going with this?" Hudson said, finishing his lunch in a few last bites.

"I'm concerned," she said. "It seems like he broke up with his girlfriend too."

"Yeah, the writing was on the wall with that one for ages, though," Hudson said, glad that she at least seemed to agree with that. "They lasted way longer than they should have, but he was really stubborn about making it work."

Amanda sent him a teasing grin. "Like his dad, huh?"

At least they could joke about it now. After twenty years, the statute of limitations was up. "Hopefully he'll learn better next time."

"Hopefully *you'll* learn better next time," she said. It was nice that they could be friendly, even as they disagreed. "You dating now?"

"Are we talking about dating lives?" he replied, surprised. "Are you dating?"

Her eyes widened. "Would you be upset if I were?"

"No, I wouldn't," he said, and truly felt it. "I would be shocked, though. When would you have the *time*?"

She laughed, looking for a second like the lively, carefree girl he'd known in high school. "Yeah, no. Dating's not on my agenda. I'm closing in on partner, which I *would* have had already if I wasn't a woman . . . but I'm not going to carp on that now. I wanted to talk to you about Jeremy, remember?"

"Still don't see what the problem is."

She pursed her lips. "Did you let him move home?"

Ah. "Yeah. When they broke up, he needed to move out. Deciding to quit was all part of it. So I told him he could have his room back." He paused when he saw the judgment in her eyes. "You know that I've told the kids they can move home any time they want, Amanda. Hell, if *you* needed a place, I'd offer it."

She huffed out a breath, regret crossing her expression. "I'm just worried. He seems so lost."

"You could talk to him about it." Hudson felt tension building between his shoulders, drawing the blades together like a vise.

"Yeah, like *that's* easy, with either of them." Her laugh was bitter. "I'm lucky I can get them to respond to texts."

He didn't say anything, trying not to blurt out *Whose fault is that?* Knowing that was too shitty a response, but there had to have been something in his face that showed. She looked wounded, and defensive, and defeated, which for Amanda was a rare and unpleasant expression.

"I know. I *know*," she repeated, a note of pleading in her voice. "You probably don't feel like I have any right to worry about the kids because I abandoned them."

His sigh was deep. "It's not the choice I would've made," he said carefully. Obviously. It *wasn't* the choice he'd made. "But you did the best you could, and I tried to make sure the kids didn't hate you."

"You think I don't know?" Her voice, while low, was impassioned. "I love them just as much as you. But I *never should've been a mother*. I don't know how to make those two facts balance out, you know?"

They'd had variations of this talk too many times in the past, once they'd started talking again. When she'd first asked for the divorce, the twins were two and a half. They were barely making ends meet, and they had lived with his parents. Her parents had been furious that she'd managed to get herself pregnant and had cut off contact with her, so there was no support from that side—they'd gone so far as to move away, too ashamed and angry to stay on the island. The rest of the island, on the other hand, had been completely supportive, probably because the Clarks had been such a big part of island society for so long.

After a quickie court wedding and a Clark family barbecue, the kids had been born, burning them both out. She'd withdrawn, barely speaking to him or anyone. He'd find her crying behind the barn, or in the meadow by a copse of pine trees. After a while, she seemed to float through the farmhouse like a ghost.

He'd thought it was just postpartum depression.

Turned out it was more than that.

"You know if I stayed," she said, bringing him back to the present, "we would've been miserable. *They* would've been miserable. They would've known. And it would've been worse."

She said the words confidently, but he saw the persistent question in her eyes: *I made the right choice . . . Didn't I? Did I?*

"I actually do know that," he said, giving her hand a quick squeeze. "After almost twenty years. I'm a slow learner, but I got that much."

"Don't do that. Don't play dumb," she said, scowling at him. "You're a smart man, and you know it."

"Eh. I'm okay." He thought of Willa, with her degree, all her life experience. Not that it should matter that they were different. He was happy with his life on the island.

Now who's questioning things?

Amanda kept pushing, though. "We *both* know the kids are smart. Really, really smart."

"They are," he agreed.

"So what are they *doing* with that?" Her voice got strident, and she looked around, noticing that some other lunch diners were staring. She collected herself. "Kimber's got a degree in agriculture from U Dub, and she's just . . . just playing with goats on your parents' retirement-hobby farm. Making soap and jam like it's just one big, pretty Instagram account. And Jeremy's just popping between retail jobs and playing at God knows what, video games and making silly shorts. I don't even know what his associate's degree is in, but whatever it is, I don't know why he bothered. I don't even know what he wants!"

"What does this have to do with *you*?" Hudson shot back in a low voice. "And what the hell do you want me to do about it?"

"They're stalled out, Hud!" she hissed. "They just think that they can float around through life, and if anything goes wrong, they can always go crash at Gram and Gramps's, and it'll be fine. What happens if they don't have that?"

He huffed out a breath.

"They'll always have me, unless I'm dead," he said. "I will always be there for the kids. You know that."

"I do," she said, rubbing her temples. She looked woeful.

"Maybe they'd like to know they have *you* too," he said.

"I don't want them to have to *need* either of us," she growled back. "Are we really helping them if they do need us forever? Or are we knee-capping them?"

He clenched his teeth, slowing his breathing. This was a familiar fight, one he didn't want to dive into.

"I don't have an answer," he finally said in a low voice. "I think that they're strong enough to figure out what they want, and I think they're more capable than you're giving them credit for. I also think that they'll figure it out, one way or another."

She started to protest, but he cut across it.

"But if they need time and a soft place to land while they *do* figure it out, I am going to fucking be there for them," he said. "While I get what you're saying . . . you can't complain to me about feeling like a shitty mom, and that they won't talk to you, if they know you're not someone they can turn to when they're in trouble. No matter what your reasons are."

She flinched like he'd slapped her, and remorse punched him back. Still, he also knew that the twins harbored a grudge against the mother who'd left, who didn't share custody, who paid for things as she went higher on the career ladder but hadn't *been* there—not for recitals or 4-H shows or power outages that left them scared in lightning storms. By the time they were old enough that she felt she could relate to or talk to them, they were distinctly cold. Both had gotten scholarships, turning down her offers to help with any college stuff. They certainly hadn't consulted with her before deciding their courses of study.

They'd moved on, and none of them knew how to reconcile that.

"You made the best choice you could," he said. "Even thought it was a hard choice. But they're making the best choices for them. You can't expect them to accept your choices if you don't accept theirs, even if you don't like them."

"I really do love them," Amanda rasped, her eyes glassy with the tears she was fighting.

"I know that. I do."

"But I don't want them to get stuck in a life they don't like. You gave up on your dreams. You can tell me you like living on the island and being a handyman all you like. But you told me you wanted to travel, a long time ago. You wanted to restore things. You even had that crazy clock idea." She smiled softly. "And you just . . . stayed on the island."

When she put it that way, yeah, it did sound defeatist. He hadn't dwelled on the things he'd put aside, figuring they were just dreams.

Then he thought about what Willa had done. What she was *still* doing.

Being a freelance cookbook writer, not holding down a nine-to-five job, wasn't stable by any stretch. Sometimes, he wondered if she was even happy. But she had a *fire* about her that he hadn't felt in . . . he couldn't remember how long.

"Do you want the kids to do the same?" she asked. "I know I screwed up. They think I'm so ambitious that I didn't even love them.

They think that being passionate and driven about something means you turn your back on the people you care about, and that's my fault. I just . . . I don't know how to *fix* that."

He sighed. "I don't know that I can either," he said. "But . . . I promise. I'll try."

CHAPTER 32

The talk with Sam had been surprisingly helpful. They'd been emailing a bit back and forth since, which went better because Thorn wasn't setting a time limit or interfering. She was very happy with both the book's organization and the recipes. Now she was just testing. Ordinarily, she'd want a number of rounds, both to replicate the recipe and ensure the amounts were spot on, and then give it to a few beta testers to make sure that home cooks could also both understand the instructions and repeat the results.

Unfortunately, her house still smelled heavily of eau de skunk, so she was camped out at Hudson's house, hijacking their kitchen.

She also had an audience. Mari and Kimber were at the dining table culling berries and cherries into boxes for the farm stand. She felt a stab of guilt, since she was taking up their countertops and any workable kitchen space.

"What's this going to be?" Jeremy asked her from a chair in the corner where he was fiddling with his phone. He'd seemed at loose ends since she'd met him. Hudson told her that he'd quit his job and now had moved back to live with them, but he had no idea what Jeremy was planning to do past that.

Same, Jeremy. Same.

"Homemade tagliatelle with lobster, in a Meyer lemon cream sauce," she said. "It's a wider pasta, so you can just cut from the sheets, no fancy pasta machine required. The lobster? That's the luxury element.

And the lemon and butter in the cream sauce echoes what you'd normally eat with lobster, with the fresh thyme and shallots adding a nice counterpoint."

Jeremy sighed happily. "Can you stay forever?"

She sent him an awkward smile. "Guess you like the food!" she chirped, playing it off.

"If you're gonna sit here," Kimber shot at him, "at least be useful, Jem."

Jeremy rolled his eyes but got to work.

"What's your next cookbook going to be?" Mari asked as she piled the berries in the boxes with a quickness and care that showed just how much practice she had.

"Not sure. It depends on what I'm assigned." She rolled out the pasta, thinking through the order of the instruction list. Since it was homemade, she'd just toss the pasta in to cook with the sauce. But there was also the lobster to consider, which was delicate and could easily be overcooked. She'd parcook the tails she'd bought first, in some butter, and set them aside.

"Ever thought of writing your own cookbook?" Kimber asked.

Willa laughed as she sliced lines through the pasta, even and straight as a ruler, then moved the lot out of the way. "Nope. I'm not famous enough."

"Did you want to be?" Jeremy asked, surprising her. "I mean, did you plan on being a celebrity cook? Like Gordon Ramsay or something?"

"*God*, no," she said, but his face fell, and she realized he wasn't just asking because he was curious or trying to make conversation. He was thinking of his own position. Maybe what he'd wanted—and what hadn't worked out.

He might be twenty-three, but at half her age, he was a *baby*. He had so much time. "I did want to be a chef, though," she added, and his attention snapped back to her.

"Why didn't you become one?"

"My parents didn't want to pay for culinary school," she said. "Even though I'd always get work, it would be for crappy pay, restaurants go under all the time, and they certainly didn't think I'd be a Gordon Ramsay. I didn't even think *I* would be."

"But you're a chef now, kind of," Kimber piped up. Willa got the impression that she, too, was subtly trying to encourage her brother. "You like what you do, even if it isn't quite what you thought you'd do."

His subtle glare, the silent communication between them, suggested he knew exactly what Kimber was trying to do, no matter how innocent her returning expression.

Willa sighed. This wasn't her business, and she was hardly someone to give career counseling to *anyone*, much less the son of the guy she was . . . doing what she was doing with Hudson. But she understood feeling lost.

"I got a degree in food science, actually," she said, before the twins could devolve into silent warfare. "I thought my life would go a totally different direction. Then I met my husband, and my life went down a completely unexpected path. I didn't even get into cookbooks until . . . God, at least five years later? Something like that."

They all looked at her curiously. She zested the lemons, then juiced them, with more attention than the action required.

"We had a restaurant that went under. Before that, we did pop-up restaurants. We did a bit of catering for really weird events," she remembered with a warm smile as memories popped up. That one midnight circus pop-up. The Camellia Gala . . . God, that had been a bitch to come up with appetizers for. And of course, the infamous graveyard bash. "But sometimes, money was just tight, and I wound up taking gigs. That's how cookbooks came in. Otherwise, I helped other people create recipes, or planned seasonal or special menus for restaurants. I had a pretty good reputation."

"That sounds fascinating," Mari said.

"My parents would say flaky," she tried to joke. But somehow, it didn't quite land the way she'd hoped. "It's not an easy way to make a living. Sometimes, it's barely a way to make a living."

"Do you regret it?" Jeremy asked.

She stilled her knife, looking at him. The small, insecure part of his voice stopped her in her tracks.

"Why do you ask?"

He shrugged, looking away. "I can't just keep moving home," he said.

"The *hell you can't*," Mari said, shocked. "You are *always* welcome here!"

"Yeah, but I'm twenty-three years old," he said. Now he was packing a box of raspberries like he was packing a Fabergé egg. Obviously he didn't want to make eye contact. "Shouldn't I have it together by now?"

"Mom called you, didn't she?" Kimber's voice was edged in frost. "Jesus. Why can't she live her life and leave us alone?"

"Kimber," Mari warned, but her voice had a note of sadness.

Kimber turned to her grandmother, eyes blazing. "Just because she knew she wanted to be a lawyer from the time she was eight or whatever doesn't mean she gets to judge Jem!"

Willa got the feeling that the woman probably judged Kimber as well, and Kimber probably didn't care in the slightest. But she'd fight tooth and nail for her twin.

"Don't you think?" Kimber suddenly sprang on her, and Willa froze.

She thought about what Hudson had told her about the kids, and to a lesser extent, about his ex-wife. It wasn't her place to comment, and she ought to say so. But since the Bruno incident, she knew Kimber admired her, and according to Hudson, Kimber's good opinion was hard won.

"I've never had kids," Willa said carefully. "So maybe this isn't my place. I can only comment on the little I know."

That stopped them, and their intent focus was uncomfortable. She quickly minced some shallots, a bit of garlic, and a bit of just-picked thyme to settle herself.

"My mother came here with her family from Saigon," she said. "My father's family came to the US a few generations ago, from Poland. They're both from immigrant families. Did I wish I could've gone to culinary school? Sure. But I get why they didn't want me to go. I think sometimes people who don't live in other places don't understand what it's like . . . to not have a safety net. They think that not being supported in their dreams is, like, this horrible thing. But in Saigon, dreaming was dangerous. If you lived, you were happy, and if you had some way to keep your life stable, you went for it. My mom was looking out for me, or thought she was, when I was graduating high school. Even now. Sure, sometimes it's frustrating. But I know where she's coming from, and I appreciate that."

That struck them silent. The twins looked taken aback, while Mari looked pensive. Willa wondered if she'd overstepped.

"Do you know what your mom's family was like?"

They looked at each other and shook their heads. Mari answered instead. "They were hard people," she said. "Kept to themselves, didn't have a lot of money most of the time. Amanda didn't like talking about them. We were shocked when they cut her off like that, but I guess they thought it was a waste for her to go to college because she'd be too busy mothering, and they felt she was ungrateful, derailing their plans. Or something." The note of disapproval made it clear what Mari thought of *that*.

"Now I feel like an asshole," Jeremy said, and Mari tutted him.

"No! I don't mean—I'm not saying you should just put your head down, get a job you hate, and feel grateful you have it," Willa said, abashed. "I mean, as much as I appreciated it, I also went ahead and leaped into one of the most unstable series of gigs in one of the most temperamental industries I could find. As much as I love my parents, and I do, I also had to go my own way. You know?"

Jeremy looked at her with blue eyes, so like his father's, and nodded. He had two deep dimples instead of one, and his smile was broad.

"You know," he said, "maybe you could do your own videos for cooking. In addition to your cookbook gigs. Build your own name until you became famous enough for your own cookbook?"

She laughed, thinking of Sam. "Yeah, I've *seen* the people who go viral for cooking," she said, shaking her head. "I don't think I'm sexy enough for that!"

Jeremy and Kimber laughed too. "I don't mean those videos. There are plenty of people who just teach cooking, or have a theme, or whatever," he said. "Or you could interview other chefs or cooks or whatever—like *Chef's Table*, but more intimate."

It sounded interesting, but also overwhelming. "I don't know anything about any of that," she admitted. "Honestly, I don't know where I'd start. I'd hate to put up crappy stuff and look lame."

"Nobody's perfect right from the jump. That's the only way you start," Jeremy argued, then stopped abruptly, like he'd been goosed. His eyes widened.

Kimber, on the other hand, traded a smug look with their grandmother that Jeremy missed.

He shook himself, then looked at her intently. "If you decide you want to try doing videos," he told Willa sincerely, "I can help you. For fun even."

She bit her lip, quickly pulling the sauce together. "I don't know . . ."

"You'd be doing me a favor."

Shit.

Of course he'd play the favor card. Especially here, in their family kitchen, where she was freeloading and taking up their space and time, even if she was paying for ingredients.

"All right," she agreed, and couldn't help but smile as the twins cheered in response.

CHAPTER 33

"This is *delicious*, Willa!" Mari enthused.

Willa looked down at her plate. She'd tested a few of the recipes from the cookbook, to glowing success, if the Clark family's response was any indication. She'd stuck with an Italian theme, with some bruschetta on fresh baguettes with a side of burrata . . . kind of cheating, but it just tasted good and had Kimber considering whether she could make a goat cheese burrata. They'd talked about that as they moved easily to the salad course, with fresh sorrel greens, radish, sugar snap peas, and mint. Even Hudson's father raved about it, saying he'd never liked radish normally.

By the time they got to the stuffed gnocchi with sausage, browned butter, kale, and white beans, they were all happily chatting. None of the dishes were particularly challenging, which actually fit with Sam's target audience. And if necessary, they could be made "video sexy" with a few easy tricks: kneading the baguettes, cutting the vegetables, hand-rolling the gnocchi. Even tossing the pasta in the pan.

Willa ought to have been thrilled, and she was, but honestly . . . she was having trouble concentrating.

Mari and Dan sat at either end of the rectangular table. The twins sat on one side, which left her and Hudson on the other. It wasn't a huge table, so they were a little crowded. As everyone ate and talked, she was too aware of Hudson's thigh pressed up against hers. She thought that maybe he was manspreading a little, but when she surreptitiously glanced down, she realized . . . he was deliberately leaning toward her, maintaining contact. When she looked at him in surprise, he smiled and winked at her before crunching into the toasted baguette and bruschetta. Flustered, she tried to pick up her appetizer and promptly dropped it on the plate. When she looked up, she saw the twins watching her, Kimber with amusement, Jeremy with curiosity.

The rest of the night went along those lines. Hudson, in the midst of conversing with his father, seemed to carelessly sling his arm over the back of her chair, the warmth and weight of it resting against her. Then his thumb circled the ball of her shoulder, both comforting and strangely arousing.

When the rest of the family got into a humorous, raucous debate over who had burned a batch of cookies in a long-ago bake sale attempt, he leaned close to her ear.

"You okay?" he asked, his breath tickling the hinge of her jaw and her earlobe.

Instinctively, she turned—only to find his face right there, only inches away, his eyes staring into hers . . . before dipping, quickly but unmistakably, to her lips, then back to her eyes.

It had taken her longer than it should have to tear her gaze away. Now, it seemed like *everybody* in the Clark family was studying them. Kimber looked absolutely giddy, and Mari and Dan looked pleased. Jeremy was hiding a grin as he rolled his eyes.

"Get a room, you two."

By the time dessert rolled around—a flourless chocolate/coffee cake with fresh raspberry coulis—she felt like she could barely spell her own name, she was so unsettled. Hudson's presence, his attention, was so intent yet so subtle (well, maybe not *that* subtle) that it surrounded her like a silk net, one that tightened the more she tried to fight it, or even move.

"That was delicious," Mari said, around a long breath. "Kids? You two help me get the kitchen cleaned, all right? Dan, you can help me with the pots."

"Oh, I've got it," Willa instinctively protested, but Mari waved her off.

"You've been cooking delicious food for us, buying all the ingredients, and I know it's because you feel like you're paying rent or something. Which is ridiculous," she added with a gentle smile. "But in this house, if you cooked, you don't clean. Why don't you and Hudson take a stroll? It'll be golden hour around now, and the meadow's beautiful."

So Willa found herself going outside with Hudson. Mari was right: it was beautiful. Sunset wouldn't be until around nine, about an hour later than she was used to in Southern Cal. But the light now was gorgeous, like the world was trapped in amber.

She sighed, standing by an old tree in the middle of the overgrown meadow. To her surprise, Hudson walked up behind her, wrapping her in his arms and resting his chin on her head before pressing a kiss to the crown. "Thanks for cooking," he said.

She pulled away, then found herself turning in his arms, facing him, looking up into his eyes. He looked at her like she was something precious, she realized, and squeezed her arms.

Then she got up on her toes, pressing a kiss to his lips. "Thanks," she said, "for everything else."

He rested his forehead against hers for a long moment. "It's not just me, right?"

"What isn't just you?"

"This. Us." He paused. "What I'm feeling."

She bit her lip for a second. "I don't think so," she said, but added, "but I have to admit, I don't know for sure. It's fast, and . . . things are complicated."

"I'm okay with taking things slow," he said. "Just so you know."

She smiled. She did know. And she trusted him.

She just had so much more hope than she'd had in a long time. She tugged him down to her and kissed him harder, more insistently.

Until she yelped as something hit her hard in the butt.

She spun, and Hudson pushed her behind him, then growled. "Goddammit, Butterscotch," he scolded.

The goat seemed to grin at him, unrepentant. It did its little trilling goat war-shriek before going back into the tall grass, like a goat secret operative.

"I really hate those things," Hudson grumbled.

She laughed. "No, you don't. You act tough, but you're really a softy."

"Not at the moment," Hudson said, pulling her back to him, and she got the double entendre immediately—and thrilled to it. Still, he sighed. "Just as well. I gotta pump the brakes before I really regret things," he said, laughing against her mouth.

"Like what?"

"Like forgetting to bring condoms and lube," he muttered, and she laughed, pulling away and swatting his arm. He grinned, the dimple in full effect. "But I haven't had sex outdoors in a long time, and it's summer. That means mosquitos, and . . . yeah, no."

She cracked up, feeling lighthearted. She'd even say joyful. They walked hand in hand through the meadow, not toward her house but toward the other side of the property. She could hear the lapping waves of the sound in the distance, and it was getting chillier as the sun finally started going down.

By the time they got back to the house, the kitchen light was on, but it was quiet. There was a note on the table. When Hudson read it, he laughed, then handed it to her.

It was written by Mari, apparently.

HUDSON & WILLA,
The kids have gone to the city—Jeremy's hanging out with friends and Kimber's staying over at Fi's. I told them I'd take care of the goats in the morning. Dad and I are down at the cabin for the night.

Do with this information what you will. And have
fun!
Love,
Mom
P.S. Be safe, too.

Willa looked at Hudson, aghast. "So they know . . . ?"

"Yeah, I'd say it was pretty obvious," Hudson said, rubbing the back
of his neck and chuckling.

"Oh, my God." Willa raised her hands to her flaming cheeks.
Somehow this was worse than the first time she'd shame-walked into
the kitchen wearing his clothes . . . because they were giving their stamp
of approval.

"You okay?"

"I want to crawl into a hole and die!" Willa said.

He laughed, tugging her until she was plastered against his chest.
"On the plus side," he said, kissing her neck and nibbling on her ear, "it
means that we've got the place to ourselves for the night."

She blinked.

Then she raced him to the bedroom.

CHAPTER 34

"I still can't believe it doesn't smell like skunk," Willa marveled as she clattered around by the stove.

He sat at the kitchen table, watching her, just in his jeans. Willa was wearing his T-shirt over a pair of panties that peeked out flirtatiously every time she stretched up to reach something from a high cabinet. She was barefoot and cooking something that smelled delicious.

Technically, there was no reason for him to be there. He'd finally finished the last of her punch list, and she'd insisted on paying him, even though by that point, he hadn't cared. The house was successfully deskunkified. No, he was there because they both wanted to be together. After putting in a day of work troubleshooting a finicky freezer at the grocery store, he'd showered, stuffed some clothes in a duffel, and then headed over to Willa's.

When she opened the door, her smile had been wide and bright as a floodlight. "Guess who finished her cookbook?"

"Congratulations," he'd said, before sweeping her up in a kiss that left them both breathless. "Guess *somebody* gets a reward, huh?"

Which he'd then proceeded to give her. Several times. In a couple of rooms.

Honestly, he was having more sex with her, in his forties, than he'd had with anyone in his twenties or thirties. It was kind of amazing. And anyone who thought that women in their forties somehow put sex aside? Ought to meet Willa, because the woman was wearing *him* out in the best way.

Actually, they shouldn't. He wanted to keep the woman to himself.

Now, it was close to ten o'clock, and they were both ravenous. She brought bowls over, graceful as always, putting them on the table before sitting herself. "You sure you're okay with spicy?"

"I used to drown stuff in sriracha, I'm sure I'll be fine," he said. "Smells great, by the way."

"I order Korean ramen from Amazon when I can't get to Asian markets," she said. "Trust me, once you have it, you won't go back to those block things again."

"You're ruining me," he said, and the truth of the words sank in a little. He stared at the bowl instead. There were noodles, yes, but also a poached egg and a sprinkling of green onions. He took a sip of the broth. "It's good."

Then the heat hit, and even though he tried to suppress it, he couldn't help but cough and reach for his water.

She laughed, shaking her head. "Don't worry. My dad can't eat spicy food either. And there's a little hack—I learned it on TikTok, actually." She got up, walking to the fridge and grabbing a narrow white bottle that she put next to him. "Kewpie mayo. You can put it in the noodles. It'll tame the heat a bit."

"Mayonnaise?" he said, uncertainty clear in his voice.

"Just try it."

He did. And unbelievably, it was delicious. He started eating for real, digging in with his fork, watching her eat the noodles enthusiastically with her chopsticks. *I should learn how to do that.*

"I have to ask. Why the degree in food science? What even *is* that?"

"It's, like, figuring out how to make french fries more addictive," she said. "The evil side of it, anyway. It can be about how to make things taste like different things, or how to make things have better mouthfeel. How to make things sweeter, or saltier, or more pleasing."

"Huh. I didn't even know that was a thing."

"I didn't either," she admitted. "Until my parents basically said that there was no way I was going to culinary school. They said that if I did, I'd be in dead-end jobs for the rest of my life, until I was too old to stand up and cook, and then I'd live under a bridge."

He widened his eyes. It was too uncomfortably close to Amanda's mindset, honestly. *Don't they need to take care of themselves? Are we doing them any favors?*

Unaware of the turn of his thoughts, Willa kept going, a small, amused smile on her face. "So I convinced them that food science was basically biochem—which, honestly, it kinda is—and that I'd be able to get a lab job. Science, they could get behind. And I still got to work with food, so I thought I was set."

He studied her. "Then what happened?"

"Well, then Steven happened," she said. "I was interning at a restaurant where his friend worked, studying . . . I don't even remember. But we met, and it was like a lightning bolt. He swept me off my feet. When he knew that I didn't want to work for some big corporation, making sawdust taste like Parmesan cheese, he told me to work with his friends. Introduced me to chefs, and vintners, and artisanal-food makers. It was amazing, and I didn't look back."

"And your parents?"

"Super, super pissed," she said, with a rueful laugh. "What about you? Did you go to college?"

He stopped eating. He knew that she wasn't asking with any kind of malice or judgment. At least, he hoped there wasn't judgment. But she'd gotten a degree in something that, despite her downplaying it, was really hard . . . and her parents obviously had high expectations. "I didn't want to go to college," he said. "I'd had enough of school, honestly. Paper writing, the whole thing. I wanted to work with my hands."

"That makes sense," she said, and he felt his stomach unknot as tension left his body. "You're good at it."

"Thank you," he said. "But all you've seen is me being a handyman, honestly. That's not exactly brain surgery."

"You told me you're a contractor. I've seen people build restaurants, and we worked with a contractor getting ours up and running. I know what that entails," she corrected. "And even if you were 'just a handyman,' like you say—that's still harder than you're making it sound. Do you think Patrick would know how to shut off breakers and fix a dead outlet, or patch drywall, or . . . I don't know, any of those other things? Or even deskunkify a house?"

He grinned, his chest warming.

"You help people stay where they want to stay. You fix the most important place in their lives. You make things better. That's not nothing either."

He felt amazingly comforted. His family had always encouraged him, tried to validate him—but on some level he'd written it off because they were family and they were supposed to be supportive. Willa didn't have to say any of those things, yet she still *got* him.

Still . . . he realized, especially after his talk with Amanda, that it didn't cover everything either.

"You know, I wanted to specialize more in remodeling and restoration," he said. "I like antiques, and old houses. Stuff like that."

Her eyes glowed. "You'd be great at that, I bet," she said.

"How can you tell?"

"Because you like fixing things, but preserving them too. Like this place."

He sighed. She just . . . she *got* him. "There's one thing I was obsessed with," he finally said.

He hadn't told this to anyone, outside his family and Amanda, back when they were young and foolish and thought sex and love were the same thing. Willa looked at him expectantly, eating noodles like he wasn't going to admit the biggest dream of his heart.

"I wanted to be a horologist." He laughed, because it just seemed so ridiculous now. Like a kid wanting to be an astronaut.

She blinked. Then she frowned. "That's . . . like a clock . . . something. Right?"

Of course she'd know. She was so fucking smart, it was gorgeous. "Yeah. Clock specialist. Repair, restoration. Design, sometimes. Clockmaker."

She rested her cheek on her hand. "How did you get into that?" she said, turning the question on him.

"My grandfather—my mom's dad—loved clocks," he said. "He took me around to garage sales and estate sales, made it like a treasure hunt. And then he let me open one up. I couldn't believe how everything worked together so perfectly. It was like a secret little world, the best puzzle I'd ever seen."

She smiled at him. "That's awesome."

"I think I was the only kid in middle school to have a subscription to *Horology Monthly*," he admitted, and her laugh was sweet, not mocking. "After he died, I didn't go out and find clocks that much, even though I still really like them. Then after the twins were born—well. Things just got too busy, you know? My life had a different focus."

She made a sympathetic noise. He knew that she, more than anyone, would understand the need to shift from dreams to survival. From making things up to making shit *work*.

"The twins are awesome," she said slowly. "But . . . do you ever think about what you'd have done if you hadn't had them? Is there any dream you would've wanted?"

He froze. Was this Amanda all over again? Was she saying that she didn't want to just be with a handyman?

"I'm happy with where I am," he said, and his voice was harsh.

Was he convincing her, though? Or himself?

She put a hand on his forearm. "I'm not saying you should be anything other than what and who you are," she said, clear and calming. "I'm just asking because you strike me as someone who's put other people before himself for a long time."

Of course she'd think that. Of course she'd say that. He stroked her cheek with one hand, then leaned over and kissed her softly.

"There was a thing—you can take a yearlong course, in Bern, Switzerland," he said. "It's with Jaquet Fonjallaz-Debayle. They're a world-famous clockmaker. Like, their clocks are tens of thousands of dollars to buy. Some of the antiques have gone for over a hundred thousand."

She blinked, looking stunned. "Wow. That's . . . *wow*."

"And they're *amazing*," he enthused, feeling like the biggest dork but not caring because Willa didn't seem to mind.

"And you learn to make them?"

"It would take longer than a year," he said. "But you'd learn how to repair them, restore them. You'd be learning from basically the greatest horologists in the world."

"How hard is it to get in?"

He shifted. "Well . . ." He cleared his throat. "I kinda took a class. A few years ago, when the kids first went to college. Got certified in basic clock repair."

God. He hadn't even told his parents that.

"But I didn't do anything with it. It's just a hobby."

"But one you love." She said it.

Fuck it. "In a perfect world," he admitted in a scratchy voice, "I'd still be a handyman, sure. I love the island, and they need me. And I love being around my family. I'm not ashamed of that, no matter how weird or whatever people might think it is . . ."

"It isn't," she said staunchly.

He took a deep breath. "I'd probably still do the contracting too. But I would love to have, as a side hustle I guess . . . I'd want to restore more houses on the island to their past glory because we've got some beauties that are being torn down for McMansions by people trying to move in and drive up prices. And I'd really, *really* love to be a certified Jaquet Fonjallaz-Debayle repairman. Maybe even design clocks at some point, after I retire." He smirked at himself. "Probably sounds ridiculous."

She pushed the bowls aside, then moved to him, straddling his lap. She framed his face with her hands, kissing him.

"Steven once told me, after a restaurant he and his friends had opened basically flamed out in under a year, that it hurt like hell but that it was worth it," she said. "Because the dream was always worth it. Even if it hurts, if you don't feel anything, if you don't *go* for it . . . what's the point?"

He kissed her throat, then pulled back to look at her. Her eyes shone with so much faith in him, it was almost blinding.

"I'm not saying you have to do anything," she added, stroking his bangs out of his eyes. "But whatever you *do* want to do . . . I'm saying I believe in you."

He kissed her hard, and she melted into him with a soft, happy sigh.

As they moved against each other, the kiss deepening, he couldn't help but wonder what she'd say if she knew that right now, the biggest dream in his life . . .

Was her.

CHAPTER 35

Willa felt excited and a little nervous. She hadn't gotten feedback since she'd turned in the completed cookbook. She wasn't sure if that was good news or bad news. Did they like what she'd come up with? Did it fit Sam's persona? Did it fit what the publisher wanted?

She knew the recipes were solid, if nothing else. For the first time in a long time, she'd felt thrilled with what she'd come up with. By the end of the process, she'd actually *enjoyed* conceptualizing them, testing them, even eating them. It was incredible how a project that seemed so daunting, so wrong for her, had led to this new sense of possibility. It felt like she'd been eating plain oatmeal for years and now tastes were exploding on her tongue, the aromas filling her nose, the feel in her mouth a mix of textures that made her want to dance in her seat. She'd forgotten, and now the pleasure of it was almost overwhelming.

She had the feeling it was tied to Hudson. Not just the sex, although that definitely was a contributing factor. It was more that the things he did gave her space to just focus on creating. It had been longer than she could remember since she'd had that, she realized.

In fact, she may never have had it.

When she'd been growing up, her life had been all about focus: the drive to get scholarships, to get top grades, to go to college. But she knew now that she'd always wanted to be a chef, but being a food scientist had been her "ghost profession"—the one she took as an adjacent to what she'd truly desired. The nonalcoholic beer as opposed to the artisanal pale ale.

Then she'd met Steven, and he'd encouraged her to finally move away from caution and take a leap with him. The problem, she'd realized later, was that they *both* always leaped, usually without much looking. It had been exciting and nerve racking. Steven had been able to laugh off their failures for the most part, writing them off as experiments and learning experiences. She'd nodded . . . and then quietly cushioned him from the day-to-day realities of the aftermath. The bills, the paperwork, the legal pitfalls. She'd loved him enough to do that.

She was also starting to realize, even without the help of therapy, that a part of her had resented him, but guilt had kept that part locked tight and buried deep.

It'd be foolish to think somehow, after this short period of time, that Hudson loved her enough to protect her in the same way she'd once buffered Steven. She wasn't even sure that was what she wanted. But she was sure that she wanted to see where they *did* go, if possible.

Her phone rang, and when she saw it was Vanessa, her heart pounded with excitement. "Hi there," she said cheerfully. "It's good to hear from you."

"Hi, Willa."

Was it paranoia, or did Vanessa sound subdued? Willa pushed past it. "Were you able to read the cookbook? What did you think?"

A small sigh.

Now her worry meter was rising exponentially. "I can always change recipes, if something's not working." She realized there was that note of desperation in her voice and dialed it back. "I mean, I was really inspired on this project. I even have several alternates, so if you can tell me what you think might work better, or how you want the concept tweaked, I can change gears and have something new in almost no time . . ."

"They canceled the cookbook."

She went still, the words not processing. "What?" she whispered.

"They canceled it." Vanessa's voice was mournful.

"But . . . why?" Willa asked. It just didn't compute.

"Because word somehow leaked online that Sam was using an 'old lady' to ghostwrite it," Vanessa said bitterly. "He's already catching backlash. Lots of negative comments. Losing followers. He's hitting a downward spiral, and his manager's trying to stem the worst of the damage."

While Willa felt a pang of remorse for Sam, she couldn't help but be focused on the problem at hand. "But . . . I finished it, on time, to specifications."

"I know. It was good work, Willa."

But not good enough.

"I was able to convince them to let you keep the signing half of the contract, though," Vanessa said.

"If I remember correctly, the ghost contract wasn't about publication. It was about turning in an acceptable project." Willa found herself arguing, something she rarely did. "I'm not angry with you, Vanessa. I'm just trying to understand this."

Vanessa sighed. "I know. I'm not thrilled about this either," she admitted. "Between you, me, and the tree . . . the new management team they put in has been making really questionable decisions, and I don't like them."

Well, Willa *really* didn't like them. "So I'm not getting the rest of my fee? The on-completion?"

"I'm sorry," Vanessa said, and she truly sounded pained.

"What if I fight this?"

"They said that you signed an NDA," she answered. "Also—again, this is in-the-vault, under-the-dome stuff—basically that they've got more money, so if you decided to, ah, make this public or decide to fight them legally . . . well, it'd be a bad idea. It's a war of attrition, and you're lucky you got to keep the initial."

"Wait, are you saying they're *accusing* me of leaking that I'm the ghostwriter on Sam's cookbook?" Willa said, her voice rising.

Vanessa was simply silent, and it was answer enough.

"Motherfucker!" Willa spat out, then winced. "I'm sorry."

"No. I truly understand how you feel." Vanessa's unhappiness was palpable. "I just wish I could do more."

Willa laughed woodenly. "I suppose that they're not offering any more contracts either," she said. Not that she wanted to work for them, but dammit, she'd counted on using this as her entry point, getting back to what she'd once been good at. Yes, it was freelance, and yes, it was uncertain, but it had been fun, once upon a time. Even better, it let her live life on her own terms: setting her own hours, picking her own projects, working her own way.

"No," Vanessa said. "They are trying to make it seem like you're somehow unreliable, when I'll bet somebody internally let it slip to somebody they shouldn't and then screwed their own deal, so they needed a scapegoat to cut loose, paying the remainder to you *and* to Sam."

Another slice of guilt. Sam would be all right, she felt sure, but still, it would be a blow. She sighed. "I really wanted this," she said to Vanessa. "Do you know anybody else, at any other house or publisher, that's looking for a ghost?"

"I can see who might be looking," Vanessa answered, but Willa could hear in her voice that it was a sop, and a pity one at that. "But with all the freelancers out there, accepting cutthroat rates, and all the food vloggers and such . . . it's just really hard. I can't make any promises."

"Thanks, Vanessa. I appreciate it."

"Hang in there."

Willa sighed. "You too."

They hung up, and Willa looked at her phone.

She used to think midlife crises were something that happened to middle-class American men. Ones who wondered where the horny dreams of their youth went as they realized they'd never be that baseball player with the hot trophy wife and then desperately tried to reroute their trajectories with ill-advised sports cars and maybe hair plugs.

Now, she realized that the crisis was real, and she was having one.

It wasn't that she hadn't pursued her dreams and regretted it. It was that she *had* pursued her dreams . . . and now wondered, perhaps too late, if she'd made the wrong choices all along and would pay for them dearly in whatever was left of her life.

Numb, she made her way up to her bedroom, pulling off the handmade quilt and slipping between it and the blanket, bare feet be damned. She closed her eyes.

Her parents had warned her, so very long ago, that she'd regret marrying Steven. That she was putting herself on a path to ruin for choosing such an unstable profession. And she'd ignored it, even when the restaurant went under, and when she'd had to work late into the night. When they'd had their house in San Mateo foreclosed on, and they'd moved back to LA to be around Steven's family. Her parents had been thankfully quiet when Steven had gotten truly sick, and felt truly sad for her when she'd lost him. She'd felt rather than heard their litany of worry. Now, here she was. Nearly fifty, with no clear path forward. She was fortunate, she knew, to have inherited this house, rather than simply bills. But she also knew that at forty-six, with her lack of previous focused experience, her career choices were limited or nonexistent. It wasn't like she was going to be working the line at a restaurant until two in the morning. She could probably land a line cook job in a diner somewhere, but that'd be the best of it, and she doubted there was anything like that on the island. Her body could handle it for a while, she supposed, but not that long—and the pay would not cover what she needed it to. If they'd even hire her when there were so many young, eager, fierce cooks out there, willing to stage for free, willing to work for shit pay so they could pursue their passion. A passion that, this week notwithstanding, she hadn't had burn in her for too long.

She curled on her side, the tears starting to slip hot down her cheeks. This was what it meant to question your life, she realized.

And wonder what to do if you'd truly chosen wrong.

CHAPTER 36

Hudson knew immediately that something wasn't right. He'd walked into Willa's house—she'd turned islander enough to leave the doors unlocked—and he hadn't heard music. This was like a church.

Or like a tomb.

"Willa?" he asked, carefully heading for the kitchen.

Red flag number two: she wasn't in the kitchen. Even after turning in the cookbook, she'd gravitated there, playing with the leftover ingredients she had, humming to herself.

What the hell was going on?

"Up here," she finally called from the bedroom.

He headed up the stairs, then paused for a second in the bedroom doorway. She was curled up in a ball on the bed, turned away from him. "You okay—"

As soon as she turned, he knew immediately that she *wasn't.* Her eyes were puffy from crying, and her face was splotched red. Her normally immaculate hair was tousled, probably from the pillow.

"Oh, sweetheart," he breathed, rushing to her side and stroking her cheek. It was still a little damp, and she sniffled. "What happened? Are you all right?"

"They canceled the book," she said. "They aren't publishing it."

He jerked. "They *what?*"

"I know," she moaned, trying to turn her face into the pillow.

"Why? Why the hell would they do that?" he said, nudging her to look at him.

"I guess it leaked that he had a ghostwriter, or something? An old, unsexy one."

He felt like his blood was boiling. "That is the *biggest bunch of bullshit . . .*"

He stopped immediately when he saw that his anger wasn't helping the situation, just making her expression sadder.

"Sorry," he quickly added. He was sure she felt worse about it than he ever would. "I'm just upset for you. And even if it's a bullshit excuse, that still hurts."

"I honestly don't care if they think I'm ugly and old," she said, and he believed it. "I kind of care that they're trying to act like I somehow broke my NDA, though. Mostly because they're using it as a reason not to pay me the remainder of my contract."

"*They're* . . ." He gritted his teeth, took a deep breath, and counted to five as he stroked her arm encouragingly. Support for her, not irritation. "They can do that?" he said, more quietly.

"Yes. They really, really emphasized secrecy. I'm not even sure who leaked it. It screws both me *and* Sam," she said. "But let's face it: he's still got possibilities for endorsements. He's still got his following on all his platforms, even if there's some unsubscribes. But I'm not getting another contract from this publisher, and it's hard to crack into *any* of them. For me, this is . . . kind of the end of the line."

She sounded so defeated, and her eyes welled with tears. He felt it in his chest, like someone had hit him with a hammer.

"God, I am so sorry," he said, even though it frustrated him that this was all he could do, all he could say. He knew how important this was to her.

"I was putting a lot of faith in this," she said, sitting up, wiping at her eyes with the heels of her palms. "But hey, at least the house is fixed."

He froze. "What are you talking about?"

Her long exhale was like her soul leaving her body, and she turned wet brown eyes to him. "Selling the house was always the fallback. I hate it, you have no idea. But that will buy me some time as I figure out what the hell I'm doing next."

He scooped her up, putting her on his lap, nudging her head against his shoulder. "I can help with that," he said gently, feeling panic prick at him, then rocked/shook her a tiny bit when she let out a watery snicker. "I mean that. I know how much you hate accepting help, but this is serious."

It was too early to say he loved her, wasn't it? Was he even sure that's what it was? It was hardly like he had a track record on this sort of thing. He had had one real relationship that had ended with two amazing kids and a dinged sense of self-worth—he was aware enough to know that. He'd made excuses and shied away from anything serious.

But he wanted something different with Willa. He was attracted to her, and the sex was hot—but she listened, and she shared. She didn't look down on him: if anything, she actually cared enough to help him see what his dreams were and encouraged him to follow them. Most of all, she wasn't trying to fix him, or save him, or bring him around. If anything, she had her own issues, her own *life*.

He wanted to help her, especially since it seemed like she let so few people support her.

"You've helped me so much already," she said with a small smile, bringing him back to the conversation and out of his haywire thoughts. "The living room looks gorgeous. And everything else . . . well, I'm sure there are a few things I can do, like maybe paint in neutral colors or something, to help sell the house. But it's not crucial. And the housing market's been so hot . . ."

She still sounded lost, defeated. His chest clenched.

"I really love the island," she added with a small, bittersweet laugh. "Even this quickly."

"You could move in with me," he blurted out.

Her eyes widened, her laugh turning into something more natural, if surprised. "The last thing you need is another living creature on Marigold Farm."

"I mean," he said, stroking her cheek, "you could *move in with me.* Be . . . with me."

He took a deep breath and held it.

Now she tilted her head, studying him, really weighing his words. *I didn't think I'd stay on this island . . .*

He gritted his teeth. Nope. He was *not* going down that route at this point.

"You mean it." It wasn't a question. She breathed it, sounding stunned.

He kissed her gently, then tilted her head so she was looking into his eyes, hoping she could see that he had no doubts. "Absolutely."

Now it was her turn to take a deep breath. She let it out in a low, long sigh. "I can't."

It hit like a punch. "Why not?" he said, trying not to press but unable to keep the note of hurt out of his voice. "If it's because you don't like to accept help . . . this isn't that. This isn't me giving you a hand or doing a favor. This is because I feel more about you than I've felt about anyone in a long time. Maybe ever. I don't want to lose you."

Another tear crept from her eye, trailing down her cheek. She smiled anyway, though.

"You're not going to lose me," she said. "But you're not going to lose yourself either."

He shifted to sit on the bed with her, cuddling her. "I want to do this," he said, his voice firm. "I'm a grown man, and I know my mind."

"I know." She snuggled into his chest. "Trust me, I know. But you're also . . . well, you're doing the thing."

"What thing?"

"You're figuring out everyone else's problems," she said. "You're coming up with a solution that puts your needs last."

"You," he said, kissing her nose, "are a fine one to talk."

251

"That's why I know." She sighed against him, molding herself to him, and he cradled her, breathing in her scent . . . clean laundry and citrus, summer sun and spice. "We both did this, Hud. You got married too young—for good reasons, and the twins are amazing—but then you just put everything into keeping the twins okay and the farm afloat, and all your dreams just got pushed aside."

"I made peace with that," he protested, but she put a soft finger on his lips.

"Listen to me," she instructed, resting herself on his chest and looking up at him. "You're only forty-two, and those dreams are still there. You don't need to figure out how to take care of me. I'm forty-six. I can take care of myself."

"Yeah, and how well has that been going?" He saw the moment the words hit her, and he wanted to kick his own ass. "That . . . I didn't mean it like that. I meant—"

"It's okay," she interrupted, even though the stern set of her face told him it probably wasn't. "And you're right, in a lot of ways. I haven't asked for help. I haven't let people in. I have reasons for that. Probably some unhealthy ones, and my former therapist had a few choice words . . . but the point is, I can and will figure this out. That doesn't mean you need to ride to my rescue."

"Then what does it mean?" he said, anger warring with loss. "We're just . . . I don't even know what we were, but we're just *done*?"

Goddammit. *This* was why he never got in relationships. It felt like she'd hit his sternum with a goddamned sledgehammer.

"What this means," she said softly, her face still sad, "is that I'm going down to Irvine to see my family, and to . . . figure some things out. Then, I'll come back up here and get the house ready for sale, more than likely. But as far as we're concerned: do you want this?"

"*Yes.*" Hadn't he said as much?

"Then maybe you need to think about going to the internship in Bern."

He stared at her. "What the fuck?" It came out sharper than he'd intended. "You want us to be together, but you want me to *go to Switzerland?*"

"I want us to be together," she said, just as sharp, her brown eyes glowing like whisky in firelight. "But not if it means that you're keeping yourself small or using me as a fucking excuse for not pursuing your dreams. I don't want that for you, and I sure as hell don't want it for myself. I was support staff for a man I loved for too long to be okay watching *you* decide to take on that role."

He sucked in a breath with a soft hiss. She spoke softly . . . but she also pulled no punches.

"I'm going to go to California for a bit," she said. "Check on my parents. My dad sprained his ankle this week, and I want to make sure they're okay. Then I need to think about what my next steps are. I think you should do the same. And when you're ready . . . call me."

He kissed her. She kissed him back. He held her, stroking her hair. She nuzzled his chest. Eventually they undressed each other, having sex like they had all the time in the world, like they'd been together forever and like they'd never made love before in their lives. Gentle, passionate, soft and harsh and complete.

But he didn't sleep that night, knowing that in a few days, she'd be gone . . . and however long after that, she'd maybe be far away, and he'd be dealing with his shit, one way or another.

CHAPTER 37

It was like stepping into a time capsule, walking into her parents' small house in Irvine. They'd managed to buy it when housing prices weren't tremendous and the neighborhood wasn't considered very good, but it had been in an excellent school district, and that ultimately was all that had mattered to her mother especially. Now, many of the houses around them had been rebuilt or remodeled, and the tone of the neighborhood was a lot more expensive.

That hadn't changed her parents, though. Walking in, she found it still smelled like she was used to—a combination of her mother's goji-berry-and-chamomile tea, her mushroom broth for the chicken soup she cooked with Costco rotisserie chickens. There was a plastic bag stuffed with other plastic bags hanging by the door. A faint medicinal odor from whatever ointment her mother used for her arthritis. Her father's photos of his family were hanging alongside pictures of her mother's, in plastic frames they'd gotten on sale at HomeGoods, the photos casual and even slightly blurry, not Instagram ideal but still perfect. There was a too-generous coating of dust on some plastic flowers that had been that way for as long as she could remember. There were boxes of bulk items in an industrial-stainless set of shelves in the living room, and the couch in front of the television sagged visibly, its orange-and-scarlet flower pattern faded from the sun.

It wasn't that they couldn't afford new items—Willa knew that. The TV itself was a slim large-screen that they'd proudly purchased (also at

Costco, also on sale) so her mother could watch her beloved K-dramas. This was a habit her mother had previously made fun of. Now she watched and gossiped over the shows with her Vietnamese friends. Her father just shook his head at her, but it hadn't stopped him from watching the World Cup on it and cheering his butt off.

"Did you eat?" her mother asked her immediately as she kicked her shoes off and changed into her house slippers.

"A little." Actually, she hadn't, but she knew that she would. Eating was like breathing at her parents' house. Her mother had gone down to the airport to pick her up, but she'd taken over, driving them back to the house. Her father was sitting on the couch, smiling at her, his foot elevated on the coffee table and wrapped up. "How are you feeling, Dad?"

He make a *pssht* sound. "Just a sprain, can you believe? All that fuss."

Her mother made a worried-hen noise at him, and he rolled his eyes, but his smile was still fond as he swatted at her butt. "I'm heating up soup," her mother announced. "Do you know what you want for dinner? I'll take stuff out of the freezer."

Willa glanced at the clock. It was barely eleven. But at the same time, it was, again, just as she remembered. Food had been such a central part of her existence. Even when they were broke, her mother insisted that they eat as well as possible. They had a garden—her father, thankfully, had a green thumb, and her mother wasn't bad herself. Her mother shopped at three different markets and worked the circulars, making a dollar stretch until it screamed. Willa hadn't even realized how tight they'd been financially until she was an adult and her mother had cautioned her about choosing such an irresponsible career.

Which made this visit all the harder.

"I can make potato-and-cheese pierogi," Willa volunteered, and her father's eyes lit up, but her mother made a dismissive noise.

"We have plenty of food, no need to go through all that trouble!" Seeing the disappointment in her husband's face, her mother then added, "I'll get out the steaks instead," which cheered him back up.

After all these years, her parents still loved each other. It was tangible. Visible. She envied it, in a lot of ways. It had always been what she'd wanted. And for a brief time, she'd had it, with Steven. It hadn't been perfect, and it had been hard, but at times, it had been incandescently beautiful.

She had doubted she'd get another chance at it. Hadn't anticipated it. Until Hudson.

"How long are you staying?" her mother called out from the kitchen, the sound of her bustling around clear.

"Just for the week," Willa responded, following her and leaning against the archway where she could watch her mother work. This, too, was exactly the same. Her mother pulled out a large pot from the dishwasher, which Willa knew had not been used to wash the dishes in decades. It was essentially a really expensive cabinet at this point.

"I see." Her mother put the soup broth on the stovetop to heat. Judging by the look and scent, it was some variation on súp nui gà, a very simple Vietnamese chicken noodle soup. It was comfort food, she knew. As if her mother seemed to instinctively know that her daughter was going to need comforting, even if she'd only booked the trip to check in on her injured father.

When the soup was ready, they took bowls out to the living room. Her father slurped it, sighing happily, and Willa tucked in. Her mother, on the other hand, put her bowl on the plastic place mat on the coffee table and fixed Willa with a sharp stare.

"So," she coaxed. "How did the cookbook you were telling us about go?"

How did she know? She was like Alexa: she seemed to hear every damned thing, and knew even more.

"There were some issues."

"Did you get paid?"

Willa sighed. "Some."

"Some?" Her mother's tone was incensed. "Why? What happened?"

"There was a problem with the author. It doesn't matter," Willa said, cutting off the line of inquiry. She had no idea how she was going to explain influencer culture and NDAs to her mother, who, despite being a very intelligent woman, cultivated a very deliberate aversion to most things on the internet.

Her mother took this in. Her father, as usual, was quiet but listening intently. "What are you going to do now, then?"

Willa took a deep breath. "I'm still thinking through my plans."

Her mother made a little noise at this, and even though it wasn't fully verbalized, Willa had heard it enough to know what it meant: *I am dubious, but I am not going to say that out loud.*

Which didn't surprise her, since essentially, ever since Steven's death, she'd felt like the largest "I told you so" in history had been brewing between her and her parents, like a ticking time bomb.

"What kind of plans?" her mother asked instead.

This was the tricky part. "I have some ideas," she said, but knew immediately that wasn't going to be enough when her mother leaned forward. "I'm going to stop over in the Bay Area after this, before I go back to the island."

Her mother looked surprised. "Oh? Does someone there have a job, maybe? It's expensive to live there, though."

Her father made a grunt of agreement.

"Not a job exactly," she said slowly.

She'd come up with the plan, or the vague sketch of a plan, on the plane. Ever since she'd talked with Hudson and emphasized that he had the support he needed to pursue his dream, she'd had a smack of clarity.

She'd always had the dream.

What she'd ignored was the *support*.

"I'm going to talk with Nat and some of my old friends from the industry," she said. "They've got a big network of contacts . . . I'm sure that some of them will extend to the Seattle area. And there are lots of things I can do online that maybe they can help with."

Her mother's eyes grew wider as Willa spoke. Then she looked at her father with something like panic. "You aren't selling the house?" she finally blurted out.

Willa sighed. "Not if I can help it."

Her father now harrumphed loudly. "This," he said, "is a terrible idea."

She winced. If her nearly silent father decided to weigh in . . . well, that time bomb was going off now, from the looks of it. "Dad . . ."

"No!" He glared at her. "I was silent when you married that man, even though you *know* it was a bad idea. You were a baby, and he was ten years older, and he dazzled you and dragged you along into debt and exhaustion. I got to *watch* you turn yourself inside out for whatever he wanted. I don't even think you liked cooking—"

"Now, you *know* that's not true," she shot back. "I wanted to be a cook, but you both said I had to get a college degree! In something *real!*"

Her mother sighed. "Maybe we should have let you go to culinary school," she said. "You could have taught . . ."

"No," her father argued. "We should have insisted she get the degree in chemistry. Then, at least, she could have a real job. With regular paychecks."

As they squabbled, Willa fought the desire to tug her hair. How could two people in their seventies reduce someone in her forties to someone in her teens?

"I know," Willa finally broke in. "I *know*. I know you don't approve of what I chose or how I lived my life. I know you feel like I'm a failure. And I'm sorry, but . . . I'm also not sorry. Because as draining as it was, I will never regret marrying Steven." She felt tears stinging her eyes, but she kept moving. "Every moment, even the hard ones, was worth it, because I really, really loved him. Every crazy idea, every over-the-top dream, everything. I loved him, and I loved who I became when I was with him, and on some level, I'm going to miss him every day of my life."

It was like opening a floodgate, and the tears came pouring out, but she kept going.

"He taught me how to dream, not just suffer," she said. "But I learned something recently. It's never just your dream. Or rather . . . you can have a dream, but you can't get it all alone. Everybody needs help sometimes. You just have to be brave enough to ask."

Her father looked angry. Her mother looked troubled but was surprisingly quiet. "So you'll beg people for help? Let them know what has happened and expect other people to make things all right? We raised you better than that."

"It's not like that," she said, and didn't cower at her father's stubborn glare. "Not for me, anyway. I know that's how you were raised, and Mom too. But I feel like it's different. It's not showing weakness or begging for help. It's loving people and letting people love you."

"They aren't family," he snapped.

"No, they aren't," she said. "But Harold put Great-Aunt Caroline in a rest home and then rented out her house and, I'm pretty sure, pocketed the profits. That's why she left it to me."

His mouth shut abruptly, and he went pale. He let out a soft curse in Polish.

"I'm not saying that family can't be trusted," she finished, giving his arm a comforting squeeze. "I'm just saying, there are different kinds of family, and if people love each other, I think that's one kind. I'm still leaning on family. Just . . . different family."

"I am calling that son of a bitch . . . ," he growled.

"Honey," her mother said, and Willa looked at her. "Do . . . do you really think we think you're a failure?"

Willa wiped at her tears. "Well. You could hardly call me a success."

"I never cared about that," her mother said, getting up and sitting by her on the couch, putting her arm around her shoulder. "Never."

She grinned, giving a watery laugh. "Sure you didn't. Immigrant Asian mom," she teased.

But her mother didn't go along with it, even though it had been a running joke for years. "I just hated seeing you kill yourself for his dream," she said. "I hated seeing my only daughter so exhausted, working so hard, and we couldn't do anything to stop you. I didn't want this life for you."

Willa gave her a hug, tucking her mother's head against her shoulder. She'd misunderstood, so hard. The words were a comfort.

"I'm doing what I can to turn that around," Willa said, with as much confidence as she could.

"How?"

Basically, she was going to take a leap of faith. Only this time, she was doing it on her own—for her own dreams.

CHAPTER 38

Willa stood outside the restaurant for a second, taking a deep breath. She'd told her parents that she was going to take the risk, no matter how scary it was. She was going to make her living freelancing as a foodie, essentially, or die trying—even at her age, even in her situation. Despite all odds.

But the real risk, she realized, wasn't going for a contract or competing in the content-generating machine of social media or anything like that. It was reaching out for help, something that seemed as impossible as crossing the Grand Canyon on a tightrope. And equally terrifying, if she was honest with herself.

She squared her shoulders. She'd been working harder, just trying to survive, for too long. Steven had always been the dreamer, and she'd never begrudged him. Now, it was her turn to dream. Which meant it was her turn to open up.

"You gonna block the door, or what?"

She startled, then looked over her shoulder. Nat was grinning at her, and she grinned back, immediately giving her a big hug. "Missed you," Willa said immediately, her throat clogging for a moment.

"Yeah, well, whose fault is that?" Nat said, but there was no heat behind it. "C'mon. The gang's all here."

Willa let herself be led into the restaurant. It hadn't opened yet—Tuesdays were dinner only, no lunch service—but the staff was moving like a dance company, a blur of well-choreographed motion that had a beauty all its own. Chef Marceline had always played French music, a throwback to her home country. Willa found herself crooning under her breath and smiling.

"C'mon. Chef said we could use one of her private rooms," Nat said, tugging her along.

"What? She didn't have to do that," Willa reflexively protested.

"She wanted to," Nat said. They went down a dark wood-paneled hallway before Nat opened a door.

Willa was greeted with a burst of excited chatter and happiness. As she stepped in, overwhelmed, she recognized faces that she hadn't seen in years. Chefs who had worked the line at Fox Lair, Steven's restaurant, or the Cloisters, or any number of other restaurants she knew of through Steven and through her own days helping create menus. Friends from college. Even the Sexy Chef himself, Sam, had come up from LA. He looked overwhelmed but happy to be included. They cheered, calling out her name.

She made her way around the table, threading through the small crowd, hugging people and fighting tears. "Thank you," she said more than once. She'd hoped that people would be able to show up, but she hadn't expected *this*.

When things finally settled down, they sat at the table with her at the head. Nat sat at her right side. Chef had even prepared some nibbles for them, ridiculously beautiful-looking appetizers and snacks, which Willa hoped she'd let Willa pay for. The assembled group looked at her expectantly.

She took another deep breath, closing her eyes, trying to get her balance.

Sometimes, it's a different kind of family. She let the breath out, slowly, letting the shame and the echo of clawing desperation ebb with it. This was it. The leap of faith.

She had nothing left but to jump.

"I guess you're wondering why I called you all here today," she said, in her best mocking business tone, and was gratified when they laughed. "Seriously, though. It's been . . . well, it's been a rough few years."

She then sketched out what had happened. Steven's progressing illness and her struggles with being a caretaker, pulling her out of cookbook ghostwriting for the most part. His medical debt. She didn't touch on the strain to her emotionally, or to their relationship, but from the understanding looks they were trading with each other, she got the feeling they read between the lines whether she wanted them to or not. She finished with her moving to the island, to Aunt Caroline's. Finally, she took a drink of water. This was probably more than she'd said to a group in years.

"What can we do to help?" Rene, the sous chef who was now an executive chef in his own right, asked while she paused.

She saw the rest of them nodding, talking among themselves . . . except for Sam. He was looking at her nervously.

"You okay?" she asked before she could think about it.

"I feel guilty," he said. "I mean . . . I didn't know. It's not your fault that word got out that the cookbook was being ghostwritten. My agent said that some other guy, one who was angling for a contract, was bent because of my deal and went in to deliberately screw me. I didn't think of how it would screw you to be taken off the project." He bit his lip, looking, as usual, his fully adorable yet sexy self. "I, um, think that they're using some of your recipes for another chef. They might even adapt the entire concept. With some changes, obviously."

Now another explosion of chatter, angry this time. Most of them being *"Sue their asses!"* or similar. She sighed.

"You can't copyright recipes," she said, cutting through the din. "You guys know that, right?"

The shouts bubbled down to a dark mutter.

"Anyway . . . I'm disappointed, and I'll definitely be mentioning it," she said, "and I'll go over my contract again."

"You'll contact a lawyer."

Now there was silence as Chef Marceline walked through the door and made her pronouncement in a ringing voice. She glanced at the person sitting at the opposite end of the table from Willa, and they immediately stood, giving her the seat and standing against the wall with a few others.

"I will help you pay for it if need be," Marceline added with a nod, "and you can pay me back if you feel you must, but we all know this is criminal, and I for one won't stand for it. Especially given your current situation. That's unacceptable, and it will be addressed immédiatement."

There was a low chorus of "Yes, Chef" from those who had worked with Marceline or had simply worked in a restaurant and knew of her. Sam, Willa noticed, was staring at her with wide, uncertain eyes.

"What else do you have in mind?" Marceline said. Well, perhaps more like *demanded*.

Willa pulled out her phone, looking at her list. "In a perfect world, I want to stay on the island," she said, her voice low. Then she gritted her teeth for a second.

Confident. Take the leap. Ask for what you want.

"That means I want to take on gigs where I can work remote," she said. "I'm not looking to work a line, that's never been my thing. But I can help with menu development. I can write recipes. I can write cookbooks. I've never done video content," she said, looking at Sam, "and I sincerely doubt I'd be good at it, but at this point, I'm willing to try anything. And the kids of a friend of mine had some good suggestions on that front."

Sam nodded at her encouragingly. "I can help with that."

"So if any of you need anything in that realm, anything at all . . . I'm looking for work."

There. Was it embarrassing? Yes. Her mother would probably want to die of shame, listening to her air her private problems so bluntly, and her father would be mortified. But dammit, this was her life, and she needed to do what she had to.

They were quiet, and for a second, she wanted to die. It was one thing to say *What do you need?* Or *How can I help?* But it was another to actually offer help. She'd wanted so badly to be self-sufficient. To not need anyone. To not *show* that she needed anyone. It seemed to prove weakness. To prove that, as her family had feared, she was somehow fundamentally broken . . . that she could not survive on her own, that she'd managed to screw up the very quintessential job of being an adult.

She waited, still as a statue.

Marceline looked deep in thought, and the others were also pensive. Then Nat broke the silence, pulling out her purse.

"I'm going to contact BluGrow."

Willa blinked. "Who or what is BluGrow?"

"They're a vegetable brand," she said. "Big agro, sure, but they're always looking for recipes, and they pay pretty well. They reach out every year, looking for new stuff."

"That's . . . thank you," Willa said.

Just like that, it was like the floodgates opened. There were other recipe-writing opportunities. One or two of the chefs worked the line at bigger restaurants and knew they were looking for ways to promote them, so fun food content might work for them if she could produce it. The ideas were flying fast and furious.

She felt overwhelmed with gratitude, almost dizzy with it. She'd leaped, and they'd done more than provide a safety net . . . they were actively building a bridge for her to walk across the chasm on.

She knew, realistically, that not all the ideas would work out. It wasn't like her future was suddenly assured. But the fact that she had people who wouldn't shame her, that she could count on . . . tears pricked at her eyes, and she tried to surreptitiously dab at the corners with the napkin in front of her.

She caught Marceline looking at her. The chef held her hand up, and silence hit.

"I have been considering a cookbook myself, for many years," she said, as casually as if she'd considered getting a haircut.

Willa couldn't help it. She gaped at her.

"I simply do not have the patience to write it," Marceline continued. "It might be a fun project for the two of us. And I have been irritated with you for being away for so long. You come see me. We'll drink too much wine and go over some memories, and perhaps we can sell this thing."

"I . . ." She stopped herself from saying *I couldn't, this is too much.* She'd said that too often in the past. She'd cut herself off from any chances, or from reaching out. Now, someone was reaching out to her, and she was grabbing on with both hands. So instead, she simply nodded. "I would love to, Marceline."

Marceline toasted her with the water glass in front of her. "Now, let's see what else we can come up with . . ."

CHAPTER 39

"Okay, this is ridiculous," his mother finally said, almost a week after Willa had gone down to California. It was Sunday, and now that both twins were home, his mother was making brunch. Hudson had tried to duck out, but she'd basically collared him as he'd headed for the door. "What is going on with you? You're living on coffee and irritation lately, and I for one am sick of it."

He gritted his teeth. She had a point. He knew he was being a dick. "Just have a lot on my mind."

Which was true. Since Willa had told him to think over what to do next, he'd truly been thinking about it.

The first thing he'd thought: that she, just like Amanda, didn't want to just be with some handyman on a Podunk island. Which had pissed him off and depressed him.

But the more he'd thought about it, the more he'd realized that in Amanda's case, it really wasn't about him—and the sooner he let that go, the better, for everybody involved. Even after their relatively short time together, he *knew* Willa. He wasn't sure if it was because he'd taken the time to get to know her on a deeper level or because he was older and had more life experience, but he thought it through. She wouldn't tell him she cared about him and then insist that he change, not after everything she'd been through.

She wasn't forcing him to do anything here. She was telling him to think about it, rather than act on impulse as he'd done in the past, charging in to save the day. She wasn't in need of a white knight, and it wasn't her stubborn insistence on independence. It was because he was trying to just come up with a solution blindly, not really taking into account what she wanted or needed.

It also would mean that, yet again, he'd push his dreams of restoration, repairing clocks . . . even just seeing the world, now that he thought of it . . . even further into the distance until they went away entirely.

He'd been postponing relationships and falling in love to protect his kids—but really to protect himself. He'd been pushing his dream of restoration away because the island needed him, and his family did too.

But did they? Or was he just using it as a shield?

Would he resent them, when it finally struck him that he'd run out of time?

"Does it have to do with Willa?" Kimber tacked on, looking worried. "She hasn't been around. Is her family all right?"

"They're okay." He'd spoken with Willa only briefly, but he'd called or texted her every night. He didn't want to lose that connection. "We just need to think some things over."

Jeremy shook his head. "That's right up there with 'We need to talk' on the relationship disaster scale," he said. "Sorry, Dad."

"No, she was right on this one," Hudson said immediately, defending her. "We're not kids, and relationships aren't easy, no matter how old you are. If we're going to make this work, we need to be on the same page."

His father took a sip of coffee before staring him down. "Where aren't you on the same page?"

He studied his father, who weighed in when necessary but generally trusted Hudson to make up his own mind. "You're getting involved in this?"

"If I'm thinking you're going to be an idiot," his father retorted, "then I pipe up."

Hudson's mother grinned as his kids laughed. He took his seat at the table, loading his plate with scrambled eggs and bacon.

"I told you that the cookbook thing fell through for her," he said. "I guess it's a hard industry to make a living in, so she's got to regroup. She's worried about making a living and figuring that whole thing out."

They all ate and listened intently as he explained, with as little detail as possible, what her life had been like before: her husband, the restaurant, her freelancing. Her caretaking.

"So now she feels like she's starting over at forty-six," he finally said. Then he grimaced. "I . . . kind of told her that maybe we could live together. I know, I should've asked you guys first, especially if she winds up selling Ms. Caroline's house. But in the moment, it seemed like a good idea."

His mother sighed. "You've got a big heart, Hud," she said. "But sometimes, you're just . . . Ready! Fire! Aim!"

"Like you two weren't when you got married?" he countered. "You were *twenty*, for God's sake. The twins are older than you were!"

Her eyebrows jumped to her hairline. "You're talking about getting *married?*"

"What? No!" He grimaced. "We haven't talked about it, but I'm pretty sure we *are* on the same page with that one. Neither of us is looking for that. But if I'm not in love with her yet, I can almost guarantee I will be. I don't want her stressed out, and I really, really don't want her moving to California or God knows where because she's afraid of living under a bridge."

Kimber whistled low, and even Jeremy looked startled.

His mom looked at his dad. "Poor Willa," she murmured. "So . . . where does that leave you two? Did she break up with you because she feels she needs to figure this out on her own? She seems to have that kind of mindset. You know, where everything's transactional."

Hudson stared at her for a second, toast forgotten in his hand. That was it exactly. She'd been intent on making sure she didn't owe him, or anyone else, anything. Like somehow, that would make her bad, or wrong, or something.

"Not that she's a bad person," his mom quickly added. "It's just how some people are wired. I bet her family's the same way."

He nodded slowly. "She wants us to be together, just like I do," he said. "But she said I need to think it over first."

"She's got a good head on her shoulders, then," his father said approvingly. "Still . . . I'm guessing you're all in, huh?"

"Absolutely," he said, then sighed. "Except there's one thing specifically that she wants me to think about."

"Is it having more kids?"

He choked on a piece of bacon. *"No."* Even if it wasn't dangerous at her age, no matter what kind of medical advances they had, he didn't want more kids. She didn't want any kids, period. "We're not interested in that."

His mother grimaced, and he watched in real time as her dream of him having a happy marriage and half-siblings for the twins evaporated. She let out a slow, deep breath. "I'm sorry for pushing you," she finally said. "I just . . . you were so young, and so unhappily married, with the twins. You're still young, and I would've loved to see you get a second chance there. But that's *my* dream, not yours."

He nodded. Then he burst out: "Willa wants me to go to Switzerland."

The table fell silent in shock.

"With her?" his father finally spluttered, like he'd said that Willa wanted him to go to Antarctica. "Why? Does she have a job opportunity there or something?"

"No. She wants me to go there on my own," he said, which shocked them even more. "There's a clock internship at Jaquet Fonjallaz-Debayle, the famous clockmakers. You can sign up and do a one-year or three-year course and be certified as either a master repairman or a master restorer. There aren't many in the world, and those clocks are works of art. They cost thousands of dollars each."

"You've always been obsessed with clocks," his mother said with wonder. "But I didn't know this class was something you were even thinking about."

"Why didn't you go for it before?" his father followed up.

He looked over at the twins, who were looking at each other sorrowfully.

"Because of us," Kimber finally said, Jeremy nodding in agreement. "Because you always put everything on hold for us."

"No," he quickly said. "I wanted to be with you two, and I wouldn't have left if you were younger. But you're amazing, and you're both adults, and the handyman business has been going great for years. I could've left years before now, but I made excuses."

"So Willa's calling you on your bullshit?" his father said, cutting to the chase.

Hudson barked out a laugh. "Guess she is." He grinned a little. "Mostly, she doesn't want me to use her as an excuse. She also doesn't want me to resent her if she is one."

"Do you resent us?" Jeremy asked.

"No," he quickly said. He was glad this was all coming out in the open, and as usual, talking things through with his family was his source of strength. It made things clearer, and it helped to know that they always had his back. "You two kids are the absolute best things in my life, and I couldn't love you more if I tried. Willa loved her husband, too, though, and she still found herself making some choices that . . . well, she doesn't regret them, or she says she doesn't. But she still wonders what would've happened, and if there wasn't another way. She doesn't want that for me."

"She's a good woman," his mother said.

"I think so."

"So what are you going to do?"

He sighed, pushing food around his plate as he thought. "Still not quite sure," he said. "But . . . I think I'm leaning toward Switzerland. The one-year course."

"That's a big deal," Kimber said.

"I know. I'm going to miss you guys so much if I go," he said, and in the pit of his stomach, there was a nervous knot. "And a long-distance relationship with Willa, when we're still so new . . . that makes me a little shaky too."

His mother patted him on the shoulder. "If I believed in soulmates," she said, "I'd lay odds that you two were, honestly. I've never seen you like this with anyone."

The twins agreed, and even his father nodded.

"So . . . ," Hudson said, swallowing against the lump in his throat that had nothing to do with the brunch he'd just tried to eat. "Guess I'm going to Bern."

And then he'd see what happened from there.

CHAPTER 40

Hudson walked into the Seattle airport, Willa by his side. He was rolling the biggest luggage he'd ever owned over to get checked in. He had all the stuff Willa had insisted he needed for an international flight in his carry-on. He'd never been to Switzerland before . . . honestly, he'd never even been to the East Coast. He was feeling decidedly nervous.

"You're going to knock 'em dead," she said, squeezing his hand.

She couldn't go up to the gate with him—he knew that. She sure as hell wasn't going to fly to Switzerland with him. But he wished she could.

The past month had been a blur. It was like the fates had taken a personal interest in his case. The instructors at the clock company not only admitted him, they somehow *remembered* him from some questions he'd emailed them, back when he'd taken his courses here in Seattle. They'd liked how he thought about clockwork machinery, apparently, and someone had dropped out or something, so the position was there. Willa had a friend of a friend who helped push his visa stuff through in a miraculous amount of time. Since Willa had reconnected with her chef friends, she seemed happier, more relaxed. More confident and hopeful, which he loved.

But it also gave him the tiniest pang of concern. He'd just met her, for God's sake. They'd been together for a bit over a month, and he was now going to be gone for a year. He had some savings, and the family had assured him that they were going to be fine, but he wasn't going to be able to afford to fly home until the thing was done. Willa was going to be fighting to make herself solvent and get whatever plans she had in order. So he wasn't going to be able to physically see her for twelve whole months.

A lot could happen in twelve months.

"You know you've got this, right?" she said, the ultimate hype woman, not realizing where his true fear currently was. "They're going to love you. You're amazing, and you're going to blow them away."

He hugged her. "If you say so," he said.

"I *know* so." She snuggled against him.

"If you need anything, though," he said, resting his forehead against hers, "you're gonna tell me, right? I swear, I will be back on the next flight. And if I find out from the twins or anything that you're *not* telling me, I am going to lose my shit."

"I'm not that bad anymore," she said, squeezing around his chest. "I know my limits, and I've got more support now. But if anything comes up, I will tell you. Promise." She looked at him, and he saw his whole world in her eyes. He kissed her, gently but fervently.

"Don't wanna go," he said. "I am going to miss you. So fucking much."

"I'm going to miss you too," she said, her voice breaking a little. "But it's just a year."

His laugh was wooden. "Just a year, huh?"

"It'll . . . okay, I'm not going to lie, some of it is absolutely going to suck," she said, and his laugh turned more natural at her honesty. At least he could count on her not to pull her punches. "But we're going to get through it, you know? You're going to be busy, and you're going to be doing so many things that are awesome. Things that are going to change your life."

"So are you." He wanted that for her. He just wasn't sure if what she was going to experience was going to make her want to stay with him or show her that he was just a stepping stone—the rebound guy who got her out of her depression, the one who helped her see how to move on. Which was probably shitty, and definitely insecure, and he'd swallow his own tongue before he said it out loud.

Because even if he *was* the rebound or the transition or whatever, it would be worth it if it made her happy.

"We'll talk, or email, all the time," she said. "Now, you've got a flight to catch, and I need to get the ferry."

He nodded and started to turn. But she grabbed his shoulder and framed his face in that way he loved, with her small hands.

"Kiss me like you mean it," she whispered, and he saw the shine of tears in his eyes. "Enough to last a year."

So he did, kissing her long enough that he vaguely heard whistles and comments of disapproval. Then he pressed a few last kisses on her cheeks. "See you soon," he lied, then turned and headed for security and what he was afraid was going to be the longest year of his life.

CHAPTER 41

November

"Happy Thanksgiving, Dad!" the twins chorused at Willa's phone, and a wave of happy shouting followed. Willa couldn't help but smile at the enthusiasm, even as she felt deafened by it.

She glanced at the screen to see Hudson smiling back, even though his eyes looked tired. He waved.

The Clark kitchen was crowded with people and food. The turkey had been in the oven for a while, ready to feed their family plus a few strays like Willa, the motorcycle crew who regularly spent their holidays here, and islanders who didn't have family around. There was a chaotic cacophony of sound, cheerful ribbing, jokes.

"Did you have turkey?" his mother called, shushing people around them.

"They don't do Thanksgiving here," he reminded her. "And they don't really have turkey here either. At least, not that I could cook. They do roast birds for, like, catering and stuff."

"What? That sucks," the big biker Bruno said. "When are you coming back, again?"

"Next September." It sounded like he was trying to be cheerful, but she could hear the strain.

There were a few more questions. Then Willa said, "I'm going to take the phone outside now" and gave people a few minutes to wave and call out goodbye before she moved to the porch. It was cold, but at least it had stopped raining, and there wasn't any snow. She pulled her sweater closer around her. "Are you all right? How are classes going?"

She was gratified to see him smile, finally. "Awesome," he said. "In a my-brain-is-about-to-explode kinda way, but it's been cool. I'm still working on tribology, the theories anyway. I'm learning so much."

"I love hearing you so excited," she said. They talked every week, when possible. Sometimes it was only five or ten minutes, true. And they texted each other every day. She sent him pictures of what she was working on, or the family, or the farm. He sent her pictures of his classmates, or the clocks when he could.

Still, she knew it wasn't quite enough, for either of them. Considering he was someone she'd only been with a few months, she missed him more than she expected . . . honestly, more than she realized she could.

She'd started getting a little insomnia again too. It was something she'd reluctantly admitted, since she'd promised him that she'd be transparent. They'd both promised that they'd communicate rather than try to spare each other or make decisions based on what they thought would be best for the other person.

Being a healthy, functioning adult sucked sometimes. She smirked at herself. Better late than never, though.

"I just miss you. All of you," he said, "but especially *you*."

"I know," she answered. "I miss you too. But it's only nine months, right?"

"Nine months left." He rubbed his hand over his face, and she saw the weariness. "Nine fucking months. Sometimes I think I'm going to go out of my mind."

She hugged herself. "I know," she repeated. "Believe me, I know."

"You sleeping, sweetheart?"

She loved it when he used the pet name. "I'm sleeping a little better," she reassured him, then felt herself blush. "I, um, stole one of your shirts."

That seemed to cheer him up. "Oh?"

"And I'm using it as a pillowcase," she said. "For the pillow I hug, not the one I sleep on."

"Huh."

"I'm gonna need to wash it soon, though," she said. "So I'm probably going to steal some more, until you get home. I realize how bonkers that sounds."

He laughed, and her heart warmed, even as her chest squeezed. "I'd volunteer to mail you one, but then I'd run out," he said with a laugh. They were quiet for a moment. "Hey, Willa?"

"Yeah?"

"You know I love you, right?"

Now it felt like her heart *stopped*. It wasn't something they'd said out loud, ever. She wasn't quite sure why. Maybe because it felt so quick? They'd only been together since July. But when they'd made their agreements—to talk to each other every week, to be open, to try for a long-distance relationship, to not see other people (something that had been so evident they'd almost laughed at it)—they'd never said that they loved each other. It was hard enough to let a continent split them up as it was. If they'd said that they loved each other after only a couple of months, she wasn't sure that he'd have gone.

She wasn't sure that she would have let him.

"I love you too," she said, in a low but steady voice. "Have for a while."

"Same."

They were silent, letting that sink in.

"God, I'd do just about anything to hold you right now," he said, his voice rough with emotion.

"Same," she teased, even though she felt emotions bubbling through her like lava. As she'd hoped, he chuckled, even if it was halfhearted. "But hey, when you come back, I am going to absolutely *wreck* you."

"Oh, Christ, don't tease," he groaned, and she grinned. They'd sexted plenty of times, too . . . a new experience for her. She'd been self-conscious the first few times, but now she was getting pretty good at it, or at least she thought so. She was torn, because it was hot, but it often just made her miss him more. "I better go to bed. Give everybody hugs, okay? I'll talk to you this weekend."

"Okay," she said. "Love you," she added. Because now she could, and it seemed to want to burst out of her.

His smile was somehow both warm *and* sexy. "I love you, too, Willa," he said. Then he hung up.

She held the phone for a long time after, wondering how the hell she was going to manage nine more months of this.

CHAPTER 42

June

Hudson sat in the small studio apartment he'd been living in since arriving in Bern. He'd been lucky to get a stipend—again, that weird the-Fates-at-work luck—so it wasn't eating up all his savings. The place was small, but he didn't need much, and he was really only there to eat and sleep and do homework.

He'd been able to fully geek out on all things horology. He'd seen intricate antiques that were worth more than any car he'd ever owned. He'd learned from clockmaker masters about how they designed clocks, both in the old days and now. He hadn't really gone in for chronometers, preferring the old-fashioned clockworks.

When one of his older instructors had complimented him on his work and his understanding of the mechanisms, he'd felt like he'd won the damned lottery.

He'd also befriended a number of his fellow students, even though honestly, most of them were younger. They teased him, calling him "old man" for turning in early rather than going out drinking with them, but they'd also admired his work ethic and taught him the particular German dialect that they used in Bern. He'd never been particularly good at languages, beyond vague memories of Spanish from high school (and when Jeremy had a *Dora the Explorer* phase). He considered several of them friends, and he'd invited them out to the farm if they wanted to visit the States. He got the feeling they'd take him up on it, eager to experience it themselves after seeing the photos and the updated website that Jeremy and Kimber had pulled together, and some impressive videos that Jeremy had made.

The videos themselves kept him in the loop with what was happening at home. They showed him that Kimber had gone ahead and gotten not one but three more goats, due to "increased demand" from her working partnership with the dairy on the island. The goat cheese thing was really taking off, mostly thanks to Patrick's restaurant's growing success. He still thought the guy was a douchebag, but according to Willa, he was becoming more of an islander and had shaped up, at least.

In the meantime, he'd shared photos and videos of his own adventures, small though they were. He'd taken the high-speed train from Bern to Paris with two of his classmates, seeing the touristy stuff, the Eiffel Tower, Notre-Dame . . . and, of course, eating lots of good food, pastries, cheese. He'd also checked out the Christmas markets around Bern . . . colorful, filled with great food, mulled wine, and big tankards of beer.

Otherwise, he mostly stuck around the school, focusing on his studies. He wasn't here to have some kind of reclaimed gap year. He was here because of his passion.

Besides, all that food made him think of Willa.

He missed her, he missed her, he missed her. He missed his family, obviously, and he missed the twins . . . but they were grown, having their own adventures. He and Willa talked often, but he knew that they both were getting frayed by the lack of contact. Not in a we're-going-to-break-up kind of way. Just . . . pining. He was getting downright sappy in his emails, for one thing. She was just as bad.

It was hard enough that he was thinking of calling it on the program. He could practically hear her voice in his head, though. *Only three more months to your certification. You can still have your island life, and you won't wonder what it would've been like.*

Which was all true.

He'd even had a conversation with Amanda, strangely enough, since he'd made it to Europe. It had been around Christmas, and when he'd answered her call, she'd said, "The kids said you were in *Switzerland*?"

When he'd explained the internship and all, she'd been quiet. When she finally spoke again, she sounded apologetic.

"I love this for you, Hud. Truly," she said.

It felt like they'd closed a door, in a good way. He was happy for her, especially since she seemed to be making headway in her relationship with the twins, slow and small though those steps seemed to be. And he believed her. She was happy for him.

He heard a gentle knock on his door, and he opened it. It was his landlady, Mrs. Weber. He greeted her haltingly in German, and she smiled indulgently. "This is for you," she said, then handed him a package.

He frowned at it, confused, but thanked her profusely before closing the door and taking it to his small table. It was from the island, obviously. A care package?

From Willa.

He opened it, then grinned. There was dried fruit, with a printed label that he recognized as Kimber's design: Marigold Farm Specialty. The hard candy was watermelon-chili flavored and bore the same logo.

He knew that Willa had been working with the family on the farmstand goods, and it seemed to be taking off. It had also expanded to "merch," which was apparently what the kids were calling T-shirts and stickers and things.

The biggest thing was a photo book, though. Not just of the farm. Of things around the island. The general store. Mrs. Tennyson and a bunch of the elementary school kids. The boat launch and a squad of fishermen, grinning with their poles held up in a salute. Like a yearbook, there were people who had signed near their pictures . . . words of encouragement and support. How they admired what he was doing, and how they were behind him 100 percent. Most of all, that they were looking forward to seeing him back at home.

Any thought of abandoning the program fled. These people believed in him enough to tide him over. He couldn't do any less.

The last page was Willa, smiling at the camera shyly. She hated selfies, he knew, just like he knew she'd taken this because she knew he'd like it. Her words, in her beautiful script, took up the last blank page.

> Hudson,
> It's been a year since I met you. Can't believe that in that time, I made a home here and fell madly in love with a man I never would've seen coming in a million years. I miss you, but it's only three more months, I keep telling myself. I can wait that long.
> I'd wait longer for you. And this is going to sound cheesy, but I don't care. I'd wait for you forever.
> All my love,
> Willa

He swallowed hard. He hadn't seen her coming, either, but he was glad every day that Noodle had somehow brought them together.

Just three more months, he told himself, looking out the window. Then he'd be home with her.

CHAPTER 43

September

Noodle was curled up in the kennel she'd bought for him, tucked near her coffee table. It was raining and thundering, signaling the changing seasons.

"It's all right, Noodle," she reassured him, making sure he was tucked in with his favorite blankie. Jeremy was in the Bay Area, hanging out with Sam and friends, and since Noodle tended to get out a lot anyway, he'd been spending more time with her.

Basically, Noodle was her dog now, as the whole Clark family acknowledged, even though no one had said anything overt about it. Noodle accompanied her on her walks from her house to the farm, which was every other day or so in the summer. He liked tramping through the field as much as she did and was equally comfortable in either house.

So was she.

She'd been busy, though. Thanks to Marceline's sharklike lawyer, the publisher had given up the rest of the advance, although as she'd suspected, the bridges there were burned. She'd managed to barely coast to her next gig, a corporate holiday job for a sweet potato company, creating and testing recipes for sweet potato muffins, bread, even ravioli. She'd also worked on pitching Marceline's cookbook, although as with most things, it took three times as long as she would have hoped.

She'd also found herself working with Marigold Farm, helping Kimber expand. That had been rewarding, and fun. They'd included her in some profit sharing, and although she felt strange about it, Mari had pointed out that she had, indeed, done work there . . . she deserved to be compensated for it.

Willa was getting better at saying yes.

The most surprising source of income: she'd partnered with Sam on some video content. Since it had leaked that he was using a ghost-writer, instead of trying to deny it, they'd leaned in. They'd then created a character for her.

Auntie.

Auntie had come bursting into his kitchen, her hair in a bun, a housedress and an apron on, wielding a wooden spoon like a paddle. She'd then chastised his shirtlessness and told him where he was going wrong in his recipes.

"Why are you kissing the dough? That's unsanitary!"

"Why are you slapping the pork belly? What did it ever do to you?"

"For God's sake! Put on an apron! You are a mess!"

It was over the top, and she'd drawn a tiny bit from her own mother. When she'd first gotten out of food science school, her mother had still picked at her techniques, especially when it came to things like cooking Vietnamese food. "Why are you measuring the water for rice? *One knuckle!*"

It cracked her up now. Not that her mother was watching Sam—or at least, she hoped not. At any rate, Sam's viewers had found it hilarious, a funny little addition that gave his Sexy Chef character more dimension. He'd added more humor, thanks to brainstorming with Jeremy and Kimber, as well as his other Seattle friends. Now he had a bigger viewership than ever . . . and a new cookbook deal in the works, although that was quiet and slow. She would probably be a cowriter, fully named.

She wasn't going to count on it until it happened, though.

She now lived in Aunt Caroline's house, her house, and she loved the island. She loved being around the Clarks, who had quickly become her family. She worked hard, and for the most part, she was happy.

Except for one thing.

She kept busy because, especially at night, when her brain had time to think, she missed Hudson with a brutality that hadn't diminished with time. She hadn't gotten used to it. If anything, it had simply gotten worse.

One more week.

She'd been counting the days like a prisoner looking at a calendar of her release. He'd told her about his packing, about his certificate. How he'd made friends that might come to visit. How they'd offered him a chance to stay and complete the full three-year program to become a master clockmaker.

He'd said no, or at least, he wouldn't complete it in person. He missed his family too much . . . and he'd made it clear that included her.

One more week.

It was around eight o'clock when the power went out. She smiled. The wind was wild, and lightning flashed and thunder roared. But Noodle was cozy in the soundproofed kennel, and she had long gotten used to the weather here, just like the other islanders.

"What do you think? Should I fire up the generator?" she asked Noodle. She peeked in to find him snoozing, so she decided to just light the candles on the mantel.

She was tucking her feet under her on the couch, wondering if she should light a fire, when suddenly Noodle burst out of the kennel, the blanket trailing like a superhero's cape. He lunged at the door, barking like mad.

"Whoa! What is it? What is it?" she said. Sometimes he'd do this—if her neighbor, the restaurateur, had a get-together, for example, and there was unexpected traffic on the road. But she hadn't heard any cars, and besides, Patrick tended to invite her to those things. (Not that she

went, since she knew he was often angling to get to Marceline or trying
to pick her brain about the restaurant business.)

She grabbed Noodle's collar.

Then the door opened.

She looked up in shock.

There, standing in a nylon jacket, a waffle-weave shirt, and jeans,
was Hudson.

He shut the door behind him. In the candlelight, she could make
out all the details of him: his stubble, his bright eyes. His hair was wet,
his smile was wide, and he looked so good she wanted to cry.

She let out a little shriek, letting go of Noodle, who danced around
them as she launched herself at Hudson like a rocket. He caught her
easily, holding her so tight she could barely breathe.

"You're home," she said in disbelief. "I thought you were coming
back next week!"

"I skipped the ceremony they have for graduation," he said. "And
took a final early, and was able to get an earlier flight. I wanted to surprise you."

"You did," she said.

Noodle was also surprised by this whole business, but then there
was more thunder crackling, and he started barking at the ceiling. She
encouraged him to go back to the kennel with one of his toys and a
small treat. With the equivalent of doggy grumbling, he went, and she
shut him in, knowing it helped him feel more secure.

She felt Hudson wrap his arms around her from behind, kissing
the nape of her neck. She leaned back, luxuriating in the feel of him
enveloping her. "You're home," she almost sang.

"I missed you," he said, turning her and punctuating each word
with kisses: "So. Fucking. Much."

She laughed against his mouth. "I knew we'd make it," she said,
nuzzling against his chest.

"I did too." He sighed, holding her against him in a way that made
her feel utterly cherished. "You were right, though."

"I was?" She smiled against him, then pulled back to see his face. "About what?"

"I'm glad I went." His expression was serious. Sexy, of course, but this was important, so she focused. "I felt like it was the first time I'd done something for me. I don't know that I would have, ever, if you hadn't pointed it out. Now that I have, I can see where I was just coasting without even thinking of why. It's like a whole new world opened up, and I have you to thank for it."

She felt her cheeks heat. But instead of demurring, she nodded. "I know how you feel. I hated having you gone. But it let me really think about what *I* wanted to do with my life, and then start to figure out how to pursue that. It was important."

He smiled, tucking a lock of hair behind her ear. "Yeah. It was."

"That said," she tacked on, "let's not do that again."

His laugh was rumbly under her ear. "Nope," he said. "You're stuck with me from now on."

"Promise?" she whispered, the love in her chest feeling almost overwhelming as she looked at this man, who had changed her life in one stormy night.

When she looked at him, the candlelight made his eyes shine.

"I promise," he said, and kissed her.

Acknowledgments

I'd like to thank Ali Rosen, who was a huge help in answering my cookbook questions and helping me delve into the weird, wild world of professional chefs.

I'd also like to thank the entire Montlake team, especially Alison Dasho and Krista Stroever, who are right there for any geeky or foodie reference. You guys get me, and I can't tell you how much I appreciate it.

I'd like to thank my agent, Tricia Skinner, for talking me off the ledge on *every single project*. Seriously. Your Sith powers in author butt-kicking are strong, and I thank you. (So does the hub, by the way, since he tends to see the panic firsthand.)

Finally, I'd like to thank my husband and son, for holding down the fort and giving me the foundation I need to tell these tales.

About the Author

Cathy Yardley is an award-winning author of romance and chick lit. She has sold more than 1.2 million books with publishers like St. Martin's Press, Avon Books, and Harlequin. She writes fun, geeky, and diverse characters who believe that underdogs can make good and that sometimes being a little wrong is just right. She likes writing about quirky, crazy adventures because she's had plenty of her own: she had her own army in the Society for Creative Anachronism, she's spent New Year's on a three-day solitary vision quest in the Mojave Desert, and she had VIP access to the Viper Room in Los Angeles. Now, she spends her time writing in the wilds of eastern Washington, trying to prevent her son from learning the truth about any of said adventures, and riding herd on her two dogs (and one husband).